THE FIFTH RAPUNZEL

THE FIFTH RAPUNZEL

AN INSPECTOR MAYBRIDGE NOVEL

B. M. Gill

CHARLES SCRIBNER'S SONS
New York

MAXWELL MACMILLAN INTERNATIONAL
New York   Oxford   Singapore   Sydney

First United States Edition 1991

Charles Scribner's Sons
Macmillan Publishing Company
866 Third Avenue
New York, NY 10022

Macmillan Publishing Company is part of
the Maxwell Communication Group of Companies.

Library of Congress Cataloging-in-Publication Data

Gill, B. M.
    The fifth Rapunzel: an Inspector Maybridge novel /
B. M. Gill. — 1st U.S. ed.
    p.   cm.
    ISBN 0-684-19389-2
    I. Title.
PR6057.I538F53   1991   91-21295   CIP
823'.914—dc20

10   9   8   7   6   5   4   3   2   1

Printed in the United States of America

THE FIFTH RAPUNZEL

1

There was no time for terror. The sudden horrific impact with the oncoming lorry sent the Saab spinning off the Lovćen road like a flaming meteor into the valley of the Boka below. The cab of the lorry, sliced in two by an outjutting rock, decapitated the driver. His head was found later amongst his bloodied cargo of grain.

Had anyone been left alive, the Montenegren authorities would have found it difficult to apportion blame. The British couple in the burnt-out car might have taken the hair-pin bend too wide. The driver of the lorry, what was left of him, had smelt strongly of *šljivovica*.

The enquiry was short and uncomplicated by eye-witnesses. The charred remains of the car's number plate, together with a couple of items of jewellery, helped identification. The bodies of Professor Peter Bradshaw and his wife, Lisa, were in due course flown home.

Detective Chief Inspector Tom Maybridge attended the funeral as a colleague, neighbour and friend, and as such was invited to read a few appropriate verses from the Bible. He found choosing the verses extraordinarily difficult and eventually settled for St John, chapter 14. The words were simple and compassionate. When he reached verse 18: "I will not leave you comfortless: I will come to you", he glanced at the Bradshaws' son, Simon, seated in the front pew. Someone had given him a black tie and the knot had worked loose. It looked incongruous worn with his maroon school blazer. At eighteen, the blazer looked wrong on him, too. Sunlight filtering through the stained glass windows was making crimson pools on the surface of the pale ash of the two coffins directly in front of him. A cloudy day full of green tranquillity would have better suited the occasion. A grey soft rain would have been kinder still.

Maybridge read on: "Let not your heart be troubled, neither let it be afraid." He paused. If Simon was like his father he would conceal his emotions very tidily, as he seemed to be concealing them now. Peter Bradshaw had never appeared to be disturbed or troubled by anything. Perhaps his career as a forensic pathologist had a formalin effect, pickling the emotions. On the few occasions Maybridge had been forced to have a consultation with him during an autopsy, the professor's skilled fingers had probed the cadaver with slow rhythmic movements like a concert pianist playing Bach on a bloodied instrument. Maybridge's hands, balled into fists to stop them trembling, had been thrust behind his back. Bradshaw, noticing his discomfort, had politely pretended not to. Very polite, Peter. Very controlled. Not like his wife, Lisa, an artistically gifted woman, but deeply neurotic.

Maybridge disciplined himself to read the remaining verses without letting his thoughts stray, and then finally and with relief he came to the last verse: "But that the world may know that I love the Father; and as the Father gave me commandment, even so I do. Arise, let us go hence."

Simon, thrust into awareness by what seemed a peremptory command, half rose, then, realising it wasn't an order, sat again and blushed.

Blushing was an adolescent embarrassment, like acne. And still being a virgin. The Magdalene in her red robe up on the east window was gloriously provocative, aglow with sunlight, the colour of wine. Keeping his eyes on her most of the time made this funeral bearable. It was the first he had been to. He didn't

8

know the ropes. Words his father had spoken came back to him: "Valedictories, Simon, are the few pieces of hyperbole untinged by envy. As for funerals, let the dead bury the dead."

The dead weren't burying the dead today and the hyperbole in the tabloids would have rung the bells of heaven. The heavies were more restrained. The *Daily Telegraph* obituary was typical:

Professor Peter Bradshaw, M.A. (Oxon.), M.D. (Lond.), F.R.C.P., F.C.Path., tragically killed together with his wife, Lisa, whilst on a motoring holiday, will be greatly missed, not only by his professional colleagues who had great admiration for his skill, but also by his students at London University where he was a part-time lecturer. The professor was an academic who performed brilliantly at the practical level and was able to impart sufficient enthusiasm in his lectures to recruit other medics into the perhaps not so popular speciality of forensic pathology.

Bradshaw's recent involvement as an expert witness for the prosecution which led to the conviction of the serial strangler, Charles Hixon, brought him a high degree of publicity which he endured with quiet good humour, but obviously didn't enjoy.

Lisa Bradshaw, an art historian, will be remembered for her book on nineteenth-century illustrators of children's fairy stories in which she compared and contrasted the styles of John Tenniel, A. W. Bayes and Monro S. Orr.

The Bradshaws made their home in the Avon area, within commuting distance of London. Both were in their forty-ninth year at the time of the accident and had recently celebrated their silver wedding anniversary. They are survived by their only son, Simon.

Survival. An evocative word.

Simon moved restlessly, hemmed in by women, and tried not to think of his mother. Mrs Maybridge, on his left, smelt of scent, rather light, a sort of clover, honey clover. Mrs Sutton, the vicar's wife, on his right, smelt of peppermints and sweat and horses. She kept a couple of ponies in the paddock behind the vicarage and mucked out the stables herself. Had the vicar done the mucking out while she wrote the sermons, it might have been a better arrangement. Parts of his funeral address, or whatever it was called, were gruesome. The organ began to play. Apparently it was time to sing. He dropped his hymnbook.

It fell on Meg Maybridge's foot and she bent over and picked it up, then turned to the right page and glanced at the words before handing it back. "When our heads are bowed with woe, when our bitter tears o'erflow, when we mourn the lost, the dear, Jesu, Son of Mary, hear." Damn it, she thought, crossly and irreverently, whoever chose this ought to be shot. You don't sing hallelujah that the dead are dead, but neither should you twist the knife in those who are left behind. She looked anxiously at Simon. He smiled at her ruefully. "It's all right," he said.

But he wouldn't sing it, though he wouldn't have broken down if he had. The funeral was a charade to be endured. A public expression of private grief. But he didn't feel anything. When Kester-Evans, the headmaster, had called him out of the biology tutorial and told him that both his parents had been killed, he hadn't felt anything either. They had been words he couldn't believe. Later, when he had heard the details, he had formed a mental image of the accident in slow motion, a dream disaster in which flames lapped the car as it fell softly towards the grey smudge of the valley below. A terrible gentleness in the falling. A deep, long silence afterwards. In his imagination the car had been empty. As yet he couldn't envisage the bodies inside it. Couldn't. Wouldn't. Shock blotted out the unacceptable.

After the hymn the vicar intoned a prayer and then it was time for the bearers to approach the coffins. Simon hadn't been invited to be a bearer – out of kindness – concern – or maybe at five feet eight he was too short? He was strong enough, the same build as Maybridge who was one of them and only a couple of inches taller. The other five carrying his father's coffin were representatives of the local police, with the exception of a friend from one of the Home Office laboratories.

Of the six men carrying his mother's coffin he only knew Alan Drew, the family's solicitor, and Dr Donaldson, the medical superintendent of The Mount nursing home. Donaldson's lean, sheep-like face with its crest of thick wavy grey hair looked drawn and ill. Grief? Simon wondered. Well, yes, of course. Everyone grieved, or pretended they did. And they smiled at weddings.

The walk down the aisle was slow as the congregation shuffled out of the packed pews. The small nineteenth-century church had been designed for a small nineteenth-century village. Macklestone village in the twentieth century had expanded, but mercifully not a great deal. It still retained its rural character, despite its proximity to Bristol, mainly because the lie of the land precluded the building of large estates. The few commuters to London built their homes on the village perimeter and for the most part merged with the locals. They helped to swell the congregation, but they didn't make it burst at the seams.

That all these people were here today, these strangers, on account of his parents, or more specifically on account of his father's being hyped up by the Press, Simon found hard to understand. Ghoulish curiosity? His father had been doing clever things with genetic fingerprinting and other scientific oddities as long as he could remember and no one had taken any notice. Until the Rapunzel murders – as the Press called them. Was interest multiplied by five? Five long-haired prostitutes murdered by Charles Hixon in the space of fifteen months. The Rapunzel ratio. One murder in fifteen months would scarcely raise an eyebrow. His father had dealt with quite a few of those. Most of them ordinary. All of them nasty. When he had first discovered the nature of his father's job, he had been about nine at the time, he had refused to touch him and had voluntarily taken baths. If his father had been hurt he hadn't shown it, just waited patiently for common sense to prevail.

And now, in the porch, neatly coffined, he was waiting again. Someone had dropped a camera and it had spewed its innards over the top step. Disapproval drifted in the air like gunsmoke. If the media wanted a picture then it should be taken with decorum and at a distance, Simon heard someone mutter. His parents' dignity in death, someone else implied, had been sullied. Meg Maybridge touched his arm, "Okay? Just a bit of a holdup." Yes, he was okay, he told her, not bothered.

It was cool in the porch, verging on chilly, but very sunny. Bright enough for a good picture, perhaps. He noticed Kester-

11

Evans had pushed his way forward and was helping whoever it was who owned the camera to pick up the pieces. Typical headmaster behaviour. He'd probably quote something disapproving in Latin as he did so. Being rude in an ancient tongue was one of his foibles.

Maybridge, uncomfortably aware of the weight of the coffin on his shoulder, glanced at Superintendent Claxby who was sharing the weight with him at the front. Claxby, thin and dapper, hadn't the build or the temperament for carrying the dead. The Chief Constable had dragooned him into it, he'd complained bitterly to Maybridge. Not that he hadn't the greatest respect and liking for Bradshaw, he'd added, but six strong young p.c.s would have done just as well, or five p.c.s and the son. "What," he'd asked Maybridge, "was wrong with the son?"

Maybridge, not understanding the question, couldn't answer it. There was nothing wrong with the son other than bereavement. And that was a disease, curable eventually, that ran its own peculiar course. This double funeral would have been easier for the boy if it hadn't attracted so much attention. Maybridge wondered which of the tabloids the owner of the camera worked for. She was a woman of about thirty, dressed inappropriately in bright yellow. Only her hair looked funereal. Long and pitch black, it framed her pale face like a nun's coif. Whoever she was, she had behaved unprofessionally. She stood at last, looked closely at the flagged floor as if to make sure that no fragments were left, and then gave Kester-Evans a curt little nod and stepped back into the crowd.

Carefully, slowly, the bearers of the coffins walked to the porch doors.

Simon, aware of imminent movement, like cars revving up at amber traffic lights, spent a few moments reading the announcements on the church notice board. A light breeze rustled through them. An appeal for donations towards the cost of repairing the church roof. Lists of various duties. Flower arranging. Brass cleaning. A sponsored walk was to take place on Saturday, proceeds to go towards buying a minibus for the local senior citizens. Simon wondered where the O.A.P.s would go when they had it. A trip to the Cotswolds, perhaps. What would they sing as they went – old war songs? 'Wish me luck as you wave me goodbye'? In times of war it could be goodbye for ever – and they

12

knew it. Had his father had it in the back of his mind – a premonition, perhaps – that his goodbye to him was a final one? He had been unusually demonstrative. A warm last hug. And during the holiday he had seemed troubled – different in some indefinable way – or maybe he was imagining it.

And now it was time for the interment. He moved forward slowly with everyone else. Meg, at his side, resisted slipping her arm through his. She sensed that he was dazed rather than calm and didn't know how to help. He had no close relatives who might have taken over. His father's cousin had left his medical practice in the U.S.A. for a brief visit to assist with the identification and transporting of the bodies, but had been unable to stay on for the funeral. Grandparents would have been a godsend, though perhaps too old. She wondered how her own son, David, would cope in similar circumstances, but couldn't make the comparison. David was twenty-three and worldly wise. This boy had been incarcerated in a boarding school since the age of nine, a narrow environment which might suit some, though possibly not Simon. Facially he resembled his mother: fair haired, pale skinned, a tender mouth and eyes that were guarded.

It had rained during the night and the coffin bearers walked with care, their shoes caking with mud. Wreaths piled high on either side of the open grave shone with a sweet beauty on the artificial grass. The real stuff, Simon noticed, grew weedily and wantonly. Eventually, he supposed, the grave diggers, now discreetly out of sight, would roll up the fake turf, fill up the grave, which was deep enough for the two coffins, and collect their pay. Another day's work.

The vicar intoned the prayers of committal and then waited for Simon to throw a handful of earth on to the coffins. He hadn't been told about this part of the proceedings and thought it archaic, disrespectful, almost funny. *Ashes to ashes, dust to dust; in sure and certain hope of the Resurrection.*

Well . . . maybe. He wondered if the remains, obviously very few of them, had been placed in the right coffins. If not, would a hybrid male and female parent one day arise? Confusing. Or two parents with a swopping over of careers and personalities, perhaps? His mother performing wild and bloody autopsies. His father

13

painting pictures and performing domestic chores, calm and controlled, in a mansion in the sky.

The thought of domestic duties reminded him that after a funeral it was etiquette to provide the mourners, i.e. these people standing around looking embarrassed, with cups of tea and sandwiches at his home. He had made no provision for this, but perhaps someone else had. The villagers had rallied round ever since they'd heard the news of his parents' deaths. He appreciated their compassion, was even a little touched by it, but there were times when he wished to be left alone. The vicar was approaching, his hand outstretched. "Dear boy," he began, "dear Simon . . ." Simon backed away. The vicar's hand had traces of cemetery soil on it. So had his. He felt sick suddenly. Sweaty. Dirty. He mumbled something about it being a nice funeral – and thank you very much – but he had to go – rather quickly because – sorry, and all that, but . . .

Simon turned and ran.

He managed to reach the copse midway between the cemetery and the road to his home before flinging himself down on his knees and vomiting.

With the chief mourner suddenly taking off, the vicar wasn't sure what to do. He knew it was up to him to try to cope with the situation, but how? What should he say? The Bradshaws, though neighbours for a long time, had rarely attended church and he hadn't known them well socially. He scarcely knew their son at all. It was the Church's duty to christen, marry and bury, he believed, though some of his ecclesiastical colleagues made protesting noises about the Church being made use of by hypocritical non-believers. The Bradshaws' faith, or lack of it, in the Almighty, wasn't his concern any more; what to do about the boy was. His wife had arranged a light lunch up at the vicarage for Simon and personal friends amongst the mourners who had travelled more than a few miles to attend the funeral, but it was quite possible she had forgotten to tell him. She tended at times to be *distrait*, especially when something was wrong with one of her horses. The piebald had a bruised fetlock.

And the boy had a bruised heart. The Reverend Sutton, kind,

sentimental and totally inadequate as a pastor and leader of men, ran nervous fingers through his thick white hair while his parishioners and the strangers amongst them looked at him for guidance. He couldn't give it.

Down on the road the hearse driver switched on the ignition and crashed the gears noisily before moving off. It was the only sound in the startled air. Everyone turned and looked at it.

Rendcome, the Chief Constable, remembered booking a hearse driver for speeding once, a long time ago, when he'd been on the beat. At times of death you tend to think of your youth, not necessarily with nostalgia. Middle age was a comfortable age, emotionally. You had learnt self-control and were confident and authoritative. Unused to a passive role, he forced himself to remain passive. If anyone helped out with a sensible suggestion, such as bidding everyone a polite farewell, it would have to be one of the villagers. Maybridge, possibly, he'd lived here a long time. He turned his gaze on him.

Maybridge, aware of the mental semaphores directed towards him by his chief, ignored them. It was up to the vicar to bring the service to a close, and if he were wise he wouldn't make excuses for Simon. Excuses weren't necessary. The boy had taken off because he couldn't bear it any more. Understandable. His composure had been like a skin over a growing tumour and the skin had ruptured. The lad needed solitude for a while. In times of stress most people did. You didn't pursue them officiously and thrust your company upon them. Pursuing officially was a different matter altogether and a regrettable part of Maybridge's job. A reluctant sympathy for the felon on the run had always been difficult to quell when the man — woman — whoever it was

had finally been run to ground. He had once confessed this to Bradshaw. "Much as I'd loathe your job," he'd told him, "there are times when I'd almost be prepared to swop with you." He'd gone on to describe the lad who'd taken refuge in a cave in the Chilterns after knifing his girlfriend to death. Together with his sergeant, he'd found him cowering in the dark, very cold and hungry, his amber eyes wide and frightened like those of a cornered fox. Bradshaw's reply had been dry and laconic. "The fox wore bloodied shoes," he said, "group AB. Same as the girl's.

15

Careless of him." Bradshaw the pragmatist. And Bradshaw the father? Only Simon knew about that.

Meg was the first to see him as he left the copse and began climbing the lane towards the house that glittered with windows up on the hill. A white sugar lump of a house, large, expensive, and totally out of character with the ancient grey stone cottages that clustered nearby.

"There he is," she said.

Yes, Maybridge thought, there indeed he was, and there wasn't much they could do to help him. At least not yet. Later, he and Meg would call on the lad. Sometime this evening or tomorrow when he was more controlled. When he had first arrived from school, Meg had suggested he might like to spend a few days with them and had made up David's bed in anticipation. He had refused. He was used to being on his own, he'd said. An odd comment. There isn't much solitude in a boarding school unless you're clever enough to find it inside your head, in which case it's all right, or you're ostracised for one reason or another by your peers, in which case it certainly isn't. He hoped it was the former. He was a difficult boy to know.

Kester-Evans, Simon's headmaster for almost ten years, had agreed when Maybridge had done some gentle probing. Simon Bradshaw puzzled him, too, he'd admitted. Superficially he appeared to conform and was academically rather better than average. When younger he had been a nuisance from time to time, as most of them were. But not a spontaneous nuisance. An outsider watching herd behaviour and occasionally taking part because he thought he should, described his attitude. During the last couple of years, the difficult period of late adolescence, he had seemed to settle more into himself and let the herd go its own way. He had friends, two or three in the sixth form who, like him, had followed the same science syllabus and been promised places in medical school in the autumn, but they were friendships that didn't go deep. He hadn't wanted any of them to come to his parents' funeral. The support of his peers apparently wasn't necessary.

Kester-Evans, aware that his own support could quite easily have been dispensed with from Simon's point of view, watched the distant figure disappear round a curve on the hill. It was the first spontaneous act he had seen Simon make. An emotional, absolutely natural, escape from the unbearable. He wondered when he would be ready to return to school for the few remaining weeks of term but now wasn't the time to ask, and he couldn't wait the few tactful hours until the time was right. He had to drive back to Dorset to chair a managers' meeting at the school by five thirty. To go without taking leave of the boy seemed heartless, but someone here might deliver a verbal message for him later. Maybridge possibly. But the detective chief inspector was with the police contingent at the moment and he didn't want to intrude. The vicar, then? Or the vicar's wife, whose invitation to 'eats' up at the vicarage he had declined? 'Eats', what a crass expression! 'Funeral meats' was the old-fashioned term. What, he wondered, would future generations do to the elegant cadences of archaic and beautiful prose? Hammer it into the ground on their word processors? Kester-Evans, musing in the shadow of the church, looked at sunlight sparkling on muddied pools and was reminded of recent rain. He prudently carried his umbrella with him everywhere and before the service he had left it in the porch. He must remember to fetch it as soon as the vicar spoke whatever final words might suit the situation and release everyone from the trap of silence and embarrassment that held them so still.

The Reverend Sutton, forgetting in his confusion that he had already intoned it, raised his hand and repeated the blessing: "The grace of our Lord Jesus Christ, and the love of God, and the fellowship of the Holy Ghost, be with us all evermore. Amen."

There were a few murmured amens and then the mourners moved slowly away.

Maybridge, about to do the same, halted in surprise as his sergeant approached him, carrying one of the wreaths. Radwell, his hands shaking, was holding it at arm's length as if he were a nervous acolyte about to present an unspeakable object at a Black Mass. "I'm awfully sorry, sir," Radwell muttered. "I should have spotted it earlier." Lying semi-concealed in the circlet of flowers was a pig's trotter streaked with dried blood.

2

Rhoda Osborne was sitting on a bench in the porch eating a Mars bar when Kester-Evans returned for his umbrella. She felt light-headed due to too long a fast. She'd had nothing to eat since a cup of coffee and a biscuit at Paddington buffet before catching the Bristol train. The chocolate now was necessary. She had hoped to be emotionally detached from all that was going on here, but it hadn't been possible. The service hadn't bothered her too much; she had sat in one of the back pews and made all the usual responses with everyone else. But watching the coffins being carried down the aisle on their final inevitable journey had stripped away her calm, forcing her to grip the back of the pew in front so that she could remain standing. Later, at the graveside, she had closed her eyes and listened to a bird singing. A thrush. A sweet gentle twittering that mocked the vicar's solemn tones. Mindless, happy creatures, birds. Humans know pain, are prone to tears. Today she hadn't wept. Be thankful for that, Rhoda, she told herself. You are in control. The only stupid thing you did was to drop your camera. And now the creep who helped you pick it up has come looking for you.

She watched Kester-Evans coldly as he went over to the umbrella stand. He nodded at her politely, found his black umbrella with the carved rosewood handle, and was about to go when he noticed a fragment of lens under the table holding the prayer books. He retrieved it and handed it to her. "There is a time and place for everything," he said censoriously. "It is not good form to take photographs of the deceased at such close proximity."

She smiled faintly. "They were boxed. And no photograph was taken."

"The bearers might have tripped on the shards." Her tone annoyed him.

"In which case they would no longer have been boxed and you would have been right to censure me."

He knew he had no right under any circumstances, it was one of the weaknesses of schoolmastering to assume a right where none existed. Even so, the vision of shattered coffins was grisly. "It would have been appalling for the boy. For Simon, their son."

"But it didn't happen. And I didn't intend taking a picture. Afterwards, at the interment. Not then."

He didn't believe her, though it could have been true. When the boys lied to him he usually 'talked things through', as he put it, and the truth emerged eventually. Why he should bother about the truth now, he didn't know. It wasn't his concern. Even so, almost out of habit, he sat beside her and waited for anything else she might have to say.

She moved impatiently. Half rose, than sat again. Examined her nails, carefully manicured and painted a dark shade of maroon. Sighed.

He was a patient inquisitor, adept at silence. She broke it at last.

"He wore a black tie. For God's sake, what ghoul would give a kid like that a black tie?"

He had given it. And Simon wasn't a kid, he was a sixth former in his final term. Being called a ghoul wasn't pleasant.

"It could have been one of his father's," she said, "though I've never seen Peter wear one like that. A bow tie with a tuxedo, sometimes. Never a black lumpy monstrosity."

He was interested that she knew Professor Bradshaw that well. Perhaps she wasn't a professional photographer, after all. He was

19

about to ask her when she got up and wandered over to the door. The mourners were congregating in groups down by the cemetery gates and some were leaving in their cars. It hadn't been difficult to suss out the police amongst the bearers of Peter's coffin and they were still together, she noticed. D.C.I. Maybridge, the local man, would have been more difficult to place if she hadn't already found out who he was. When standing with his colleagues he exuded an air of authority like the rest of them, and of very obvious annoyance when she'd dropped the camera in the porch, but when reading the lesson there had been a depth of sincerity in his voice and he had looked at the boy with compassion. He might be approachable some day. So far she had had no luck with any of them.

Kester-Evans, hoping for a response, introduced himself. "John Kester-Evans, headmaster at Collingwood in Dorset. Simon's school, and his father's before him, though not in my time, of course."

She glanced at him over her shoulder. So this gangling elderly man with the straw-coloured hair was Simon's dominie. A useful link, perhaps. Worth cultivating, maybe. She went to sit beside him again. "He must have thought well of Collingwood," she said, "to send his son there." It was polite. Peter's words came back to her. "A minor public school. I found it bearable. I think Simon does. The head is a bit of a pain, but harmless. Well meaning." Harmless. A favourite adjective. He had used it frequently. Well meaning? Yes, she could believe it. She smiled at him and her smile transformed her.

Kester-Evans, a bachelor in an all-male environment, responded with some confusion. "Yes. Quite so. Thank you." He always believed first judgments to be correct, and they usually were, but now he was less sure. The hard, pure lines of her face had softened. He told her he was concerned about Simon. During the last conversation he'd had with him, just before the funeral, the boy had mumbled something about medicine being "the sickest career there is, especially my father's branch of it", and then, aware of the *double entendre*, had tried to make a joke of it. It wouldn't be funny if he refused his place at medical school. The bereaved tended to act on impulse. The sooner he returned to school for the last few

20

weeks of term, the better. He needed a guiding hand and the company of his peers.

"His friends here in the village are very helpful," he went on. "The Maybridges particularly so. But the academic relationship is important. I've guided Simon and I know his potential. He'll never be as brilliant as his father, but if he chooses another speciality in medicine he could do very well."

Brilliance, Rhoda thought, could blind. Like a diamond it had many facets. Sharp edged. Sometimes cruel. "Cadavers," she said quietly, "don't bleed."

"What?" Kester-Evans thought he had misheard her.

She let him think it and then responded in the way she believed he would want her to. Her own career as a freelance journalist was important to her, she said glibly. In retrospect she cherished her years at university and wouldn't have missed them for anything. But she understood Simon's attitude now. Grief was unbalancing. She hesitated. "Someone just a few years older than him – well, someone my age – might be able to get through to him."

Steady, she told herself, you're going too far, too fast.

Kester-Evans glanced at the camera case which was bulging in the wrong direction like a dismembered corpse in a plastic bag. And then he looked at her face again. She smiled her transforming smile.

"It was unfortunate," he said.

"Indeed, yes," she agreed.

"Expensive?" He was playing for time, making up his mind.

"Yes, but it doesn't matter. I'm sorry I was rude to you just now, but I was upset. Not about dropping it – a camera can be replaced – but dropping it where I did. I'd hoped to take a picture at the graveside, as I told you. I'm planning to write a profile of the Bradshaws for one of the Sundays – *The Times*, possibly, or the *Observer*." (Well, it seemed a good idea, impromptu but plausible.)

They were quality papers and he approved of them with just a few reservations. His reservations about her were fast disappearing. "You've known Simon's family a long time?"

"Long enough."

Maybridge might have wondered, "Long enough for what?"

21

Kester-Evans, more naive, more trusting, didn't. He explained that he had to return to Dorset for an urgent appointment at the school and wouldn't have time to call on Simon before leaving. "I've bought his rail ticket – seeing it should persuade him to use it. It's valid until the end of the month, but I don't want him to wait that long. I was hoping someone from the village, one of his friends, would hand it in and pass on a message from me." He took it out of his wallet. "I could post it, of course, and write, but a letter is too easily ignored."

She agreed that it was. "The sooner you're able to talk to him directly, the better. He needs a little gentle urging to return to Collingwood without delay."

A little gentle urging. He was so easy to mimic. Too easy.

She added hesitantly, afraid of blowing it by appearing too keen, that she didn't have to return to London until the evening and that she would be happy to call on Simon if he would like her to.

Her hesitancy won him. "It's most kind of you. I'm grateful." He handed her the ticket. "If you could give the lad just a few hours on his own before calling he might be more receptive to your good counselling."

She promised that she would and that she would be tactful. "Is there any message, apart from returning to Collingwood, that you'd like me to pass on to him?"

Kester-Evans thought about this for a moment or two. He hadn't written the usual letter of condolence. It hadn't been necessary, he had been in contact with Simon most of the time. But today, this special day, perhaps something more spiritual should be touched upon. In similar cases he had found Ovid's quotation about immortality suitable and soothing. It began '*Morte carent animae*' and was rather lengthy. In translation it might sound clumsy and even – though God forbid – a little pompous. He had genuine sympathy for the boy, so why not express it simply? "Give him my best wishes," he said rather stiffly. "Tell him I'll be in touch soon." He ran his fingers over the knob of his umbrella. Silky wood. Very smooth. "Tell him . . . tell him . . . that his father was proud of him . . . had great hopes for him . . . and . . ." He knew he should mention Simon's mother, but didn't know what to say. In all the

22

years the boy had been at Collingwood he had never met her. "And his mother, too," he finished lamely.

"Yes," Rhoda said, "his mother, too." Her voice was clear and steady, but she was careful not to look at him.

Embarrassed, a little emotional, Kester-Evans took his leave of her. It wasn't until he was musing over the day's events some while later that he realised he hadn't asked her name.

Lisa Bradshaw had loved the almond tree. She had planted it as a sapling, tended it, watched it grow. Now it cascaded its spring blossom in droplets of white on the rough orchard grass. This had been Lisa's private place, well away from the house and not seen from any of the windows. Lisa's refuge when she wanted to be alone.

And now her son's.

Simon had approached with some trepidation, as he had used to in the days when he might find her there. His sickness had gone but the pain, the natural pain, was intense. He wanted her to be there, as he had last seen her. She had been wearing slacks, blue cotton or linen, a light material, too light for winter. But the day hadn't been cold. Sunlight had slanted on her short, crisply curled hair. From a distance she had looked like a tall slim boy, not a woman in her forties. Her breasts were small and her hips very neat. Everything about her was neat. Coolly elegant. It was hard to imagine her doing anything as gross as giving birth. She could hardly bear to touch him. He flinched, remembering.

On that last day, that last day he had seen her, he had sought her out on his father's orders so that he might say goodbye to her properly. His father's words. It was his last day of the Christmas holidays and he was due back at Collingwood. His father had put the luggage in the car and they were ready to go. She had played the maternal role during breakfast, had even cooked bacon for him. And she had asked dutiful questions. Had he remembered to pack everything? Had he enough socks? Whether he had or not was patently of no interest to her. She hoped he would have a 'good term', whatever that might mean. And he had thanked her for hoping it. He had gone upstairs to fetch his anorak and, glancing through the window, had seen her walking down the garden. The maternal role, this time, hadn't included standing waiting for him in the hall. Not even a perfunctory farewell. It had hurt. It always did. But it never surprised. His father had been irritated by the omission and he had sought her out to please him. Reluctantly.

The long winter grass had muffled his footsteps as he had approached. Miserably. Silently. She was unaware that he was there and was startled when she turned and saw him. "My God," she said, "do you have to creep up on me like that?" She controlled herself, assumed the maternal role again. "I'm sorry, dear, but you startled me." She 'deared' him a lot – 'deared' most of her acquaintances, too – half the time, he guessed, she couldn't remember their names. He said he was sorry, too. She seemed to wait for more – his reason for being there. He said he'd come to say goodbye. Obviously she thought they'd already said it, but she extended her hand. "Of course, dear. Have a good journey. Remember me to that headmaster of yours with a name like a bird – Kester – Kestrel – whatever." He said he would and was careful not to point out that you can't remember someone you've never seen. It was natural, perhaps, for men who had just turned eighteen to shake hands with their mothers, rather than kiss. It hadn't been natural when he was younger. The handshake was dutiful and very brief. His father's leavetaking up at the school had been unusually demonstrative. He had hugged him. "It's okay, you know," he said. "Life's a bit of a survival course. You jump a few hurdles, knock a few down, eventually with average luck you arrive where you want to. Your mother can't help being the way she is. Don't let it bother you."

He wondered now, as he stood by the almond tree, what a normal domestic set-up would have been like. His father had planned holidays for him that took him away from home as much as possible. He had gone on various adventure courses. He could absail. Navigate. Pitch a tent. A desert island would hold no terror for him. Nothing physical bothered him. Except sex. Girls, as far as he knew, played a passive role. What if he couldn't do it?

His mother and father had been sufficiently adept, or careless, to produce him. They had been sufficiently in love – or was that too strong a word? – to celebrate twenty-five years of marriage by going abroad together. So with them it must have been all right. He wasn't quite sure what he meant by 'it'. Not just sex – more than that. Had they ever touched each other lovingly? He tried to remember occasions when they had. There had been no flinching away from each other, of that he was sure. He was the one who had to keep his distance. His father's last hug had been unexpected. He was grateful for it. Would remember it.

He touched the bole of the tree. It felt flaky and warm. Tiny insects moved busily in the angle of a branch. The air smelt greenly of sunlight on sap.

This was his place now. He could approach it boldly, more boldly as time went on. The rickety, ancient and very comfortable captain's chair in the summerhouse, just a few yards away from the tree, was his, too. She had spent hours sitting on it, writing sometimes, sketching, or just lying back with her eyes closed. Dreaming. Of what? I needed to know you, he thought. I needed to talk to you. I can't hate you. I can't love you. So why this pain now? This bloody, terrible pain?

He walked back to the house. Away from her. Trying to ward off the pain as if it were something physical outside himself. Something that wouldn't go.

The phone was ringing in the hall.

He watched it. Listened to it. Took it off the receiver. Replaced it. Removed it again before the caller could re-connect. An easy way of shutting people up. He didn't want the conversation of strangers. Not even of friends. There had been quite a few messages of condolence over the phone. Mostly from people he didn't know. And there had been a large pile of condolence cards and letters.

arranged the cards on every available flat surface in the sitting-room. The two on the television were particularly grand, large gold crosses entwined with violets. 'In loving memory of two wonderful people' had been the message on one. 'In the hands of God' had been written on the other. And there had been a verse about the mills of God grinding slowly, hand written in red ink on the opposite page. He hadn't bothered to read beyond the first line. The usual maudlin tripe, he'd thought. Now, glancing in at them from the hallway, he noticed that a draught from the window had blown several of them on to the floor. He went in and picked them up and then decided to get rid of the lot of them. The room without them would look less of a ghoulish shrine.

Maybridge, aware that Simon had deliberately disconnected the telephone, shrugged. He had phoned because Rendcome had told him to. The Chief Constable's reaction to the tampered wreath had been less than calm. Simon, he said, should be told about it. All in good time, Maybridge had thought.

Police matters were normally discussed in police stations but today was an exception. They had driven over to Maybridge's home, which was just a few minutes away from the church, and were gathered together in the living-room. The wreath, with the pig's trotter nestling in a ring of sweetly perfumed yellow roses, was on the mahogany coffee table. Meg, reasonably careful of her furniture, had placed the current issue of the *Guardian* under it. Why Rendcome hadn't just removed the trotter from the wreath she couldn't understand. Later, she supposed, she or Tom would have to take the wreath back, minus the trotter, and put it on the grave again together with the others.

The situation was disturbing but not unique. Hate mail and the occasional obscene object were all part of policing. Maybridge had been taunted by a lunatic's letter at a writers' conference some while ago. That had had its funny side. This, she conceded, hadn't.

She wondered at what stage she would be expected to invite her three unexpected guests to lunch. She had prepared cold roast pork and salad for herself and Tom. There would probably be enough for everyone. No one, just now, would be keen on the pork.

Superintendent Claxby commented drily that had Bradshaw been present he would have traced the lineage of the pig back to its distant ancestors, given a learned discourse on its claws, minutely dissected its hairs, and then named its present owner. But as he wasn't and as this was probably a final gesture from an aggrieved relative of Hixon's, the Rapunzel strangler whom Bradshaw's evidence had put behind bars, he didn't see much point in bothering with it.

"All the same," Rendcome persisted, "a final gesture or not,

26

Simon should be aware of it. We would be failing in our duty if we didn't tell him. His father would wish it."

It was easy, Meg thought, to attribute attitudes to the dead. Peter might or might not wish it. Lisa wouldn't care. "If it were David," she said, "and that wreath had been Tom's, I'd put that nasty piece of meat in the bin and not tell David a word about it."

Maybridge smiled at her. And I'd give you my celestial blessing, he thought, if I were anywhere around.

"Ah, but as David's mother that would be your prerogative," Rendcome pointed out. "If Mrs Bradshaw were here the decision would be hers."

Lisa's decisions about anything were, to put it mildly, bizarre. Obviously Rendcome hadn't known her. She felt impatient with him, and with Tom, too. Tom should have refused to make the phone call. What would he have said if Simon had answered? "Someone has desecrated the Chief Constable's wreath and he's hopping mad?" The fact that it was a wreath from the local constabulary and with a few appropriate lines written on the mourning card in Rendcome's careful script added insult to injury, she guessed. Had it been the vicar's wreath it wouldn't have rankled so much.

It crossed her mind that someone at headquarters might not have liked Bradshaw. A policeman could have been responsible. She looked thoughtfully at Sergeant Radwell, who had found it. The trotter hadn't lain on top of the rosebuds, it had been semi-concealed beneath them. Radwell must have done a little probing. Why?

Radwell, who had been sitting in silence for the last ten minutes, was debating whether or not to point out the obvious or to shut up about it. Superintendent Claxby had rightly praised Professor Bradshaw's forensic skill in his take-off of him just now, but he hadn't suggested that Bradshaw would have removed the trotter and looked at the square of greaseproof paper that was under it – as he had. None of the senior policemen, not even his immediate boss, had done so. He suggested now, rather diffidently, that he should.

Maybridge, aware that the young sergeant rarely spoke out of turn unless he had good reason to, complied. The piece of paper, grubby and distinctly unpleasant, had something scrawled on it in pencil. It was difficult to make it out. He took it over to the window and read, holding it up to the light:

Prov. Chap. 19.9.

He frowned, puzzled.

"Proverbs, chapter nineteen, verse nine." Radwell mumbled. It was embarrassing to instruct one's elders. And bad policy. He had gained his sergeant's stripes by being as tactful as possible and producing immaculate paperwork.

"Which is . . . ?" Maybridge asked.

Radwell said he didn't know. He had spent some while in theological college before discovering he hadn't the temperament to be a priest, and been teased about it by his younger colleagues from time to time. And by some of the senior ones too. Surely Maybridge didn't seriously believe he'd learnt the Bible by heart?

Maybridge, aware he'd asked a stupid question, looked around for the family Bible he'd been leafing through recently, trying to find something suitable for this morning's service, and then he remembered that Meg had tidied it away in her study upstairs – if tidied was the right word. The study, unlike the rest of the house, was in a controlled state of chaos. Meg's university notes were in a pile of manilla folders on the floor by the window. Her students' essays, separated by elastic bands, covered the surface of the antique cherry wood desk. A word processor, a gift from one of her fellow dons who had recently retired and didn't want it any more, was balanced on a blanket box by the bookcase. The bookcase spilled books like a river in full spate from the bottom shelf. But the Bible was where it usually was. On the top shelf, incongruously sandwiched between two volumes of Rousseau which happened to be the same size and held it neatly.

Maybridge returned with it to the living-room and, resisting the temptation to look it up himself, he handed the Bible to Rendcome.

Rendcome, after a little fumbling, found the right section. He read the proverb aloud: "A false witness shall not be unpunished, and he that speaketh lies shall perish."

The words were chilling.

28

No one spoke for a moment or two.

Rendcome closed the Bible and put it on the table beside the wreath. He addressed Maybridge directly. "We were both in court when Hixon was sentenced. Do you remember his words to the judge?"

Maybridge did. He had accused Spencer-Leigh of being swayed by the false evidence of the forensic expert – Professor Bradshaw. And then, before he could be stopped, he had turned to the jury and in a sing-song tone, verging on hysteria, had quoted a psalm at them. The words were memorable. Maybridge repeated them. "When he shall be judged, let him be condemned: and let his prayer become sin. Let his days be few; and let another take his office."

Bradshaw hadn't been in court at the time but had heard about it afterwards. He had called Hixon a Bible freak, unfortunately in the presence of the Press. 'Strangler sings psalms' was the *Sun*'s headline. Pithy and alliterative.

"There was more," Rendcome said, "before the judge silenced him. A biblical quotation about not extending him any mercy – or favouring his fatherless children. An overt threat to his son, wouldn't you say?"

Superintendent Claxby, less emotional than his superior, pointed out that Hixon was safely locked up and couldn't be a threat to anyone. "At least, not for a long time. In the good old days of hanging he wouldn't be a threat at all." This last remark was addressed with malice aforethought to Maybridge and his po-faced sergeant in the hope of annoying them.

Maybridge, too bothered about Simon to respond, decided a word or two – a carefully edited word or two – to the boy might not come amiss, after all. He would see him in the morning and point out as gently as possible that his father had made enemies, and that generally enemies could be ignored, but it didn't do any harm to know that they existed. Behind bars, of course.

3

Rhoda, roaming free in a territory she hadn't explored before, spent some while orientating. The village was dominated, quite gently and prettily, by the church, and over on the other side of the valley where the ground climbed up to the main road, by The Mount, which wasn't pretty but grey and rather grand like a carefully preserved monastery. A tributary of the Avon, hardly more than a brown sluggish stream, spanned by a bridge, neatly divided the village. On one side was a network of roads that seemed to meander without any serious intention of arriving anywhere and then turned corners into narrow streets of old and charming cottages. On the other side was a cluster of shops. The butcher's was approached by a path across a vegetable garden where thin little cabbage plants grew in carefully weeded umber soil. Later, they would flourish, plump and coarse leaved, in the summer sun. A general store sold groceries and farming equipment and had a sandy smell like rain on a beach. A hairdresser's next door to it displayed a faded cardboard cut-out of a blonde model in the window. Rhoda touched her long dark hair and remembered Peter's fingers touching it. A sensual man, Simon's father. This was his village, though it was hard to imagine him here. It was too silent. Too still. Like being buried in gauze.

She walked on. He had trodden these pavements, too. Called in at the local, the Avon Arms, for a pint, perhaps. She had had a ploughman's lunch there earlier, mainly to kill time, and it hadn't been bad. The barman had expected more trade after the Brad-shaws' funeral, he'd told her. A crass remark. Trade at the garage on the corner didn't seem to be doing any better. There was only one car on the forecourt, a dark blue Mercedes which the owner was filling up with petrol. Some of it spilt and the air was pungent with fumes. He replaced the hose and then glanced in her direction. She recognised him as one of the coffin bearers, the tall, bony, grey-haired one who had been carrying Lisa's. Fearing another Kester-Evans type lecture, Rhoda turned her back on him and walked briskly down one of the side roads.

Doctor Steven Donaldson watched her for a moment or two, but with little interest. She had been one of the many strangers at the funeral. The one who had dropped the camera. Just another intruder who had come to watch the show. A woman of no consequence.

No one was of any consequence, now that Lisa was dead.

Except, perhaps, Lisa's son.

"Fairy stories," Lisa had told Donaldson, all those years ago, "are not for children. They are for the old, the ugly, the wise, and the unwise." She had spoken a lot of nonsense, under sedation, and he had sat by her bedside and smiled and stroked her hand. Later, less sedated and obviously irritated, she had scratched him. Tiny globules of blood lay like red beads on his wrist. Professionally

blandly. "Lick them," she had urged. "Let's play vampires. Let's pretend I'm really and truly mad." And then she had turned her face into the pillow and wept.

Tears are cathartic. He let her get on with her weeping and went to the adjoining bathroom to wash his wrist before the blood could stain his shirt cuff.

Treating a young mother for post-natal depression was one of his less onerous chores – usually. You prescribed pills. You counselled. In The Mount, where the therapy was costly, you sat on beds and smiled. The Mount catered for a multiplicity of nervous disorders. Some serious. Lisa, he believed, would get better. Given time.

The first stage was to persuade her to leave her bed. In the first few days she had clung to it as if afraid someone would tip her out of it. Her husband, Donaldson guessed, might have been tempted, but a nursing home bed is sacrosanct, not like the marital bed. Marital beds, he mused, were the source of much trauma.

The second stage was to get her to mingle with the other patients. To discover that someone is a lot madder than you – and everyone thinks that about everyone else – restores one's equilibrium to some extent. She had ceased to cower.

The third stage was for her to see the child again. Her son, now two months old. Donaldson had warned her husband not to thrust the baby at her. "If she wants to hold him, well and good. If she doesn't, don't make a fuss. Above all, don't get angry."

Bradshaw had got angry, but not with her, with him. He hadn't displayed his anger, of course, but Donaldson had sensed it. Two professionals from different medical fields meeting on common ground and locking horns like a couple of combative bulls. A push here, a thrust there, a little ground given, a little ground lost. The psychiatrist lectured the pathologist – oh, so carefully – on how he should treat his wife and child. The pathologist listened politely and wished the psychiatrist dead. Well – not dead. But silent. Meanwhile the baby cried in his pram. And Lisa watched him cry, quite without emotion.

It was a step in the right direction, Donaldson told Bradshaw. Not caring might be a negative emotion, but at least it was safe. "I don't believe she'll hurt the baby." He didn't add "again".

Bradshaw hadn't told him in so many words that she had tried to smother the child, but he had been in the job long enough to pick up the nuances, to read between the lines, to recognise and evaluate anxiety. He had heard it all before; in some cases after the mothers had been put on the 'at risk' list by social workers.

"You understand," Bradshaw said, "that it has been serious?"

"Yes."

"I have employed a nanny and I'll keep her on as long as necessary."

"That might be for quite a long time."

"What are you trying to tell me?"

"The child needs to be loved. I don't think Lisa is capable of it yet. You will know when she is."

Bradshaw, husband and father, hoped that he would know, but at least both roles had been handed back to him. "Then I can take her home?"

"That's up to her. It depends on whether or not she feels ready to go."

Lisa, when asked, had chosen to stay another week. A few hundred pounds wouldn't hurt Bradshaw's pocket, Donaldson had guessed, and he had accepted his wife's decision with barely concealed relief.

What, Donaldson had wondered fleetingly, was the nanny like? Lisa, ill, wasn't prepossessing.

Simon hadn't intended getting drunk on the evening of his parents' funeral. He hadn't deliberately sat down with a bottle of scotch and one of his father's beer tankards and sloshed it in. The drinks cupboard held a neat assortment of appropriate glasses for various wines and spirits, but the tankard was large and handy and held a squirt or two of soda without getting overfull. Later he ignored the soda.

The trouble, he told himself, was the house. It was viciously, tauntingly bright. It shone in the evening sunlight, which seemed to enter it in low sparkling swoops as the clouds came and went and the wind blew merrily. He tried playing music on the tape recorder to diminish the sound of the wind, but all the tapes were his mother's and his mother's taste wasn't his. She had liked Scarlatti's harpsichord sonatas – thin tinkling sounds that did him no good at all. Haydn was better, but not much. His father, a self-confessed moron when it came to music, had taken him to concerts from time to time and been patently bored stiff by them. His father's sense of duty when it came to family life had been erratic. A series of father and son outings, some of which they'd both enjoyed, followed by his father's absence on a case – well, probably on a case. A lonely period spent avoiding his mother; difficult because she was avoiding him too and they tended to meet in places where they didn't expect to.

But they never met in her studio at the top of the house.

Clutching his tankard and bottle of scotch, he made his way there now. She had called it her den when he was little and had made growling noises at him which were supposed to be a joke, but weren't. Not that he had needed to be scared away from it. A couple of visits when he knew she was out in the garden had been enough.

She painted here. And she wrote here. Sometimes she slept here. The heavily patterned Welsh quilt in shades of mustard and fawn was draped neatly over the green velvet studio couch. Her easel was folded and the paints stacked on a low shelf by the washbasin. Her typewriter and reference books had been put away in the white wall cupboard. Obviously she had tidied the room before going on holiday. Or someone else had – afterwards.

The large dormer window, painted a pale blue inside, looked across the orchard. The topmost branches of the almond tree were just visible from here and looked like the tip of a white frilly parasol. The blossom wouldn't last long in the wind. Soon it would lie like snow out of season.

The room felt cold.

Simon drew the quilt over his shoulders and sat on the couch. The wall opposite was covered with a mural of fairy tale characters. Some malignant. Some delicately beautiful. None lovable. He knew nothing of Tenniel and wasn't aware that she had painted it in his style, or as near to his style as she could get. The mural didn't trouble him, but the bird with gaudy plumage sketched boldly in acrylic on a piece of stiff cardboard yellow with age, did. It was held by a couple of drawing pins pushed into the back of the door. He had seen it before. Once. And afterwards in nightmares, evolving out of the darkness, taking form and colour and then slowly disappearing. Someone, a nanny or an au-pair, had read him the Grimms' fairy story when he was five or six, but it was his mother's voice he heard in the nightmare. A voice heavy with melancholy. He heard echoes of it now:

My mother killed me;
My father grieved for me;
My sister, little Marline,
Wept under the almond-tree;
Kywitt, kywitt, what a beautiful bird am I!

In the nightmare the bird's wing had been across his face, making it hard to breathe. He took some deep breaths now and chided himself for being a fool. When you're eighteen a goddamned bird and a shitty verse from a shitty story don't frighten you. Not any more. And you don't give a damn because you're sitting here alone and don't know what the hell to do with yourself. You're free. As free as any goddamned bird that ever was. Everything is fine. Get it? Fine! Wonderful! Okay? So stop being so stupid.

A few words of consolation from himself to himself.

They didn't help much.

But the whisky did.

"A pig's trotter isn't very original," Maybridge said. "I mean, not very original as a form of abuse." He realised he was sounding rather inane, certainly quite unclear, but the conversation was proving even more difficult than he had expected. For one thing the lad was quite obviously hung-over and had only just got up. He was still in his pyjamas. Or possibly his father's. Middle-aged striped pyjamas, a size too big.

He tried again. "Rams' heads on farm gates – threats of that sort. You've probably heard of them, read of them. Lunatic actions. Actions that stop at that, usually." He paused, remember-

didn't remember it, too. "Anyone in your father's profession attracts both praise and resentment," he went on. "In his case the praise was well deserved. His testimony couldn't be faulted. Anyone put behind bars because of it has been put there justly. Someone on the outside – a misguided relative, perhaps – made a stupid gesture with the wreath. I don't know if your father had any hate mail. If he had he probably destroyed it. Regarded it with contempt. Rightly. But if you ever get any – or a stupid phone call – or, well, anything that bothers you, then tell me. Promise?"

35

Simon nodded. They were sitting at the kitchen table and the kitchen clock pointed to half past nine. The kitchen looked very neat. The pile of dishes he had last seen in the sink the night before had been washed and put away.

Maybridge asked him if he had had any breakfast.

Simon shuddered.

"You could try a prairie oyster. A raw egg in spirits." Unwise advice, perhaps, but it had worked for him from time to time in the past.

Simon said he was all right. He didn't want anything. Thanks all the same.

"How do you intend spending the day?"

Simon shrugged. He was still sleep sodden and the night had been weird.

"If you're wise you'll get some fresh air. Walk over to see Meg whenever you want to. She'll give you a bite to eat when you feel like it."

Maybridge had to drive to headquarters so couldn't have prolonged the talk even if the lad had been in a fit state to listen. Meg had mentioned the chores he would have to face at some time – an acknowledgment of the letters of condolence; a brief word or two in the local paper would probably suffice – and the disposal of his parents' clothes to a local charity. "Tell him, if the time seems right to tell him, that he can unload all that on to me if he can't face it."

The time wasn't right to tell him. And somebody else, according to the state of the kitchen, must have been looking after him, though there was no one else on the premises now. The vicar's wife had probably been around. And he'd hit the bottle after she'd gone. A natural reaction. Simon noticed the slight smile on the Chief Inspector's lips and, despite the thumping in his head, managed to smile back. A disbelieving, amazed kind of smile, Maybridge noticed. Grief was like that. It unhinged you emotionally. Tears and laughter were perilously close and suppressing them wasn't easy. And the whisky, gin, whatever it was, had probably taken the lid right off. Good therapy, but better in small doses.

"We'll talk again," Maybridge said, taking his leave.

"Yes." Simon saw him to the door.

He thought the woman had said that to him, too, but he could have been mistaken.

She had let herself in through the conservatory, she'd told him, as he hadn't answered the front door bell. He had been too far gone to question her right to let herself in. She was there, that was all he knew. And he was sitting on the bottom step of the stairs, which seemed unusually steep and were in constant motion like the companionway of a ship. He had told her that he was all at sea, which seemed a reasonable remark at the time.

She had left him sailing his turbulent ocean, returning at intervals to see if he needed anything. Her laconic "All right?" and his nod in reply was the extent of their conversation. He'd thought she was from the W.I. or the Mothers' Union until she'd helped him upstairs to bed. And put him in the wrong bedroom. He'd crawled under the duvet, fully dressed. And she'd stood over him and made him take his clothes off and put on the pyjamas she'd found under the pillow. He'd thought vaguely that it was like being dressed in a shroud – and that his father would be embarrassed – and that if he thought he couldn't do 'it', then he was wrong, but that he might not do 'it' very well because he was feeling rather muzzy. And that he liked the smell of her, but not the look of her fingernails, and that her hair had the texture of a cat's fur – a black Persian cat.

He might have told her some of this. He wasn't sure. Some time during the night she came and sat on the bed, but didn't touch him. She said "Peter", mistaking him for his father, perhaps. And then, very quietly, she had mooched around the moonlit room like an animal getting the feel of a lair. He fell asleep and dreamt of a forest, dank and dark, where the leaves fell like rain.

In the morning she was gone.

Rhoda caught the early morning train to London at Bristol Parkway station after hitching a lift in a milk lorry. She felt tired after a sleepless, busy, very profitable night. It had been extremely lucky that the boy was pissed and she could search the premises without being disturbed, though her conscience had told her to tidy up the place as a kind of reparation before leaving him. She had looked in on him when dawn was breaking, a final look in

37

case the booze had worn off or he'd been sick. He had been lying hunched up on his side, one arm supporting his head, the pillow on the floor. A restless sleeper like his father. The bed was by the window and there was enough light for her to see the growth of stubble on his chin. Peter had shaved twice a day. Once would do for the boy – for a while. He'd had an erection last night when she'd helped him undress, but hadn't seemed aware of it. Kept talking about cats.

She smiled now, remembering. He was the kind of kid you wanted to protect, not thieve from.

But stealing Lisa's diaries had been irresistible.

She had found them hidden under a couple of Irish linen table-cloths, of all things, in the bottom drawer of a chest in her study – studio – whatever the extraordinary, mural dominated room was called. The top drawers held typewritten notes on the artistic style of various illustrators of children's stories: A. W. Bayes, Monro S. Orr, Arthur B. Frost, Henry Holiday and John Tenniel. (Artistic and literary obsession with the grim works of Grimm?) The bottom drawer had been locked but the lock was loose and she had prised it open easily. The white tablecloths, a dusty beige along the folded edges, had been there a long time. And so had the diaries. She had flipped through some of the earliest ones and a few sentences had caught her attention here and there:

Nanny Ferguson loves Simon. Good. Nanny Ferguson loves Peter. Good. Good. Peter screws Nanny Ferguson. Bad. Poor Nanny Ferguson. Poor little owl.

Peter in Hull. Nasty murder. Nasty job. Simon thinks Peter's job nasty, too. Sorry for Peter. Peter needs Simon. Simon needs Peter. Can't be sorry for Simon. Wish I could.

Simon six today. Took him to The Mount to see the loonies. Peter cross. Told him Hans Andersen's mum took little Hans to see the loonies, too. Loonies played with Hans. Hans liked them. Hans' mum cleaned the loony bin and weeded the garden. The Mount loonies didn't play with Simon, but Doctor Donaldson did.

Several months later:

Steve Donaldson says I'm okay – well, almost okay – but to keep on visiting. He has a patient called Shirley, he told me, who paints another patient called Marylou. Not on canvas. On flesh. Sunflower breasts with little brown nipples. Daisy chains around her throat. Sounds fun. Wanted to see. Steve wouldn't let me. "The privacy of the patients must be respected." Okay – but why tell me? Who cleans the bath afterwards?

Later still:

Much, much better after a period of being rotten. Simon to start boarding at new school. Feel great about this. He's nine. Good for him to get away. Will drive down to school with Peter. Mother plus father plus child. Have bought new suit – dark blue. Will try to say right things to Head – but what are they? What do mothers say? Perhaps they just weep.

A week afterwards:

I didn't go. I couldn't. Looked at Simon's suitcase in the hall. His name on it. Everything very new. Simon's new shoes. Shining. Black. His hair looked very clean. Fair and straight. Melanie had washed it. Last au-pair job before leaving. Hope she will return during the holidays. Somebody must. Can't cope. Peter angry when I said he'd have to take Simon on his own. Swore at me. Simon heard. Looked upset but didn't cry. Never cries. Told him I'd post him some sweets. Must remember to do this. Hope he'll be happy. I mean this. Be happy, Simon. Please. I'll feel better if I know you're happy.

The early diaries were of no interest to Rhoda apart from sketching in Lisa's mental state, which was only relevant in a small degree to her mental state later. Which seemed to be normal. During Simon's early adolescence the diaries rarely mentioned him. There were crisp references to the research she was doing, mainly about social contacts with others with similar interests. A snide remark about Meg Maybridge caught Rhoda's eye:

39

Lunched with Meg Maybridge yesterday. She should bone up on her dates. She thought Rousseau's pal, Grimm, was one of the brothers Grimm. Laughed when I told her she was a century out. Said her attention had slipped and what did I want for dessert – lemon mousse? A hint I'm sharply acidic? Well – maybe. Do her English Lit. students ever trip her up – and does she care if they do?

Another reference to Meg was kinder and was written a few months later:

Monro S. Orr's illustrations of Grimm's fairy tales are brilliant, Meg tells me. As if I didn't know! She gave me a very early edition she'd had all her life. More use to me than to her, she said, now that her son had grown up. It's not of any use to me, I've already got all his work. Didn't tell her. She's generous. Nice. Would have made a good mother for Simon. Can't imagine her sleeping with Peter, though. She isn't his style.

Style. Rhoda caught a glimpse of her reflection in the train window and smiled a bitter little smile. He was easy with compliments, Peter. On their first meeting, in a chilly carriage on a broken-down train somewhere south of Birmingham two winters ago, they had shared coffee and sandwiches. His sandwiches – hospital canteen. Her coffee – instant. Neither good, but better than nothing. He had praised the coffee. Polite, of course. And apologised for the sandwiches. Ham, dried up and too fat. Some while later, still stranded, he had praised what he called her "patient acceptance of an appallingly long wait". If the delay had been shorter they might not have exchanged names. Hers meant nothing to him, but he said that Rhoda was charmingly old-fashioned. Greek, wasn't it? Or Latin? She had heard of him. As a freelance journalist she had covered a few crime stories and his role as forensic pathologist had been mentioned from time to time. She had asked him if he was working on anything at the moment. He was always working on something, he said, the killing instinct was inborn from the time of Cain. It kept him in bread and butter. Speaking of which, would she like another of his revolting sandwiches?

Smiling, she had declined. He had smiled back. The middle-aged, thick-set man with the stubby fingers which must have done all manner of appalling things was, she had thought then, extraordinarily attractive.

Most women, she was to discover, did. Including her sister, Clare.

His wife's last two diaries were in her holdall. Two small leather-bound books, pushed in between the remains of the camera. What use would a photograph of the coffins have been – other than a macabre reminder of a relationship that had ended? There was no clue to violence there. But the diaries might reveal something about Clare. Where she was. And if she were not alive – what had happened to her.

4

Two days after the funeral, when Simon judged himself to be of sound mind and capable of clear thinking, he wrote to the medical school and said that he wouldn't be attending as a student in the autumn. Medicine wasn't for him. What career might eventually suit him, he didn't know. Nor, at that particular time, did he care.

He kept the telephone disconnected in case Kester-Evans bothered him (time enough to tell him later when he felt strong enough to defend his action), and as there was no point in going back to school he cut the badge off his blazer and put it in the bin.

His next positive action was to buy a car. He had been given a modest little hatchback on his seventeenth birthday just over a year ago. His father's choice for him. Not a good one. He needed something fast. Until the Will was proved, or whatever the legal term was, he couldn't sell the family's second car – the Volvo – and add it to whatever he got for the hatchback, which wouldn't be much. Or he thought he couldn't. He knew he was due to inherit everything, but perhaps not immediately, so instead of purchasing a beautiful red B.M.W. coupé he made do with a second-hand, souped-up Lotus Eclat with a hefty mileage and pocketed enough on the trade-in of the hatchback to buy some suitable gear. Clothes had never interested him, but you couldn't drive that sort of car in boarding school clobber. And he was tired of sweatshirts and jeans. The lovat green suede jacket and matching cords he eventually chose might have better suited the B.M.W. A wrong choice pondered over took his mind off pain and was therapeutic. A couple of highly patterned jerseys, bright and cheerful, put colour in his cheeks and suited any kind of car. Happy for a while with the sort of trivia that puts death into perspective – a long way off for the healthy young – he roamed around Bristol, ate a highly spiced meal at an Indian restaurant, went to look at the *Great Britain*, down at the Docks and was called 'Sweetie' by a pretty little tart at the dockside. She didn't invite him to go home with her. He wondered if he would have if she had. The woman with the long dark hair lingered along the edges of his mind. She had come and gone like a dream. He only half believed in her.

A week later she came back.

Rhoda's approach this time was more carefully thought out. Simon mustn't be alarmed. She needed his co-operation and, for as long as possible, his goodwill.

He was hosing down his new car in the drive when she arrived. His back was to her and she watched him spraying the water under the wheel arches, dislodging cow muck. For a moment, and for the first time, she saw a physical resemblance to his father. The shoulder muscles, the way he flicked his wrists. When he was older, thickened out, the resemblance might become more obvious. She blanked the thought. Stay objective. He is a means to an end. Don't let memories colour anything.

And stepped smartly out of the way when he turned, startled, still hosing, and almost soaked her shoes.

He dropped the hose and water snaked across the gravel and ran into a bed of thick white alyssum, making the air pungent with the smell of flowers and wet manure. The sun shone brilliantly.

He went to turn off the tap and pressed his damp hands against his burning cheeks before returning to her. Bloody hell, why did he blush so much? When would he stop?

She said hello again – and added "Simon". And smiled her

43

winning, transforming smile. "Last time I was here," she went on smoothly, "we didn't have much opportunity to talk. I'm not at all sure I told you my name. It's Rhoda. Rhoda Osborne."

He nearly said how do you do, but that would have been too ridiculous. This woman had seen him naked – well, maybe not quite, he wasn't sure – and had put him to bed.

He mumbled something about being sorry.

"Whatever for?"

"I'd been drinking."

"And why not?"

"Even so . . ."

"It's all right."

She went over and admired the car, giving him time to compose himself. "A nippy little job. Yours?"

"Yes. A 521 twin-cam."

She made an approving noise. "Sounds good. I don't know what it means. No, don't tell me, I still wouldn't know. Pretty fast?"

"Yes. Not much chance to speed around here, though."

"But overtakes well?"

"Well enough." And you've smoothed me down enough. I think I've stopped blushing. I was wearing my father's pyjamas. Christ! And now I want to laugh. Oh, God, I mustn't.

He grinned suddenly and once again she saw his father in him. And couldn't smile back.

"Look," she said gently, "do you think we could go inside and talk awhile?"

He had been using the back entrance and she followed him directly into the kitchen which had reverted to its original state. Didn't he ever wash up? His father had been tidy. And what had possessed him to connect his father's answering machine to the telephone? Peter's rich, deep voice saying calmly that he was away at the moment, but would be back soon, and please to leave a message, had sent shock waves through her. Followed by anger. And then amusement. What kind of son had the Bradshaws spawned? Someone wickedly insensitive? Or had he merely forgotten to wipe the tape?

Lisa's voice would have interested her. The focus was on Lisa.

44

She was here to collect evidence – of what, she wasn't sure. A pattern would form. As yet the strands were nebulous, like a shadowy web building slowly in a dark recess.

Simon asked her if she would like a cup of tea – or a gin and tonic – or something?

"If the 'or something' could be coffee – black – then yes, please. And I don't mind if it's instant."

He opened one of the kitchen cupboards. "There's a percolator somewhere."

"Don't bother. It's quicker out of a jar."

"My mother . . ." he began, stopped. What he had begun to say about his mother wasn't important. One of the few good things she could do was to make good coffee. And one of the many bad things he could do was to make trite conversation, if he didn't watch himself. And fumble and mumble and drop the spoon. And . . .

And why the hell was she here?

His gaucherie warmed her towards him. She had known other boys in their late teens, smooth young sophisticates, self-assured, level-headed sixth formers about to embark on university life. Young men she'd never refer to as kids. But then the genes were different. And the environment, in Simon's case, bizarre.

"I didn't mean to call on you unannounced," she said, "but there seemed to be something wrong with my phone."

He blushed, deeply embarrassed but grateful for the lie. As a way of fobbing off Kester-Evans it had seemed amusing. It wasn't, of course, it was appalling.

He tried to explain. "I disconnected the phone, but someone
you see, I get bothered by people who think I can't manage and want to come and help, and then Kester-Evans . . . my headmaster . . . wants me back at school . . . and he's the one I particularly don't want to talk to . . . and, well, that's it, I mean . . ." He returned to the coffee making, his blush slowly subsiding. "Please do sit down." It was stiff. Very polite.

She sat at the kitchen table where Maybridge had sat not so long ago. Maybridge would have given him good counselling. Rhoda should have given him the same, plus the return ticket to school.

Instead, she accepted the coffee and asked for sugar. "Brown for preference."

"I haven't any."

"It doesn't matter. White will do."

They sat in a silence that wasn't companionable. He was aware that she was studying him and drank his coffee, which he hadn't wanted, in hot nervous gulps.

"People," she said soothingly, "don't matter a lot. I mean outsiders. They're not important enough to worry you. Ignore them. Tell them to piss off." She grinned, "Sorry, awfully rude?"

He grinned back. Relaxed. "Probably not rude enough. I'll tell them I'm rabid." He added: "Actually, I have changed the tape. Just repeated what my father said."

She shrugged. Pity. She would have liked to hear Peter's voice again.

"I've chucked in my place at medical school," he told her.

"For a good reason?"

"I never wanted to go."

"I can't think of a better."

"My father wanted it for me."

Oh no, laddie, she thought, he didn't. On the few occasions your father mentioned you he said you were battling your way through a survival course, and God knew he hoped you'd be happy at the end of it. Whatever you did.

"Your father wanted you to be happy." It was spoken on impulse, because it needed to be said.

He remembered that she had spoken his father's name that night when she had sat on his bed. "You knew my father?"

"Yes." She didn't look at him but glanced up at the shelf of dark blue pottery jugs and plates arranged for effect over the work-top. Lisa's feminine touch. "I'm really here to talk about your mother."

He froze a little. Withdrew. She noticed. This wasn't going to be easy. The well-rehearsed cover story had to be good.

That it was a witch's brew of fact and fiction, based partly on the diaries she had read, he wasn't to know. It was plausible. She was a freelance journalist, she told him. (True.) When Lisa's book on nineteenth-century illustrators had been published some while ago she had been introduced to her at a publisher's party. (False.)

46

The book had been well received, but by a limited readership. (True.) The editor of one of the Sundays had suggested to her that an article on Lisa's artistic and literary ability would be of interest, particularly now, and had invited her to write it. (False.)

"I would like to agree, Simon. But not without your permission. I would write it very sensitively. Let you see it at every stage. Your father had been a public figure most of his life but she was very much in the background. She deserved more acknowledgment than she had. Looking at it commercially, there would be renewed interest in her book. It would sell more. Good for you financially." She paused. A wrong move? Money, she sensed, wouldn't woo him. Try again. Soften it. "I would write nothing hurtful. Nothing derogatory. I'd just try to give her her rightful place – up front in the art world. A kind of memorial to a woman who was brilliant but never had the accolade she deserved." She hesitated, feeling for the right words. "People like Lisa aren't easy to know. Artists and writers are difficult people. Self-absorbed to some extent. Incapable sometimes of showing their feelings. They can be misjudged, even by their own families. It takes one to know one. I felt I knew her in that brief time we met. She said she found it difficult to express affection – that she worked out her emotions mostly on canvas."

Rhoda clenched her hands under the table. Careful. Going too far. What sort of affection was shown on that mural upstairs? Precious little. Okay – so it was in the style of someone else – but it was ninety percent Lisa. And you've read most of the early diaries. It's no use trying to tell this boy that she loved him. She was as weird as hell. And he knows it. Try putting a little guilt on him: "You've read her book, of course?"

He shook his head.

"Why not? You must be awfully proud of her?"

He was silent. She applied salve. "Possibly you were too young to appreciate it when it was published. You're not now. Read it, Simon, it's terrific." It was an exaggeration. It was a good, well-researched book, cleverly illustrated. It would bore him, probably, but it wouldn't upset him. Lisa, at the time of writing it, had been totally sane.

47

But how sane had she been when Clare had walked into her life and into Peter's bed? And then gone missing?

When the son of an old friend lets a stranger into his home there's not much you can do about it, Maybridge pointed out to his wife. "Simon is old enough to do as he likes," Meg agreed. But age couldn't be measured in years and Simon's naivety worried her. Journalists don't move in on the bereaved within a couple of weeks of the funeral – actually move in and live in the house – with some weak story about researching background. No respectable newspaper or magazine would sanction it.

Or was she, in turn, being naive? How far would the Press go for a story? Too far, she had to concede, for a story that was hot and immediate. Which this wasn't. Rhoda Osborne was a freelance journalist, Simon had told her, who wanted to write about his mother. It was convenient for her to stay with him so that she could look through his mother's art work and manuscripts. In return she would cook him his meals. It wouldn't be for long.

Meg had called to see how he was getting on and had been startled by what Simon, speaking defensively, had told her. Carefully keeping her voice neutral, she had asked if she might meet her. Sometime when she wasn't working, Simon had hedged. "She's up in my mother's studio, taking notes. I mustn't disturb her."

"My immediate response to that," Meg told Maybridge, "was to say, 'Mustn't you? In your own home, too. How odd!' And then he blushed and was so bothered about blushing that he wandered over to the window and stared out across the garden towards the orchard. 'She likes the almond tree,' he said. 'My mother liked it, too. Used to sit there a lot.' How do you follow that? With Grimm's horror story?"

Maybridge, whose knowledge of Grimm was slight, didn't know what she was talking about. He raised an enquiring eyebrow.

"A particularly nasty tale about the decapitation of a child," Meg explained. "The lid of a chest full of apples is dropped on him when he looks inside – by his villainous stepmother. Had it been his natural mother it would have been worse. The body is buried under the almond tree. A bird squawks a lament every few pages. Lisa has a painting of the bird in her studio."

"Oh," said Maybridge.

"Given Lisa's state of mind," Meg went on, "researching Grimm couldn't have done her much good. Doctor Donaldson should have fed her a diet of Enid Blyton. Safe, nice, twee, little Noddy."

Maybridge, adrift from the original subject, steered back to it. Simon might be bedding a girlfriend, he suggested, and had made up the story about the journalist. And it was handy the girl was cooking his meals. If he were being harassed, he would have said so. As for a stupid yarn about an almond tree and decapitation, what about all those blood and guts stories David had thrived on when he was a kid? They hadn't done him any harm.

"Debatable," Meg said drily. "He still reads Stephen King."

Maybridge, unwilling to be drawn into a discussion on the literary merit, or lack of it, of the horror genre – personally he liked King, too, and read him when Meg wasn't around – went out to do some gardening.

The mild spring had brought on the roses and some of the bushes needed de-budding. A necessary act of decapitation to help the survivors to bloom. Superintendent Claxby would draw an analogy there, he thought, as he snipped away with his secateurs, especially if Sergeant Radwell were around. A discussion about the overcrowding of prisons had prompted Radwell, normally tactful and reticent, to state with some heat that anyone advocating the death penalty must be sick. "Murder is the ultimate atrocity," he'd dared tell Claxby, "especially when committed by the state." Claxby, unruffled, had drawn the sign of the cross over his head and murmured: "Pax vobiscum. Now flee thee to a monastery – or call me 'sir'." The 'sir' had been whispered through gritted teeth and Claxby had smiled. "Pompous little prick," he'd said to Maybridge later. Maybridge, as always, had defended him. Mostly because he agreed with him. But how far could compassion be extended? He'd felt none for the Bible-quoting serial strangler that Bradshaw's evidence had nailed. A life sentence in Hixon's case should mean just that, and probably would.

Maybridge recalled Hixon's first murder – the strangling of a prostitute in the vault of one of Bristol's war-damaged churches, known locally to some of the winos who dossed down there as the Church of the Nazarene. The structure, beyond repair, had been left open to the sky, a grey elegance of upthrusting stones softened by ivy and clumps of sedum. The vault, in most places intact, had at one time been the repository of brasses let into the floor. These had been cleared away and the cavities filled with rubble. As a temporary shelter for tramps the vault was marginally better than sleeping under a bridge, though almost as cold. After the discovery of the body they gave it a miss for a while. Now most of them were back. A strangled prostitute called Louise, her hair plaited and tied around her neck like a noose, might still haunt the sensitive, but on a pouring wet night she was better forgotten. Old Alf Whitman had found her. "A stiff at St Naz," he'd told the desk officer at the nearest police station. The officer, who had never heard of St Naz, believed, rightly, that the old fellow was drunk. Whitman, not sufficiently drunk to stop trying and not sober enough to be lucid, had wept with exasperation, tinged with terror, before finally getting through. "And I didn't do it," he'd added. "Aw, Jeeze God – t'wasn't me."

Whitman had avoided being called as a witness at the trial by the simple expedient of dying, aged seventy-four, of a liver infection in Bristol Royal Infirmary. One of Hixon's relatives – well, probably one of Hixon's relatives – had sent a wreath. The only one. Bronze chrysanthemums. The typed message had been:

May the Lord receive you with joy.

C.H.

Maybridge smiled wryly at the recollection. Hixon mad? Well, maybe. But not mad enough to convince the psychiatrists, and not sane enough to be careful. When an insurance clerk who is also a lay preacher and an apparently happily married man embarks on a mission to rid the world of sleaze (his word), he shouldn't sample the product first. In his case, five products. All under thirty, most pretty, none deserving to die.

Doctor Donaldson, who was supposed to be an expert in matters of the mind, had attended the trial and heard Hixon's final outburst.

"The fire of fanaticism," he'd observed, "stoked by lust." It probably summed it up.

It had been no part of Rhoda's plan to sexually arouse Simon. The word 'lust' didn't occur to her – or to him. 'Sexually arouse' might be the same thing, but it sounded better. She had to accept the fact that he was sexually aroused and that the reaction was natural. She had been a fool not to anticipate it. He'd had an erection, after all, that night when he was pissed and she'd put him to bed. Now, quite sober, his masculinity was being an awful nuisance to him, and a blushing embarrassment because most of the time he couldn't hide it. Amused, she had thought of Kester-Evans. What would he have counselled? Cold showers? Physical exercise? Withdrawal from the scene of temptation?

She could hear Simon showering in the bathroom every morning – not a cold one, though. When she went in later for her bath, the window was steamed over and the towel rail blazing hot. As for exercise: he mooched. A stroll around the garden. A short walk to the dairy for milk. He didn't even go out in his car. Just looked at it as if he was rather pleased he had it – a handsome piece of machinery. And he looked at her. Differently. When the young fall in love there is a degree of pain. Rhoda, carefully avoiding the word 'love', felt her conscience kick. She tried to subdue it. A few words to Peter, inside her head, helped. "I haven't enticed Simon. Been careful not to. I saw to the domestic arrangements. They're okay. You couldn't fault them. I sleep in Lisa's studio, on her couch, with her Welsh blanket on top of me. It smells of whatever perfume she used. Sweet. She wasn't sweet, was she? But that's the way she smelled. Simon wanted me to have the guest bedroom, next to his. I told him, no. I needed to work late. And I do. And I have. If you and Lisa were able to walk in on me, Peter, you'd erupt together in one great explosion of rage. I sometimes lie in her bed and think of a great hellish thundercloud of rage. And it excites me. Pleases me. Makes me more sure that what I'm doing must be done. Digging away for the truth, all the time.

"But Simon . . . What do I do about Simon? I'm not here to hurt him."

Simon, aware of a cooling in a relationship that, on her part, had never been very warm, was mutely miserable. He had shared his home with this gut-churning, odd, beautiful, vixen-eyed woman for six days, and in that time he had pushed himself up to some sort of mountain peak, because she was up there, too. Mountain peaks are lonely places when the other person doesn't want you. You might get the message that she's rejecting you but you only get it in your brain. Your brain won't transmit it to the rest of you. Your body doesn't get it. Your body gives you hell. You can't even eat – well, you can't eat much.

He derived some comfort from the fact that she spent time cooking the evening meal for them both, doing the best she could with the contents of the deep-freeze and showing concern about his likes and dislikes. "If you don't like chicken chasseur, or whatever ridiculous name it's called, you should have said." "I do like it." "Eat it, then." "I have – most of it." "Not enough. You're a growing boy, for God's sake." "For God's sake, I'm bloody eighteen." A rueful smile from her: "Sorry. It's just that I'm bothered about you. It's not all that long since the funeral and . . ." she shrugged, "well, I think I know what you must be feeling. It takes time for everything to be normal again. I'll be gone soon – just a few more days – and then you'll have the place to yourself."

He looked at her, stricken. "A few more days?" The future was a horrid abyss, a dark crater on his mountain top. He couldn't bear it.

She collected up the plates and emptied the remains of his meal into the pedal-bin. "There's ice-cream and cherry tart."

He winced.

"What, then? What would you like?"

A tumblerful of neat whisky. An injection of any mind-numbing drug. "Nothing."

She felt extremely irritated but kept her voice level. "I may have to stay a while longer – perhaps another week." Now would the silly boy have some pudding?

He agreed he would – just a little.

Simon's apparent indifference to what she was doing up in his mother's studio, day after day, was a bonus she hadn't expected when she'd moved in. She'd hidden the diaries in a half-used box of typing paper and shoved it under the couch in case he walked in on her and picked one of them up. It didn't matter if he saw the manuscripts, they wouldn't hurt him, and she was working on them legitimately; a few pages of boring comment, turned out now and then in case he asked about progress. She'd asked him if he'd ever gone through his mother's papers – anything she might have written – or any letters – or even postcards that she might have received. "When someone dies, there's usually correspondence to be got rid of. If you haven't done that, could you let me have a quick glance? There might be something relevant to the profile I'm writing. Editors like the human touch." He said there weren't any letters. His mother never kept them. And his father didn't either. "What about art, then? Most of her sketches relate to her work. Did she never do sketches of her friends?" The possibility obviously surprised him. "No, she never painted living people." Her art, he explained, was other people's art – re-done. Though she might have some sketch books she'd put away somewhere. He didn't know. He'd never asked. Art and literature – if writing books about art was literature – weren't his 'thing'. Any more than forensic pathology was. "We don't necessarily like what our parents like," he'd added, his gaze lingering on her hair as if he longed to touch it.

Well, sometimes we do, she'd thought.

Why did most men like long hair?

Why had Lisa bought a wig?

The entry was in Lisa's penultimate diary:

Bought a switch of hair in a little shop near the university. Light blonde. Divided it into two plaits. Dressed for dinner in the dark blue bust-clinging frock. Like hers. Well, almost. She's more busty than me. Let the two plaits swing forward and form a loop, then went down to Peter in the dining-room. He was decanting brandy. Nothing straight from the bottle for him. Oh, no. Good crystal. Have it. Use it. Have women. Use them, too. "They're calling them the Rapunzel murders," I told him, "the Press. And what do you call your long-haired lady? Di-aneme? Like Herrick?" He kept on decanting. Didn't spill a single drop. Then turned and looked at me. Eyes like ice. Smiled.

53

"Need another session at The Mount with Donaldson, Lisa? Or just some stronger pills?"

The writing had trailed off there, to be resumed after a few empty pages:

Dianeme, in Herrick's poem, had ruby ear-rings. If the poor little tart in the church vault wore ear-rings, they'd be glass. What would Peter's Dianeme wear? Pearls? All they had in common was their hair. And Peter. Hands on the living. Hands on the dead.

Rhoda shivered and pushed the diary aside. All the murdered women had had long hair. Clare's hair had been long, too. And blonde.

And who was Peter's Dianeme?

5

"The Mount is a rest home," Simon told Rhoda. "My mother went there to rest." He had known for some years that the bland description was misleading but preferred it to the truth. "Why can't she rest in her own bed at home?" he had asked his father during one of the school holidays when he was about eleven or so. "Why do slimmers go to health farms," his father had hedged, "when they can diet just as well in their own kitchens?" It was no answer and he'd tried to provide his own. "To resist temptation." His father had smiled and rumpled his hair in a rough gesture of affection. "Temptation comes in many guises, Simon. Bed and food probably run the lot. Stop worrying about your mother

Steven Donaldson is an expert on mothers. Especially yours." He had been too young then to understand the irony, but the words were clear in his mind now as he looked at Rhoda. She was a lot older than he, but no more a mother figure than his mother had been. Why this thought should occur to him, he didn't know. She had come into the small book-lined room off the hall which his father had used as his study and found him reading a Rider Haggard, or rather, leafing through it – the title *She* had appealed. Was there any poetry on the shelves? Rhoda wanted to know.

Anything by Herrick, for instance? He'd found a *Golden Treasury* and given it to her. She'd sat in silence, turning the pages, and then discovered whatever she was looking for. "Ah," she said. "Dianeme. So that's where she got it." "Got what?" "It doesn't matter. Just a reference."

He noticed she had washed her hair for the second time that day. One of the green guest towels was draped over the shoulders of her white sweatshirt. Perhaps her hair had got dusty when she had been in the attic. He had heard her pulling down the Slingsby ladder but had resisted following her. There was nothing of interest up there. Just suitcases. Perhaps one of the smaller ones had his mother's name on it and the address of The Mount, though it seemed unlikely. The Mount, after all, was local, just a few minutes away by car. He asked her how she knew about it.

She was evasive. "Well, it does rather loom over the village – it's not the sort of place you can ignore. Someone may have mentioned it to me. I can't remember. What's the name of the man who runs it?"

"Donaldson – he's the medical superintendent."

"A colleague of your father's? Or a friend, perhaps?"

Simon wasn't sure that either word had applied to his father's relationship with Donaldson. Both men were doctors but colleagues implied a shared speciality – psychiatry was far removed from pathology. As for friendship . . . he had only been in their company a few times and they had been coldly polite. Donaldson and his mother – that was different. Professionalism plus what . . . ? He looked thoughtfully at Rhoda. Plus . . . *that*? No, it couldn't have been. Donaldson was old – at least fifty.

He wasn't sure how to answer the question, but managed to get near the truth. "Doctor Donaldson has mostly acquaintances. Everyone knows him. I don't know if he visits much socially, but he encourages visits to The Mount. He has Bridge parties sometimes – and musical evenings. The Maybridges and the vicar, people like that, go along. It's mainly for the patients though, those who want to attend. A way of getting them back amongst people again." He was sorry he had used the word 'patient' and added quickly: "Some of the villagers call it a psychiatric hospital – it isn't – it's a private nursing home. People go there to escape

56

. . . well, pressure . . . a job that worries them . . . or any other sort of bother. Donaldson lets them do their own thing. Nothing at all, if that's what they want. A man called Paul Creggan lives in a tepee in the grounds for a few weeks now and then, and then goes back to being an accountant – or whatever." Creggan living in a tepee was one of the stories about Donaldson's methods that had stayed in his mind. And reassured him to some extent. At least his mother hadn't lived in a tent. On the whole she had been pretty normal.

"My mother wasn't neurotic," he said. "Just couldn't cope sometimes. Couldn't sleep. Got on edge. There are a lot of people like that. There was nothing wrong with her mentally. Donaldson could tell you that."

As soon as he had spoken the words he regretted them. He didn't mind her probing here but he didn't want her to go probing there. There was no knowing what Donaldson might tell her.

"Must we keep talking about my mother?" he burst out irritably. "Can't you understand that I'm stuck here while you spend hours upstairs? There are times when I wish you'd never started whatever it is you're doing – your article – your profile. You never talk to me. Not properly. Just ask questions. Not about me. About her. I'm a person, not a bloody cipher. I *exist!*"

It was petulant. But it was justified, too. How to soothe the boy, Rhoda wondered, without taking him to bed? A careful caress? A light touch of fingers on his cheek? No, his mood was too volatile. They'd be rolling around on the carpet within minutes.

– to Bristol, perhaps?

He thought it a rotten idea. What was she proposing? To take him to the zoo – to throw peanuts at the monkeys – suck a lollipop? He wanted to go to London with her – to her flat or wherever it was she lived. He wanted to see where she ate and slept. To open her wardrobe. Feel her clothes. She was as nebulous as a mirage. As unknown as a refugee in an empty landscape. He wanted to know her. In every sense, *know* her.

His silence perturbed her. There was a quality of maturity in his glance now that reminded her of his father. He was a boy/man, and at this moment there was no childishness in him at all.

"I need to go in to do some shopping," she told him briskly, "and to get a book in one of the antiquarian book shops. One that was mentioned in your mother's . . ." She broke off. His mother as a topic was taboo for a while. "Though that's not urgent. We can have a meal somewhere. And then you can show me the sights – your favourite parts of Bristol – the modern precincts – or the historical areas – anything."

He had no favourite parts of Bristol, though it was a pleasant enough city. He imagined the two of them trekking around like a couple of tourists and ending up in the crypt of St Nicholas's, seated at one of the long trestle tables, doing brass rubbings. Or maybe in the vault of that other place with the odd name that didn't sound C. of E. at all. The place where the tramps went at night – and where his father had been called out by the police to look at the body of a murdered girl.

He told her decisively, as his father would have told her, that he would rather take her to Gloucester. "You can shop there."

For a while the man was in the ascendancy and she didn't argue.

A visit of condolence, Donaldson believed, was obligatory. He had put it off as long as possible and was relieved not to find Simon in. The possibility that he might be down in the orchard, in the summerhouse, occurred to him but he preferred not to look. He went back to his car and wrote a note on one of his address cards: "Sorry to have missed you. If there is anything I can do, then please call on me." It looked curt but there wasn't room for more. He hesitated before putting the card through the letterbox. He had written a letter of sympathy a couple of weeks ago – the usual words about grief – loss – fond memory and so on – but it had seemed shallow and conventional – a parroting of emotions and he had torn it up. He knew how he felt. How Lisa's son felt was no business of his – professionally or any other way. There had been too much involvement in the past. Clinical detachment where Lisa had been concerned had been a sick joke. Detachment from her son was prerequisite to a return to normal life. Or as normal as any life can be.

"Happy insanity," one of his patients had joked, "is vastly preferable to being sadly sane. How dare you cure me? I don't want to go home."

Quite a lot of them didn't.

Including Lisa.

"Discretion," he reminded his staff from time to time, "is as vital as good nursing. The patients must trust you. Encourage them to talk, talking is therapeutic, then forget what they've told you, unless it's relevant. If it is, tell me." He could have said, more simply, "Don't gossip," but that would have been insulting. On the whole, he had what he thought of as a good team. They batted on an easy wicket and were well paid. The non-professional staff, who kept the place clean and saw to the other domestic chores, tended to come and go. None was local. The cook, Mrs Mackay, a taciturn Scotswoman, had been with him eight years, which was exceptional. She had recently bought a cottage on the outskirts of the village and with luck would remain up to retirement age. Or perhaps beyond. "If music is the food of love," a grateful patient had commented, "and the converse is equally true, then she plays one hell of a good sonata with her Grampian roast." She wasn't at all bad at more exotic dishes either, but she refused to give them fancy names. French and Italian words describing anything she cooked were taboo. Bouillabaisse appeared on her menu as fish soup, and a fricassé as stewed mince. Caviare, served occasionally as a starter, was listed as fish roes. New patients, expecting the worst and sunk in gloom at the prospect of a terrible meal, were pleasantly surprised. Shock therapy by a Cordon Bleu electrified their tastebuds. Only the anorexic were slow to respond.

And Paul Creggan.

Creggan liked a soft boiled egg, white bread and butter, canned soup and strong cheese. The food was carried down to him in his tepee and placed on a tin tray on an upturned tea-chest. He drank bottled water and weak beer. When he had first visited Donaldson for a consultation and a request to be admitted, he had arrived in a chauffeur-driven Daimler and worn an immaculately tailored grey suit the same shade as his well-groomed hair. Donaldson, who had had no prior warning of the visit, had pointed out that he would need a referral from Mr Creggan's general practitioner.

59

Creggan had told him that it was on its way – would arrive soon – but not soon enough if Donaldson sent him back home again. "Have you ever experienced despair, Doctor? The big black dog? In my case a big blonde bitch." Creggan's matrimonial kennel was a large luxury flat in Maida Vale. "Sumptuous," he described it, "to the point of suffocation." His companion (wife, mistress, he didn't say) was of the best bloodstock – beautifully bred. "But yaps like a demented terrier, Doctor. All the time. The canine species can be legally put down. I don't wish to break the law, Doctor. If you send me back I shall be sorely tempted."

Donaldson, not impressed, had suggested he should take a holiday.

Creggan, not impressed with the advice, had started taking off his clothes.

Donaldson had taken an empty syringe out of his desk drawer and handled it thoughtfully.

Creggan had dressed again.

The saga of Creggan's eventual admittance to The Mount covered several pages of case history. A letter from his G.P. had urged it and also, surprisingly, a letter from one of The Mount's ex-patients, a stockbroker. "Give him a break," he wrote, "he needs it. When the market collapsed, made me suicidal, you helped a lot. He's a harmless eccentric, if that's not too unscientific a description, and domestic problems are making him worse. He needs a period of calm. I told him you'd see he got it. Don't let me down."

The doctor's note had omitted any diagnostic analysis. He wasn't an expert, he said, but when patients cried for help he believed they needed it. He would be grateful if Donaldson would listen and, if necessary, treat.

Both letters were persuasive. But Creggan's attempted bribe, over the phone, offering to double the fee, wasn't. A second phone call, apologising and asking if he could bring his tent, had surprised Donaldson into laughter. He had been even more surprised later to discover it wasn't a joke.

The tent, a brown canvas tepee, lacked a few Indian feathers at the top to be totally bizarre, but was bizarre enough to attract amused comment. Donaldson allowed it to be set up in a wild area of garden that was near enough to the main building for convenience but not too obvious from the road. He had dealt with a few extraordinary obsessions in his professional life, and the only rule he laid down about this one was that Creggan should use one of The Mount's bedrooms which had been set aside for him so that he might keep himself clean in the ensuite bathroom and use the lavatory. Whether or not he slept in the bed or on the trestle bed in the tepee was up to him. Creggan chose the latter unless the weather was exceptionally bad. He had come to find peace, he said rather plaintively. He hadn't come to fraternise with people who might be just a little peculiar. Resisting psychotherapy and medication of any kind, which Donaldson was honest enough not to push but felt he had to offer to justify the fee, he spent a few weeks every now and then in self-imposed isolation. A retreat in a Trappist monastery would have been less expensive, but perhaps more rigorous. In The Mount he could use his time however he liked. Casually dressed in khaki shorts and a shabby brown pullover, with a tweed jacket over his shoulders if it were chilly, he spent hours reading detective and western paperbacks and listening to the radio through earphones. When he got bored, he slept. In the night he took long walks when the moon was high, or in the early dawn when there was enough light to see by.

Donaldson had alerted Maybridge to the walks, assuring him that Creggan was harmless. "He's perfectly safe. Don't let any of your eager p.c.s hassle him." Maybridge, not one to take advice, especially in a case like this, had him tailed for a while and finally agreed with Donaldson that he wasn't a threat to anyone. Just a man who preferred the night to the day – quiet moonlit fields – no personal encounters. A man who wanted to be on his own.

But not all the time.

Creggan had attended the funeral of Peter and Lisa Bradshaw. That the mole should emerge into bright sunlight, to mourn the passing of a couple he didn't know, had startled Donaldson. Creggan had stood at the back of the church, sombrely dressed in his London clothes, and had averted his eyes from Donaldson's when the coffins were carried out. Before the interment, and just after the camera had been dropped, he had returned to The Mount, packed his bag, left a note to say he would be away for a couple

61

of weeks, and taken a taxi back home. Or back somewhere.

His sudden departure after attending the funeral was disquieting.

Rhoda might like roses, Simon thought.

The visit to Gloucester was better in some respects, and worse in others, than he had expected. Better insofar as she talked to him as one polite adult to another, mainly about the architecture of the cathedral, the décor of the restaurant where they had lunch and the quality of the wine which she had chosen and allowed him to buy (a cheap white medium-dry French). The main meal was her treat, she'd insisted, what would he like? As he guessed she hadn't much cash he'd decided against Chicken Kiev (it had garlic, anyway, and he didn't want to breathe fumes over her) and opted for a hamburger. She had chosen Chicken Kiev.

The not so good parts weren't anything he could complain about. They weren't her fault. She was about an inch taller than he and it was obvious when they walked side by side. In the house it wasn't noticeable. Out here in the busy street, noisy with traffic, he was conscious that her mouth was on a level with his ear and while he heard everything she said, she didn't always hear him. Had suggested, politely, that he mumbled.

And she couldn't help the way she looked. Beautiful. Tight yellow jersey. Tight jeans. They'd looked looser when she'd worn them at the funeral. Perhaps they'd shrunk. A couple of yobs of about his age had whistled at her. They'd both shaved themselves bald apart from a knob of hair at the top, tied with bootlaces, and looked disgusting. She'd agreed with him when he'd said so, but had seemed rather amused.

She had left him a couple of times to shop and suggested that he might like to shop, too. Did he want a razor, or anything? He'd thought this might be a hint that he looked scruffy and had felt his chin, which hadn't grown any stubble since the morning. His father's stubble had been black. His was blond. Unfortunately. Blond stubble wasn't macho. He told her that he had an electric razor and that it shaved quite close. He didn't need another.

She had left him again, just a few minutes ago, to go to the pharmacy across the road and he had wandered over to look at the window of a florist. He wanted to give her something and flowers

62

seemed appropriate. He'd feel an absolute idiot buying them, but most men probably did. If you let embarrassment stop you, you wouldn't do anything. He paid seven pounds fifty for a small bunch of tightly budded pink roses and an extra quid for the wrapping. He should have brought more money out with him. He had no idea things were so expensive. The assistant had teased him about having a girlfriend, and the bloody woman had made him blush.

When Rhoda had told him she was going to the pharmacy to buy tampons he hadn't blushed. It had sounded matter-of-fact. Part of adult conversation. Woman to man. He didn't think she had said it to put him off. It occurred to him that her withdrawal during the last few days might have had something to do with her periods. The menstrual cycle, according to the biology lecture in school last term, lasted for a few days once a month. Some women suffered from pre-menstrual tension. If a woman was regularly on the contraceptive pill her periods stopped for a while. Now that AIDS was a threat it was better for a lover to wear a condom. The word 'lover' had amused Simon's fellow sixth formers and he had grinned sardonically along with the rest of them. Now it didn't amuse him. It no longer seemed sentimental or stupid. He wished he could be Rhoda's lover and wear one of the sheaths he had carried around for some time. Did sheaths ever go off? Rot? Form holes? "Be honourable in your dealings with women," Kester-Evans had intoned from the back of the lecture hall where he had been listening with the boys. "Treat them with the respect with which you would treat your own mothers." That the remark was unintentionally incestuous obviously hadn't occurred to him. The lecturer had pretended to busy himself with his lecture notes before adding a few innocuous sentences and bringing the lecture to a close. The boys had suppressed their mirth until he had left the rostrum and Kester-Evans had followed him out. And then they'd erupted. They were all experienced, Simon believed. Not a virgin amongst them. Virile and confident, not the least bit scared.

Rhoda, about to emerge from the pharmacy, held the swing door open for a woman with a couple of large bulky parcels, and in that moment glanced outside and saw Simon's bouquet. And then she saw him looking at her and tried to look pleasantly back. By Christ, but you can't control your expression all in a moment! But you have to. Go out. Greet him with a smile. Coolly. He's bought the wretched things for you. Peter's gift was usually his favourite brand of Scotch. To share – pre bed. Forget Peter. His kid has gone all sentimental. Roses, oh God! A frill of white paper around them, like a paper doily. And cellophane.

She was gearing herself to play the scene – older sister, perhaps – slightly maternal, perhaps – when the woman dropped her parcel. A bottle of cough linctus smashed and spattered its yellow viscous contents over a large box of cotton wool and over Rhoda's shoes.

A delay. Apologies. Cleaning up. "It's all right. Just old trainers. I'll sponge them when I get home. Not to worry. Mind you don't cut your fingers on the glass." And then – stepping out smartly to greet Simon.

He wasn't there.

There was no rubbish bin in the vicinity. Untidy Britain was meagre with its rubbish bins. Simon walked quickly, looking for one, and then pushed the roses between a pile of cardboard boxes and a crate in an alley near the car park. Her first unguarded expression had seared him.

Some while later Rhoda found him sitting in the car. His face was hard with embarrassment, his eyes dark and evasive. She wondered what he had done with the flowers. And wanted to hug him as she would a child. Console him. Tell him it didn't matter.

But it did matter. It mattered one hell of a lot. The scene was getting increasingly difficult to play.

They spoke very little on the drive back. The creamy yellow Cotswold villages seemed to him as old as time, and as dreary as time. Heavy dark skies would have suited his mood, but the sun shone. When they reached the main road he drove faster, then faster still. His parents had died in a car, he mused, what had it been like for them, that sudden end? Rhoda, beside him, was breathing quickly. Scared? He hoped so. He wished she would beg him to slow down, but she didn't. Eventually he eased his foot off the accelerator and was pleased when she sighed with relief.

"Pretty powerful," she told him, "and you handle it well."

He was young enough to appreciate the compliment, but not quite old enough to receive it graciously.

"Any fool," he said bitterly, "can drive a car."

"Here's one fool," she lied tactfully, "who can't." Lies were becoming a habit. She tried to soothe him with another. "It has been a good day out. I've enjoyed it."

He glanced at her but didn't answer.

6

Grief can be assuaged to some degree by photographs of the dead, Maybridge mused, as he examined the photograph of Lisa that Meg had found. You hold on to memories. An image propped up on a mantelpiece. On a bedroom dressing-table that catches the morning light. Framed on a living-room wall. When the pain eases you look at it less often. The wound heals partly, in some cases completely.

His contact with the bereaved in the course of his police work was always traumatic, all deaths unnatural, no soothing inevitability about any of them. On a few later visits, when shock had been blunted by time, the photographs had appeared. The victims (children, some of them, and those were the most heartbreaking), were shown as they had been, unmarked by violence. Mary Luce, the youngest of Hixon's victims, had been photographed on her eighteenth birthday, a few months before she was murdered. The studio portrait had been handed to him by Mary's mother.

"Look," she'd said. "Just look." And then, after a pause, "She looks back at you, doesn't she? Innocent. Trusting. Do whores look like that? Well – do they? That animal raped her. She'd never been with a man before."

66

It wasn't true. She had been at the trial and heard all the forensic evidence relating to Mary and the other victims, but when those you love are dead you have to protect your memory of them, and if that means pushing the truth around until it is almost acceptable, then that's what you have to do. The horror of Mary's death by strangulation couldn't be articulated; the shock of discovering her daughter's whoring could be – and denied. Maybridge had said, sadly and honestly, that she had been a pretty young woman. A lovely photograph. Encouraged, she had brought out an album of snaps and shown him many more. Mary at school. On holiday. At a disco. Different phases of growing up. Happy moments caught for ever and proudly displayed.

The photo of Lisa, a snapshot, was a good one. Very clear.

"Yes," Maybridge said, handing it back to Meg, "you're right. Simon would like to have it. It will mean more to him than to anyone. Especially now."

The evening was pleasantly cool after a very hot day. He had been watering the bedding plants at the base of the patio and the soil smelt sharp, like ginger. Soon it would be time for their evening tipple – Guinness for him and a small brandy for Meg. A quiet period together, he watching *Sports Night* on the telly and Meg catching up on some letters she had to write. She had come across the photo when she had been looking for an address book in the bureau a few minutes ago and had called him in from the garden to see it. He asked her where it had been taken.

"At the opening ceremony of the childrens' library. Up at the school. She'd done a mural for it – oh, a very harmless, childish one. I'd warned her and it was okay. Very good in fact. Alice the Mad Hatter's tea-party. Everyone looking rather sweet."

Lisa producing anything remotely sweet was hard to imagine. "You should have taken her standing in front of the mural. On her own. This is outside. It's a pity she's one of a crowd."

Meg agreed. "But everyone is standing behind her, luckily. She's in a prominent position. Peter is in there somewhere." She looked for him and found him. "Here – at the back. I should have asked him to move forward but I was focusing on Lisa. She looked so natural. Not posing. The snap could be enlarged and the background cut away. Should I have that done, do you think? Or give it to Simon as it is?"

"As it is. He'd rather have his father in it."

"It's odd he doesn't have a single photograph of his parents anywhere. At a time like this they're usually put on display. They're needed."

Which was precisely what Maybridge had been thinking.

Meg, in most matters very honest, didn't tell her husband that taking the snap to Simon was partly a pretext to suss out the woman who was living with him. She guessed Tom knew, of course, and half expected to be told to tread gently, that she wasn't on her own domestic territory. When she had heard from a social worker about David's crazy alliance with a pot-smoking unmarried mother of four he'd met in a squat, she had been so dismayed she had jack-booted tact into the ground and her son hadn't come home again for almost a year. His first visit back, on his nineteenth birthday, had been a period of unvoiced mutual apologies. A carpet slipper approach to everything. His new girlfriend, sharp, glossy, a non-smoker of anything and too bright to get pregnant, hadn't been Meg's ideal of a soul mate, either. But she had smiled and shut up. This time, not emotionally or maternally involved, to smile should come more easily and careful comment was just a matter of being polite.

Meg visited mid-afternoon on Friday, the day when she had no tutorials at the university. It was blustery, with a hint of rain in the air, and she wore a thick blue handknitted jersey over a navy blue pleated skirt. The wicker basket she carried contained a couple of jars of raspberry jam and a jar of Indian chutney, products bought at the church fête. Also in the basket was one of Lisa's books, A. E. Houseman's *A Shropshire Lad*. And, on top of it, a carton of six free-range eggs.

It didn't occur to her that she looked like a stereotyped country housewife. Bland. Tending towards plumpness. Reassuringly ordinary.

And it didn't occur to Rhoda, who opened the door dressed in an old green caftan of Lisa's, that she looked like a mediaeval looter of clothes of the dead.

Meg, recognising the caftan as the one Lisa used to wear when she was painting, and the woman inside it as the one who had dropped the camera in the church porch, felt a hot rage burn up in her cheeks and for a moment she couldn't speak. How dare this woman come here and take possession?

Rhoda, mistaking the flush of anger for a blush of shyness, was reminded of Simon. She asked the caller with the basket of goodies if she had called to see him. Meg, still speechless, nodded.

Rhoda graciously asked her in. "Simon's down in the orchard doing some scything. Apparently there used to be a regular gardener but he hasn't been recently. Shall we go through to the kitchen?" She led the way and suggested that Meg should put the basket on the table. "All those nice things. That chutney looks lovely. Everyone is so kind to him."

"Are they?" said Meg drily. Not overtly hostile. But almost. She introduced herself. "I'm Meg Maybridge. My husband and I have been friends with Simon and his parents for many years."

Rhoda began emptying the basket while she reassessed the situation. One of the eggs rolled out of the carton and cracked. She picked it up and wiped the slight ooze with her forefinger. Maybridge. One of the policemen who carried Peter's coffin. "Your husband is the superintendent who gave the address at the funeral?"

"Detective Chief Inspector. And – yes – he read the excerpt from the Bible."

"Very sympathetically. It was well chosen." No gush this time. Total honesty.

Meg relaxed a little. "It was important to choose something that wouldn't hurt Simon. Some passages are too full of doom and damnation. It's an Eastern ethos, of course. Difficult to relate to." Mentally she cautioned herself: Don't be sidetracked. She hasn't told you her name yet. You're not supposed to know it. See if her story tallies with Simon's.

"And you are?"

Rhoda removed the jam. "Home made? He'll enjoy it."

Meg smiled. Said nothing.

Rhoda stopped stalling. "Rhoda Osborne. I'm a journalist. I thought Simon had told you last time you called. Or maybe it was another visitor." Simon had referred to her as Meg and she hadn't made the connection. This lady was no pussycat. A little gentle stroking wouldn't do. Her position here would have to be made tenable – somehow.

The kitchen smelt of soup spilt on to the electric burner. It had splashed on to her jeans and shirt, too, but luckily hadn't scalded her. Her clothes were tossing on the rotary drier in view of the window. She indicated them and explained. "That's why I'm wearing this. With Simon's permission, of course. I haven't brought much in the way of spare clothes – didn't intend staying more than a few days. The caftan happened to be handy – it was up in the studio where I'm working." Stalling an immediate analysis of her 'work', she hurried on. "I've never worn anything of Lisa's before. You must have thought it shockingly insensitive of me, but there wasn't any option. I think her clothes and Peter's should be packed away and given to a charity. Would it be crass of me to suggest it? Would it be more acceptable coming from you?"

A neatly turned conversation. A necessary statement made.

Meg, not fooled but mollified, went along with it. The trespasser trespassed within limits. "It wouldn't be crass coming from either of us, but it's up to Simon to say who's to do it – and when. How long have you known him?"

It was the obvious question and she had been expecting it. As far as Simon was concerned, it had to be honest. "Briefly. His father used to mention him quite a lot – Lisa, not so much. I suppose you know he's not going back to Collingwood – and he's not taking up his place in medical school?"

Meg hadn't known. She sensed it was another devious twist in the conversation away from Rhoda, but was genuinely upset by what she had been told. David had chucked university, too, and had been in and out of jobs ever since. A stint on an oil rig. A season on a trawler. Courier with a travel firm. And now, and for the first time, an indoor job portering for Christie's. Humping antiques, he called it, a prelude to selling them at a million a bid.

"Does Kester-Evans, Simon's headmaster, know?"

"I couldn't say. I haven't discussed it with Simon. He just told me he'd written to the medical school – Barts, or wherever – and that was that. It's his life. His decision. He'll be happy in his own way. Eventually." She noticed the book in the bottom of the basket. "Is this for Simon?"

"It was his mother's. I suggest we take it to Peter's study and put it with the rest of the books. Perhaps you know Houseman's poems?"

Rhoda didn't. "Quite jolly little country pieces," she said, flipping through the pages, scarcely glancing at them. "Should cheer him up."

Meg looked at her thoughtfully. If this woman were the journalist she professed to be, then her knowledge of literature was sadly lacking. Or was she, Meg, being unfair? What had journalism to do with literature, anyway? Precious little. Some of the poems were deeply depressing. Death on the gallows and dust to dust – and so on – and so on. If Rhoda had been one of her students she would have told her so. "Not as happy as they might seem," was all she could politely say. "He might like to read them later on. Not yet."

The two women were in the study when Simon came in from the garden, hot and sweaty, with wet grass on his shoes. Rhoda was leaning against his father's desk, her head tilted back, her long hair brushing against a silver penholder. There was nothing aggressive in her attitude; she was, in fact, smiling. Meg, seated, looking up at her – a disadvantaged position – was smiling, too. There was an aura of combat in the air. "Lisa," Meg was saying, "was a very private person. It's hard to imagine she'd want to be featured in a magazine or newspaper – or whatever you intend. She shunned publicity when her book was published. She's that kind of person.

"*Was*," Rhoda reminded her softly. "Simon will have the last word about this when the profile of his mother is completed." She turned and saw him standing by the door. "My being here isn't bothering you too much, is it Simon? Mrs Maybridge thinks perhaps it is. That the whole idea upsets you."

Meg, about to protest that she had said nothing of the sort, bit her lip and was silent. She hadn't said it, but obviously she had implied it. She waited for Simon's answer.

His anger grew slowly as he realised what was happening. Meg

71

Maybridge had come here to pry. She had come to get Rhoda out. "No," he said, trying to keep his voice calm, "I'm not upset. Not about anything. This was my parents' home. Now it's mine. I say who is to come and who is to go. You don't have to worry about me. Rhoda is here because I want her to be here. What she is doing is okay."

He turned away from Meg and went over to stand by Rhoda. A declaration of alliance. "You'll knock it over." He moved the penholder and touched her hair. An excuse to touch it. He could smell her scent and his own sweat. At this worst of moments, fuelled by anger, embarrassment and sheer proximity, he found it hard to control himself.

Oh, God, Meg thought, observing him, he's in love with the bitch!

Rhoda took a few paces away from him and picked up the penholder. "Engraved. 'P.B.' Peter Bradshaw. Nice present from someone. Your mother, perhaps." She put it down again. "Go along and get yourself cleaned up, Simon. You're walking grass and mud into the carpet. And when your hands are clean, put the kettle on. I'm sure Mrs Maybridge would like a cup of tea."

It was brusquely dismissing. The bubble of emotion pricked with a sharp pin.

"It must have hurt him," Meg told Tom later. "She could have been kinder but at least she's not leading him on." She had declined the tea, making an excuse of having to do some shopping. "I went to fetch my basket from the kitchen, hoping to see him, but he wasn't there. He'd left the study, looking abject like a kicked dog. I wanted to give him the photo, but not in front of her. Luckily he was on his own, doing something to the car, when I was leaving, and I handed it to him then. It was in an envelope. He looked at it as if it were a subpoena, he was still very uptight, but he took it graciously enough when I explained. I told him to come round and visit us sometime. And have a talk. I suppose I should have said for a meal – or a drink – or a round of golf with you. The word 'talk' seemed to shrivel him up. He hardly said goodbye."

Maybridge tried not to smile. Meg's 'talks' could spark off bonfires. He wondered what was worse – a frigid indifference to other people or too much concern. "You can't wade in and sort

72

out his love life for him," he told her. "If his parents were around, they couldn't either. At eighteen, an obsession with an older woman isn't unusual. She's probably harmless. If she isn't, it's up to him to sort her out. And if he can't then he can come to me and I'll do all I can. But he must come to me first. Friends can be too intrusive. As for his chucking medicine as a career, he's probably right. It amazes me how he got through the interview. Candidly, if I were mortally ill in hospital, seeing Simon approaching with a stethoscope around his neck would hasten the end."

Meg, who hadn't been expecting that sort of response, was annoyed. If students had academic ability, and Simon had, it was enough to be going on with, she pointed out. Students grew into their chosen profession as time went by. All they needed was a chance to start. "He's sabotaging his future, and she knows about it and doesn't care. I can't help being worried."

Maybridge didn't answer. He'd had rather a bloody day. Literally. A lad of fourteen had stolen a motorbike and crashed it through a plate glass window. When you arrive on that sort of scene you tend to put other matters into perspective. At that particular time, Simon's affairs seemed of little consequence.

Later that evening Simon showed Rhoda the photo. It was a gesture of reconciliation. Her gesture had been to pour him a large whisky on the rocks. It had always soothed his father and though it might not be a good idea in Simon's case it was, by implication, a man's drink and she couldn't think of anything else. She was sorry she had belittled him in front of the Maybridge woman, but it had seemed the only thing to do at the time. In retrospect she should have handled the visit better. In retrospect one can usually do most things better. She had changed out of the caftan as soon as her jeans and shirt were dry. It was a pity Mrs Maybridge had seen her wearing it. The wolf in grandma's gear. Red Riding Hood, alias Simon sexually transformed, standing by her bedside, anxious to jump in.

Not so anxious now, thank God. They were sitting looking at a nineteen-forties Western on television. He on the sofa. She on the chair that had probably been Lisa's, a squashy fawn-coloured recliner. Peter would have favoured the upright brown leather, more supportive for his back. Lumbago, he had told her, was an occupational hazard of pathologists and missionaries. Bending over countless cadavers or recumbent ladies in old-fashioned positions took its toll. She had liked his humour – wry – not always kind. His son showed no vestige of humour whatsoever. But, given the cirumstances, what could she expect?

He got up and turned the television sound down before handing her the photo. "My parents," he said laconically. And then he turned up the sound again so that the room was filled with the rattle of gunshot, thudding of hooves and blaring music. He closed his eyes, listening to the din, being anaesthetised by it. He should have felt some pain on seeing the photo – or, perhaps, pleasure – instead he felt guilt. His mother had looked very trim and young in a green dress and matching shoes, the same dark green as the grass. His father, three rows behind, had his head turned towards a blonde woman, a little shorter than he, standing next to him and at the end of the row. It was windy and she was clutching a red straw hat. The only one there with a hat. And the only one he didn't recognise. The others were local people. Teachers from the village school. A couple of librarians. Doctor and Mrs Francome. The vicar and his wife. Steven Donaldson. He couldn't think why they were all grouped there together. Some village event, probably, and his mother seemed to be the star of it, whatever it was. Or Meg Maybridge must have thought so when she'd taken the snap. She stood out from the rest and seemed confident though unsmiling. The centre of attention. Why couldn't she have been calm like that all the time? Socialised. Been ordinary. What had been wrong with her?

Rhoda was saying something and he couldn't hear above the din. Didn't want to hear. Consoling words, probably. He had carried the photograph around in the pocket of his jeans for some while before deciding to show it to her. His mother's manuscripts hadn't meant very much to him. It hadn't mattered that she was reading them. To him they hadn't felt personal. This was the only photograph of his parents he had; if there were others he'd never seen them, and he had been reluctant to share it. Even with Rhoda.

She turned the television off and her voice was sharp in the silence. "Is this your mother standing in the front?"

74

The question surprised him. It was a good likeness. She had met his mother, hadn't she, at a publisher's party?

'Yes. I thought you would have recognised her."

"I do, of course . . . but . . ."

He noticed her hand holding the photograph was trembling. "What's the matter?"

She ignored the question. "This was taken here in Macklestone, wasn't it?"

"Yes, by Meg Maybridge. She gave it to me when she called."

"Meg Maybridge," Rhoda said softly. "The wife of the local detective chief inspector. How apt."

She walked out of the room, still carrying the photograph, and Simon heard her going upstairs and into his mother's studio. Alarmed for her, she had looked odd and seemed to be talking rubbish, he followed her.

He stood outside the door on the landing and spoke her name tentatively. She didn't answer.

He tried the door. It was locked.

"Rhoda, what's the matter? Are you all right?"

"Go away, Simon. Leave me. Just go away."

Echoes of his mother's voice. *Go away, Simon. Go away. Go away.*

Rhoda left the next morning for London. She borrowed Simon's car and left it in the station car park. She had been gone an hour when Simon got up shortly after nine.

He found a note from her propped up against the milk jug:
Have to go home for a few days. You'll find your car in Bristol Parkway near the taxi rank. Yes, I can drive. I won't wreck it. Sorry if I deceived you. Rhoda."

He was appalled she had gone. And then, gradually getting used to the fact, he calmed down. The house without her felt boringly normal. The air was scentless, her perfume removed. He was no longer thrust into an emotional strait-jacket. His body, quiescent in her absence, behaved. No longer in a state of sexual turmoil, he was able to eat. A couple of rashers of bacon. One of Mrs Maybridge's eggs, fried hard. Toast. Strong tea. She had liked hers milkless, sugarless and weak. Afterwards he dumped all the dirty dishes in the sink and turned the tap on them and left them to soak. She had been tidy. "Without a woman to look after you," she had told him, "you'd turn the place into a piggery." Well, maybe. Pigs were placid creatures. He wasn't placid now but he'd stopped feeling as if his insides were being gouged out with a knife. Pain was ebbing.

He wondered if she had left the car key in the ignition. If so, would someone have stolen it? Why had she said she couldn't drive when she could? Were women always that devious?

He took the local bus to the station and was relieved to see the car still there. The ignition key wasn't visible but, after a panicky search, he found it in the map compartment. On the way back home he put the radio on loud. She didn't like music in the car. On the drive to Gloucester she had turned it off. Without asking. What was married life like? he wondered. Apart from going to bed and having sex whenever you wanted it, what was the point? Did one partner always dominate the other? Rhoda was dominating him. All the time. It was hands off – stay at arm's length – don't dare come close.

Going back into the empty house was more difficult than leaving it. It was lonely. Unwelcoming. He went upstairs to the studio and sat on the couch. Rhoda's nightdress, short white cotton with sprigs of flowers on it, was on the pillow. A virginal-looking nightdress, not at all what he would have expected her to wear. He had always imagined her lying naked. He fondled it, sniffed its musky smell, then put it back on the pillow. She had never spoken of any other man in her life. But there must have been. He didn't want to know. Didn't want to think about it.

The morning sun was blazing into the room, making it hot. The rays spotlighted in the picture of the multicoloured bird pinned next to the mural. He imagined it burning then, phoenix-like, rising from the flames with its melancholy cry: Kywitt, kywitt, what a beautiful bird am I! The bird of his nightmares, mocking him.

He went over and ripped it from the wall. Tore it up.

And then he began looking around the room to try to find the photograph. She had brought it up here yesterday. He needed to look at it again. A happy picture of his parents in a group of happy ordinary people. No dark images.

He searched for a long time without success, turning over the papers of the manuscripts, pushing aside the pile of books on the floor by the cupboard, looking in the cupboard where the typewriter and reference books were kept, and then by chance he glimpsed the blue cardboard box half-hidden under the couch. The photograph wasn't there either, but three small books he hadn't seen before took his attention. He had found his mother's diaries.

7

Rhoda's conscience was an unbiddable animal. It roamed free. When she had moved in on Simon it was over the horizon somewhere, comfortably out of sight, but when she had left him it was snapping at her heels. She kept remembering his anxious voice outside the studio door. "Rhoda, what's the matter? Are you all right?"

No, she wasn't all right. Far from it. She had come to seek and she had found. And it was appalling and frightening and she'd had to get away and plan what to do – if anything could be done. All her anxieties were focused on her missing sister and what might have happened to her. She couldn't carry the extra burden of Peter's son.

In the days when she and Peter were together, sharing his flat for a while, he had accused her of having an exaggerated sense of duty towards Clare. "She's not your everlasting responsibility," he'd pointed out. "When your parents died you quit college so that you could get a job and pay her school fees – for God's sake, what was wrong with the state system? Okay, with an eight-year age gap between you, you felt responsible, I understand that. But she isn't a child any more. Your duty is done." He'd got it all wrong, she'd told him. She hadn't behaved the way she had out of a sense of duty. She had never felt dutiful to anyone. It was a blood tie, but not the sibling stranglehold he imagined. She hadn't used the word love to Peter. It wasn't a word that came naturally to her. Caring for Clare had been a mixture of resentment, exasperation, tenderness, even a touch of maternalism on account of the age gap. When Clare went off on her own and started messing up her life by marrying a ski instructor with better biceps than brains, there hadn't been much she could do about it. But when she had divorced him a couple of years later and had needed a roof over her head for a while and someone to be with her, Rhoda had moved back to her own flat and invited her to stay. Peter had been furious.

His attitude had changed when he met her. Her siren songs were sweet and persuasive and – more surprisingly – she meant them. Clare besotted? Undoubtedly. Peter captivated? It seemed so. She had started hinting to Rhoda – maybe to Peter, too – that she should move into his life permanently. Being with him when he came up to London to lecture at the university wasn't enough. How Peter had responded had been hard to guess. He rarely mentioned his family, but his description of Lisa as 'slightly disturbed' had sounded like an ominous euphemism. It was unlikely he would leave her. Rhoda had warned Clare to watch what she was doing. Peter's domestic set-up with his wife and son was private territory. Keep away.

But Clare had trespassed. Shortly before the Bradshaws' silver wedding anniversary, according to the date Mrs Maybridge had scribbled on the back of the photograph, she had moved right in on to Lisa's home ground.

Lisa's anger must have been intense when she had painted the picture of the long-haired blonde with red slashes of paint across her head and running in long streaks from her throat to her thighs like wounds. When Rhoda had come across it in the loft, it had just seemed an artist's dissatisfaction with a crude piece of work – a crossing-out in crimson. But the photo had given it significance. Clare, in her red hat and red and black striped dress, standing next to Peter. A provocative, daring, stupid statement of involvement. Lisa, standing at the front of the group. Alone.

79

Rhoda's going and not coming back, despite her saying it would be just for a few days, was hard for Simon to come to terms with. At first her absence was bearable. He got out. Went for long drives. Drove fast. The weather was blowy and the air smelt good. He felt as if his emotions had been vacuumed and everything inside his head was very neat. And then the weather closed in, rain clouds obscured the sun, the wind no longer blew. The house was grey and murky and Rhoda-less. He longed to smell her musky perfume. Touch the warm skin of her hands. Listen to her voice, exasperated, bossing him. He took her nightdress to bed, wrapped it around one of the pillows and hugged it to him. Dreamed of making love to her. And succeeded. In the morning, ashamed, embarrassed, he washed the nightdress sketchily and dried it indoors. Rhoda. Rhoda. Rhoda.

It was during a period of dull despair that he started reading his mother's diaries. They were the three early ones when Lisa had been at her worst and referred directly to him. He read them in the summerhouse with the doors closed against the rain that was slanting down through the leaves of the almond tree, frail leaves that fell soggily into the sodden grass.

He read them guiltily, apprehensively, and with a growing awareness of the maternal bond that would be there for ever, no matter what. In some aspects of her he saw Rhoda, but she overshadowed Rhoda. Her diaries made flesh of the shadow as if she were alive again. Alive and indifferent to him. Or alive and accusing. The bland, smiling, bored, trying hard to be maternal and failing presence was hard to exorcise. Talking about her to Donaldson might help. His note: "If there is anything I can do, then please call on me," had been polite rather than warm, but he might have meant it. Perhaps he could see her medical records – if he dared to ask for them – if he dared to know.

He couldn't remember his last visit to The Mount. His mother's garbled account of taking him there on his sixth birthday was a confusion of anecdotes concerning Hans Andersen and the 'loonies' who wouldn't play with him. His mother's world in those days had been an extraordinary place in which the centuries merged and the past became a grotesque, fairy-tale present. Writers like Andersen and Grimm were a peculiar breed, and illustrators of their sick dreams were probably worse. And she had revelled in them. Caught their virus, perhaps, as she had studied their work. Had she done something else, followed a different career, would she have been all right? And what did he mean by 'all right'? She had been all right, hadn't she, most of the time? Probably all the time when he wasn't around. So the fault must lie with him, mustn't it? There must have been a reason for rejecting him. Had he looked different, had a different personality, would he have passed whatever test she had set?

And would he have passed whatever test Rhoda had set?

Confused, longing for Rhoda, and with his self-esteem about as low as it could be, he walked up the long gravelled drive to The Mount's pseudo-Gothic front door.

And Sally let him in.

Sallys are nice girls. Cheerful girls. Therapeutic girls. They bring sunshine into psychiatric hospitals and are a joy to all.

Or almost all.

Steven Donaldson had started having reservations about Sally Loreto a few weeks after employing her. She had done nothing wrong. On the contrary, she had done everything right. Her domestic duties weren't performed to perfection, but were performed well enough. The domestic staff liked her. The professional staff liked her, too. And so did the patients. Especially Creggan. Possibly it was Creggan's warmth towards her that had made Donaldson uneasy. "An attractive young woman," Creggan had said, "but where did she get her surname from – a convent or a saint?" Donaldson had replied brusquely that as far as he knew she wasn't a Catholic. An illogical response to a silly question. There were times when he felt as irrational as his patients. Creggan had smiled at him with a degree of sympathy.

Sally was twenty-two years old and looked younger. She was small, narrow hipped, but with well rounded breasts which were bra-less. Her hair, albino fair, almost white, crisply curled at the nape of her neck, and her eyes by contrast were a deep turquoise blue. She jogged around the grounds every morning before the day's chores and then sat for a few minutes on the bench in the hall, her arms crossed over her chest and her head bowed. Not a

81

yoga position, just a rather graceful slump that probably eased her pectoral muscles. Later, rested, she changed out of her green and white jogging suit into a floral overall and brought the patients their morning cups of tea.

Creggan's morning cup of tea, taken off the premises in his tepee, took rather longer to deliver. Just how much longer was reasonable was difficult for Donaldson to assess. Sex before breakfast might be good therapy for Creggan but it wasn't part of The Mount's therapy and he had a duty to protect Sally. He had been a fool to employ anyone so young, but there hadn't been anyone else. Domestic work in a psychiatric hospital – or nursing home as he had described it in the advertisement – doesn't attract applicants. He had believed he'd been lucky to get her. He wished he could still believe it. A growing anxiety neurosis was an occupational hazard and external events of the last few months hadn't helped. Physicians might heal themselves if they suffered from organic disease, psychiatrists had a harder time trying. Here, where the lush came to be dried, it was folly to be seen seeking solace in neat whisky. Vodka and tonic, however, was almost as good and didn't linger on the breath. To seem to practise what he preached was vital. He owed that much to his patients.

And he owed Simon a courteous reception when Sally showed him into his consulting room. Which she shouldn't have done. An open invitation to his patients to come and chat any time wasn't open to visitors. They first encountered his secretary, Miss Bailey, who informed him they were there, or told them he wasn't there, or otherwise engaged.

"Miss Bailey has gone to the dentist's," Sally told him and smiled her little girl smile at him, "so I brought him straight along." She eyed his glass of vodka and tonic on the desk, not fleetingly but for several seconds. "Is there anything I can get you, Doctor? Would your guest like some coffee?"

Simon said quickly that he wouldn't.

The air zinged with irritation.

Donaldson knew that Brenda Bailey had gone to the dentist's, but Sally should have left Simon in the outer office. And she shouldn't look at his drink like that or act the gracious hostess, offering coffee to his *guest*. She was a domestic, damn it. He

82

thanked her crisply and waited for her to close the door after her before offering Simon a chair.

"I'm sorry you were out when I called on you, Simon. I should have called again. I'm really delighted you've come to see me."

Delighted – no. Disconcerted – yes. He bore more than just a fleeting resemblance to his mother. It was impossible to look at him and not see her. He felt very tired, suddenly. Why had he come? What did he want?

He remembered asking Lisa the same questions just a few months ago. She had walked in unannounced on a rainy afternoon, seated herself in the same tub chair in the window recess and gazed out across the garden, silently. Her face had been in profile and her brown and cream headscarf, very damp, was slowly working loose from its knot and slipping on to the collar of her mack. She'd seemed withdrawn, hardly aware of her surroundings. He'd thought she might be close to tears and had asked the questions gently and with concern, but when she had turned and looked at him, her eyes had been very bright and clear. "Soon," she said, "Peter and I celebrate our silver wedding anniversary. Marvellous, isn't it? He wants me to go to the Istrian Peninsula with him – where we went for our honeymoon. Who is he running from, do you suppose? The latest lady love getting too close – like that other bitch, Trudy Morrison? Or is it the male menopause? A change of heart?"

Questions that couldn't be answered were better ignored. Bradshaw's lady love, as she had so quaintly put it, had been the girl in the red hat who had turned up at the opening ceremony of the new library extension looking as if she were attending Ascot.

There had been rumours that she had something to do with the art world and had come as a guest of Lisa's. Other rumours had, correctly, linked her with Peter. His attitude towards her had been carefully cool, his face a stiff expressionless mask as if he'd had a night of heavy boozing and was nursing a hangover. Peter had the knack of putting his emotions on ice, according to Lisa, but could be lethally charming when warmed up. A sardonic appraisal of a husband she had never stopped loving.

Love – a trick of nature to procreate.

But Lisa hadn't wanted a child.

Donaldson started talking to her son. Inconsequential talk. A spider's web of words to stem the bleeding of an old wound. The wound, he knew, couldn't fail to be there. The ills of most of his patients went back to childhood days, to sexual abuse in some cases, neglect in others. There were more problem parents than problem children. The former, unfortunately, produced the latter, but it didn't always show until adolescence. Sometimes a lot later.

He asked Simon if he was looking forward to a career in medicine.

"No."

"You'd rather do something else?"

"Yes."

"Any idea what?"

"No."

Donaldson hesitated before asking the next question. A leading one. "Are you troubled about anything?"

'Troubled' is a down-beat word. He used it frequently, along with 'a little concerned', 'rather bothered', 'somewhat worried'. A soothing approach followed by a period of silence, carefully calculated. If properly timed the patient opened up. If he'd got it wrong, he clammed up. In this case, getting it wrong might be getting it right. Simon wasn't the type to make a social call so he had come for information of some kind and was finding it almost impossible to voice his question. He was rigid with tension. It might be better not voiced. Donaldson sat back in his chair. Waited. Had Simon been anyone else, his professional instinct would have nudged him to grab the moment before it was too late; instead he stayed silent, glanced at the diary on his desk, pushed it to one side. When he looked at Simon again, he saw he'd calculated it perfectly. The boy's hands were no longer clenched into fists and he wasn't breathing so rapidly. His resolve to speak had ebbed. Whatever it was he'd come to say, he'd thought better of it. A possible indiscretion had been averted. What would Simon have asked him? he wondered. "Was my mother paranoid?" "Can paranoia be inherited?" Or would he have come out with the less traumatic worries of adolescence, more easily assuaged by a calming speech about the human con-

84

dition being a mixture of moods and reactions suffered by everyone in different degrees and at different times, all perfectly normal? A glib, meaningless word, normal. But soothing.

Simon said he wasn't troubled about anything. He had realised in the last few minutes that a request to look at his mother's medical file would have been refused. Donaldson would have said that it was private. Or destroyed. It probably had been, and it was better so. Why keep records of the dead? It was difficult to imagine his mother having anything to do with this elderly goat-like man with his long bony head crammed with psychiatric jargon. Had he let his defences down, asked him anything, told him anything, he would have spouted Freud at him. Or ferreted away until he had dug up his sexual fantasies and – worse – his making love to Rhoda's nightdress. It had been pointless coming here. He got up to leave.

Donaldson, slightly guilty about the way he'd opted out professionally, felt he should make more effort socially and suggested that Simon might like to have a look over the premises. It would ease the boy, he thought, if he had preconceived disturbing notions of the place.

The Mount externally was a sombre mish-mash of the eighteenth and nineteenth centuries with a twentieth-century extension at the back which would have induced neurosis in an architectural purist, though a thick coat of ivy helped to disguise the worst of it. Inside were craft areas and a heated swimming pool where scantily clad patients, or staff, they all looked the same to Simon, seemed to be enjoying themselves, some in the water, others seated in loungers. In the main building there was a music room, a billiard room, a library and several small sitting-rooms, all cheerfully furnished like a middle quality hotel. Patients – staff? – sat in groups mostly, though a few loners roamed around, or sat alone reading, or just sat.

Simon, expecting something more clinical, asked about ECT. Most visitors did. Donaldson said he didn't believe in it. Simon warmed to him a little. It couldn't have been all that bad for his mother. Perhaps not bad at all. Just a place to rest, as he had told Rhoda. He asked if he could see her room.

Donaldson told him smoothly that no particular room had been

85

set aside for her, she had visited very rarely, just now and again when domestic pressures, that sort of thing, got her down briefly, but he would show him the room she'd had last time she was here. And then he remembered that Corinne Sinclair, a sixty-year-old manic depressive, had gouged out chunks of plaster from the wall with the metal-tipped heel of her shoe the previous night and was now deeply sedated in the 'quiet wing', the only part of The Mount that remotely resembled a hospital. Instead, he showed Simon one of the other bedrooms and said it had been Lisa's. It had a wide window facing the lawn and the shrubby area beyond, where Creggan's tent was. The crazy, cheerful little tepee, viewed from up here, didn't look sinister enough to worry anybody. Simon tried to imagine his mother standing by the window, looking out. She probably wouldn't have liked the yellow chintz curtains, they would have been too flowery for her, not modern enough. Apart from that it was a nice enough room. He wouldn't have minded sleeping here himself.

Donaldson's private accommodation was a three-roomed flat on the top floor, carefully and appropriately furnished. The first time he had entertained Lisa up there, she had looked around it with amusement and told him it was phoney. "Who are you trying to con, Steven? This isn't you." She had been referring to the book-lined walls, all the books in their pristine jackets and most un-read. Poetry. The classics. History. Modern fiction, but not a lot. The family photographs – his sister's family – hadn't been too prominent, but made a quiet statement. A bachelor needs a little help. The one photograph that had meant anything to him, and had been taken a long time ago when they were undergraduates at Cambridge, had been placed a little behind the others. Lisa had alighted on it. "Hush, hush, whisper who dares," she had teased. Lisa had the ability to annoy. And arouse stronger emotions, too.

He decided not to show his flat to her son.

On the way out they met Sally coming in. "Mr Creggan is back," she told Donaldson, "and he's brought a dog. A pooch. A sort of middle sized mongrel. He said he saw a programme about geriatrics petting dogs and getting better. Dog therapy. He said it should work at any age. If you don't want it, Bob Millington up at the farm will probably take it for a while until Mr Creggan goes again." She smiled. "You do get lumbered with problems, Doctor Donaldson, and you keep so calm."

If Donaldson could have sacked her there and then for her veiled insolence, he would have done. And if he could have booted Creggan out without losing his fee he would have done that, too. Creggan was paying well over the odds and money mattered. He excused himself to Simon and strode off in the direction of Creggan's tent.

And left Simon and Sally standing together within touching distance.

Sally duly touched him, her fingers lightly resting on his wrist. It wasn't a Rhoda touch, but it was warm enough to be pleasant. "I knew your mum," she told him. "Last time she was here, I'd only just come. I cleaned her room out for her and she gave me something when she was leaving. I'll give it to you if you'll take me for a run in your car. I have a free afternoon tomorrow."

For the first time for months Simon felt mildly happy. He asked her her name.

"Sally," she told him, giving his wrist a gentle squeeze.

Sally was the sort of name he associated with a milk-shake with a lot of sugar in it. A bit boring. Not like Rhoda. He asked what his mother had given her, but she wouldn't tell him.

"You'll see."

He noticed that when she smiled her eyes were coolly appraising. Her eyes and her lips didn't match. Her boobs, however, were a beautiful pair. His eyes lingered on them and she giggled. "Tomorrow's okay, then? About half past two? I'll come down to your place."

8

Max Cormack, a young Irish pathologist, took over Peter Bradshaw's job with some trepidation. He had the right qualifications and sufficient experience not to do anything stupid; even so, he felt like a raw understudy stepping into the leading actor's shoes. How was it that dabbling with the dead fired the imagination of the living? Crime stories sold newspapers. And books. And plays. Othello strangling Desdemona still sent thrills of horror down the spine. Intimations of mortality, other people's mortality, churned the stomach but were exciting, too. The public wanted to know more. And more. Forensic science, as opposed to other sciences, had some readable bits like excerpts from a 'whodunnit'. Genetic fingerprinting, for instance, had featured in quite a few articles in the Press. The Press coverage of Bradshaw had been very high profile, to use the current jargon. Getting himself killed so spectacularly had probably helped.

Easy on there, Cormack chided himself, cynicism will get you nowhere. Bradshaw was a competent pathologist and, according to his colleagues, a likeable bloke. And his colleagues, the senior policemen he'd met after being appointed, seemed likeable, too.

Not the type to go in for practical jokes, though at first he'd thought one of them was taking the mickey.

The pink envelope had been placed on his desk next to a couple of folders full of Bradshaw's unfinished business and a single sheet of paper, typed by his secretary, outlining the general set-up and pointing out what was urgent and what wasn't. A competent girl, Sofia. Pretty, too. Asian, he guessed. Skin the colour of milky coffee and dark brown eyes. She was eyeing him now as he fingered the envelope. It was fully addressed and stamped and had come through the post.

He opened it. The card inside was pink, too. *Congratulations on your new job* was the printed message. And under it the picture of a Scottie dog wearing a tartan cap and smoking a pipe. Anthropomorphic. Very twee. An Irish leprechaun doing a jig on a mortuary slab would be more in keeping.

He turned the page. And saw closely written in a small cramped hand: *Look at Rapunzel Number Five, Doctor Cormack, and look hard. May the good Lord guide you to the truth while Bradshaw rots in hell.* It wasn't signed. It took him a few moments to recognise the handwriting and remember where he'd seen it before. Photocopied on the Hixon file. Not a joke. Not even an execrable one.

"What's Hixon trying to do," he asked, tossing the card over to Sofia, "trying to prove he's mad?"

"Only a lunatic would want to go to Broadmoor," she said and then, realising what she'd said, giggled. She examined the card and passed it back. "Professor Bradshaw had a lot of this sort of thing. Only worse. Obituary cards – some of them. Very stark. He tore them up."

put the card in the desk drawer. D.C.I. Maybridge was meeting him for a drink that evening. He'd been part of the Rapunzel team, too, and had probably been badgered in the same way. He wondered if Maybridge would object to talking shop over a couple of pints.

They were due to meet at the small pub near the docks at eight thirty. He would have preferred a different venue. The corpse of an elderly man, drowned a few days previously, had been caught in the propeller of a motorboat and brought ashore like a gutted fish. Hardened to his job, he had gone through the usual routine while one of the young constables, Radwell, he thought his name was, had crouched behind a bollard and been sick. Maybridge hadn't been present.

By eight thirty the small section of dockside had been washed clean. The evening sun shone on the mullioned windows of The Bell and on Maybridge, nattily dressed in a lightweight grey suit, who was standing by the entrance. He had arrived early. "Look," he said, without preamble, "if you'd rather go somewhere else, they serve good draught ale and a bar snack, if you want it, a couple of streets away. Radwell told me things were pretty messy over there."

"Pathologists, like policemen," Cormack assured him, "have selective memories. Just now everything is looking pretty good. The Bell will suit me fine."

Maybridge, who hadn't a selective memory and was plagued by horrific visions of violent death for quite a while after each case, thought he could detect bravado in Cormack's response. "Well, if you're sure."

"Quite sure."

But the pathologist chose a table away from the window, Maybridge noticed. There are degrees of professional toughness. Age, in some cases, hardened the carapace, though mostly it was a matter of temperament.

When a newcomer joins a team you try to help him to settle in. Extending the hand of friendship to Peter's successor had been easier than Maybridge had expected. Peter himself would have approved of the appointment; there would be no stealing of his thunder. Cormack had a quality of Irish charm that was difficult to define and was probably best summed up as being easy with people. He was highly competent, but not aggressively so. Peter, at times, showed off. Played to the gallery. Part of his professorial role. Cormack wasn't professorial material and had no ambition to go in that direction. He hoped to stay put, he told Maybridge. He liked this part of the country. He had put his house in Sheffield on the market and was on the look-out for something not too big, but large enough for a family home. He and his girlfriend were planning to marry in a year or so when she returned from the

States. She was nursing in a Chicago hospital. In the meantime he was living in digs and trudging around estate agents in his spare time. So far he hadn't seen anything that appealed. Or if it appealed, he couldn't afford it.

Over a second pint of Guinness he broached the subject again. "Your village, Macklestone, reminds me of a hamlet near Derry where I was brought up. If anything comes on the market there, would you let me know?"

Maybridge, guessing he had Peter's house in mind, explained the situation. "Bradshaw's son, Simon, has inherited the property – or is about to. It's much too large for a lad on his own, but it's too soon to approach him about selling up."

Cormack, who did have it in mind, was embarrassed. "Sure it is. No way would I worry him. God, I'd be no better than a bloody vulture if I did. But maybe later . . . when he's had time to think . . ."

Maybridge wondered to what degree thinking about it would hurt. Would it be turning the knife in the wound if Simon met his father's successor with a view to selling his home to him? Would it hurt less to sell it to someone else? Or would he be glad to be rid of it? Cormack seemed a decent enough bloke. Not insensitive. They could meet casually perhaps and the property needn't be mentioned until both were more sure about it. Simon might want to stay put. He suggested that Cormack might like to have digs in the village. "I could give you the addresses of a couple of farms that do B. and B. and an evening meal. It would give you a chance to have a proper look around. Something else might turn up in the meantime. Everything should be clearer in a few months."

Cormack, pleased with the idea, thanked him. There was no great hurry. The future, with average good luck, should last a long time. Simon's parents, he reminded himself, had probably thought the same. And the chap who had been fished out of the dock this morning. And all those unfortunate little tarts that Hixon had raped and strangled.

He mentioned Hixon's card but didn't show it. A cosy chat about an eminent predecessor's home and his son couldn't be concluded with Hixon's purple prose about Bradshaw's rotting in hell. A glossing over the contents, however, didn't fool May-bridge.

"Derogatory about Bradshaw, and that's probably putting it very mildly. Did he threaten you?"

"No. Just pointed me in the direction of the fifth Rapunzel. Obviously likes the name the Press have tagged on to his victims. Seems to imply that she wasn't his victim and wants me to do something about it."

Maybridge was watching him keenly, his hand of friendship momentarily not quite so firm. "Your reaction?"

Cormack answered thoughtfully. "You tell a hoaxer to get lost. Someone who is dangerously paranoid, no matter what the shrinks might say, you ignore. I have no doubt whatsoever that the professor's forensic evidence was one hundred percent correct in all five cases." It was tempting to ask why Hixon should have settled on just that one case, but perhaps not politic. Instead he asked how Hixon had got hold of a card like that in the nick, written that sort of rubbish on it and got it past the censor.

"The same way he desecrated the wreath at the Bradshaw's funeral." Maybridge told him about it. "Someone on the outside does it for him."

"And someone on the outside informed him about my appoint-ment – that's how he got my name?"

"Could be. Or he could have read about it in the local paper. Newspapers aren't banned in the nick. Most of what is reported in the Press is correct, though some information is withheld when it's a murder investigation. Afterwards, when the case is closed and it can be safely released, it is."

"Safely?"

Maybridge took a few sips of Guinness before replying. "Serial murders usually have method in common – one particular way of doing it. Or a bizarre way of signing off. If it's a knifing, a hieroglyphic in blood, perhaps, somewhere on the victim's body. A signature can be copied. It confuses the evidence. So the police keep quiet about it. But you must know all this. It's part of your job."

Cormack did, of course. But most of the cadavers he'd investi-gated had been straightforward killings. Run of the mill murders, the majority domestic, and reported freely during the Press conference. The Rapunzel murders had been unique. The common denominator: manual strangulation of five long-haired prostitutes, their hair plaited and tied tightly around their necks afterwards – like a noose. According to Bradshaw's reports.

"My job," he told Maybridge amicably, "is dealing with anything the police land on me. You haven't landed anything bizarre on me yet. No one has written a billet-doux on any of my cadavers' bellies. All has been sweet and simple. Or maybe simple but not sweet. You catch the murdering buggers at some risk to yourselves. I make a further mess of their victims at the autopsy, then bung off everything relevant to the forensic science laboratory. The experts get going with traces of semen, blood, hair fibres, human and otherwise, nail scrapings, etc, etc. They analyse this and that, feed the computers with data, and, hey presto, get an answer. Usually correct. But no acclaim whatsoever. Nice job, though. Not messy. Good if you want a quiet life."

"Hm," said Maybridge. Peter hadn't. He'd probably appreciated his back-up team, but he'd been standing out there well in front and obviously enjoying every minute of it. Simon doing a back-room job was easy to imagine. He might have his father's genes, but he certainly hadn't his temperament.

Genes. Genetic engineering. D.N.A. fingerprinting. All up-front words in common use bandied around by lay-men as well as professionals. Cormack had used the phrase 'usually correct' just now. Rightly. Even an exact science has a margin of error. D.N.A. fingerprinting had been ruled unsafe in a recent murder enquiry in the U.S.A. The fifth Rapunzel case had been particularly difficult. Unlike the others. He was relieved, however, that Cormack had dismissed Hixon's insinuation as paranoid. It was, of course.

It's easy to play the fool and get away with it if your audience is made up of amateurs. If they're a team of professionals, headed by a professional, it becomes rather difficult. The Mount's medical staff guessed that Donaldson was being well paid for turning a blind eye on Creggan and risked sounding him out about it at one of the staff meetings. Sue Raudsley, a psychotherapist who had only been on the staff a few months and didn't care if she were sacked, was spokeswoman and junior enough to sound naive. "What, if anything, is wrong with Paul Creggan?" she asked. Donaldson, anticipating the question at some stage, but not just then when he wasn't in the mood to answer it, had snapped back: "His desire to pitch a tent in the grounds of a psychiatric hospital, sleep on a trestle bed and eat appalling food. Normal behaviour, would you say?" The Raudsley woman, to his annoyance, had pressed on: Was Creggan suffering from stress, failure to respond to the parasympathetic nervous system, perhaps? Or could his night walks be linked with depression and diurnal variation of mood? If so, why wasn't he on medication? Valid questions. Donaldson, furious that his ethical credibility was being impugned, had congratulated her drily on her text-book knowledge and suggested that she might learn to apply it more effectively when she had more clinical experience. It hadn't been a comfortable session and he had brought it to an abrupt end.

He was thinking about it now as he approached Creggan's tent. Creggan had his back to the tent flap, which was open, and was pulling a jersey over his head. His suit was on the floor, gathering dust from the tarpaulin and the sisal matting. The tent smelt of grass and Creggan's after-shave, which he wouldn't use again until he was back in London.

Donaldson greeted him coldly. "Welcome back. You left on impulse, perhaps. Your note was very brief. I would have appreciated being told. A few minutes of your time in my consulting room wouldn't have delayed you too much."

Creggan apologised. "You're right. It was discourteous of me. I attended the funeral and then . . ." he spread his hands, shrugged. "It was upsetting. I didn't stop to think." He picked the suit up from the floor and put it on the bed. "Do sit down. It's good to see you again. Good to be here."

"I wasn't aware you knew the Bradshaws." Donaldson sat on the only chair there. It was made of wicker but with a thickly padded back and seat.

"No," Creggan said. "Put it this way, I joined the party like a great many more. The lady with the camera spoilt the show – or added more interest to it, depending on your point of view."

94

Had all The Mount patients attended, Donaldson felt like telling him, Press interest would have been intense, the villagers would have been outraged and he would have been reported to the G.M.C. for unprofessional conduct.

Creggan's answer to his question about knowing the Bradshaws hadn't been a clear negative. Donaldson put it to him again. "I wondered if you had met Mrs Bradshaw – Lisa – during one of her visits here."

"Here – to my tepee?" Creggan deliberately misunderstood him. "Oh, no, Doctor Donaldson. Far too primitive. Not at all the right surroundings for the lady – any lady. Fine for me, of course. And for my dog." He clicked his fingers. "Come on, boy, come and be introduced."

The animal, part basset, part rough-haired terrier of some sort, had been curled up asleep behind a wooden crate containing a dozen bottles of Dom Perignon champagne. Creggan's gift of appeasement.

"Champers from us both," he told Donaldson. "For you and your staff. Or just for you." He fondled the dog's silky ears. "He's called Perignon, too. Perry for short. Your delectable little Sally has suggested that he stays at White Oak Farm, if the farmer agrees and you won't have him. He has kennels, she tells me, and a cattery. I can collect him there for walkies."

Donaldson eyed the dog dubiously. It eyed him back, yawned, then wagged its tail. A cheerful animal. He remembered Creggan's allusion to the black dog of despair during the first interview. And his later attempt to bribe his way in. The champagne now was a bribe. How would pompous Miss Raudsley react to that? More importantly, how should he?

"I can't allow a dog on the premises," at least he could be definite about that, "and if you tried keeping it out here it could still wander indoors and be a nuisance to the patients. As for keeping it at Millington's farm – that would be all right by day – but going up there and collecting it at night and taking it on night walks in the country where there are sheep . . ."

Creggan interrupted him. "On a lead, Steven. And not always at night. I promise you there'll be no trouble."

It was the first time Creggan had used his Christian name. It didn't signify anything, most of the older members of staff used it. Even so . . . a growing familiarity? Or a touch of contempt?

"Medication might help you," he suggested, resuming the dominant role, "if you have trouble sleeping."

"Ah, but I do sleep," Creggan pointed out, "whenever I feel like it. Just as Perry sleeps whenever he feels like it. Look at him now." The dog had slumped down again and was resting its muzzle on its paws. Its eyes were closing. "Your therapy might seem unorthodox to some, but you've helped me enormously," Creggan went on, unaware that he couldn't have said anything more apposite. "It would help even more if I could have a companion on my walks. If you'd allow it I'd be immensely grateful."

Donaldson remembered a wet patch on the ceiling of his flat where the roof leaked. How grateful? Possibly that grateful? Creggan's attempt to bribe his way into The Mount had annoyed him. His conscience these days was less tender.

And he might have known Lisa. If so, he might be persuaded to talk about her, and that could be revealing.

As for the dog . . . more unorthodox therapy? On the contrary. "All right," he conceded. "I'll try and fix things up with the farmer on your behalf. If Millington agrees, then the dog can stay."

Creggan, very relieved, tried not to show it. He had done enough reconnoitring on his own, surveying possible sites. Lush, soft, spongy ground. All he needed was the help of four strong paws and a muzzle that could pick up the right scent.

Max Cormack and Creggan's dog moved into White Oak Farm on the same day. Millington accorded them both a similar welcome – not effusive. He didn't like dogs but the kennels and cattery were a source of income, badly needed. As for having Bradshaw's successor as a paying guest, he would rather have had someone else, had anyone else wanted to come. But there wasn't anyone and Maybridge had recommended him. If he refused to have him he'd upset Maybridge, and that might not be wise. Maybridge had sensed his reluctance and made a feeble joke about the Pope and the Archbishop of Canterbury being pally these days. An accusation of bigotry he resented. He was a staunch Nonconformist, but having an Irish Catholic in his home didn't worry him.

He didn't have to go to his church any more than he had to go to the local C. of E. where his wife played the organ. He just didn't like Cormack's job. He had heard he was working on a wino who had fallen into the docks and drowned. Not that Cormack had said he was a wino, one just assumed it. It could have been suicide, of course. He imagined a white whale-like body on a slab with flippers for fingers. How could it be fingerprinted if the skin had all come off? Would Cormack have to rely on the teeth for identification? What if the corpse was toothless and the dentures lost?

On a more personal level, would this young doctor resent a question about the hernia operation that his G.P. had recommended and had gone wrong? Or did he only deal with the dead?

Millington put Cormack's suitcase down in the large, white painted, sun filled bedroom on the top floor and told him that he wore a truss. Cormack, delighted with the bedroom, said he was sorry to hear it. He had offered to carry the case himself but the wiry little farmer, ruddy cheeked like a garden gnome, had insisted on taking it from him. He asked him, unwisely, why a truss in these enlightened days, and Millington told him – at length. Cormack mumbled something appropriate about mishaps not always being avoidable.

"They're mishaps when they happen to other people," Millington stated bitterly. "How would you like it to happen to you?"

Not an auspicious start in new digs. Cormack wondered if he had been unwise leaving the old ones. But this room looked out over acres of spring-green countryside, and the house itself was superb. Old, creaky, uneven walls, beams, probably damp, but glorious for all that. Packed full of history. Bradshaw's place, as yet seen only from the outside, couldn't be more different. Modern. Functional. But, of the two, Josie would probably prefer it. He would be glad when she came back to Britain. He wanted to settle down. Have kids.

He changed the subject by asking Millington if he had any family. Millington said he had a brother farming in France and wouldn't mind selling up and joining him. "What good has the E.E.C. done the farmers over here, tell me that? At least he makes a living over there. My wife wouldn't go, though, that's the trouble. Likes being here, she says. Born in Macklestone. Has put down roots. You have to be born in a place to put down roots. You're not accepted otherwise. You're tolerated, that's all. I've been here twenty years and I'm tolerated. Nothing more."

Cormack saw it as a back-handed compliment to the villagers. A very tolerant lot, obviously. Millington amused him, but in small doses only. Macklestone, like all villages, might have barren soil here and there, and if you want to put down roots you have to nourish it to some extent. Like being sociable. He invited him to have a drink with him in the local when he'd unpacked.

Millington declined. He had to be around, he explained bitterly, to give a key to the kennels to a man called Creggan who went on night walks with a dog. And that was the fault of the Common Agricultural Policy, too. In the old days you weren't so skint that you had to pander to lunatics.

Cormack raised his eyebrows and waited for more.

Millington wasn't forthcoming. His wife would have supper on the table by seven, he told him. In about half an hour. The dining-room was to the left of the front door, across the hall from the sitting-room. The sitting-room was for him to use any time he wanted to. There weren't any other paying guests at the moment. He could go in there and read. Or play the harmonium, if he wanted to, but not late at night. Cormack thanked him, said he wasn't musical but liked to read, and would be down shortly. He clenched his jaws against laughter until Millington had gone.

Mrs Millington's Christian name was Dawn and she urged Cormack to use it. He found it extremely difficult. She was too old to be called Dawn, the golden flush of youth long gone. She was in her late forties, he guessed, a heavily built woman with dark brown eyes, greying hair worn in an old-fashioned chignon, and thick strong farming hands. Hands, he was to discover, that could play the harmonium with great tenderness and skill. She spent an hour every Saturday evening practising the voluntary for the church service on Sunday. Usually she chose a time when Cormack was out. It was by chance that he returned early from a visit to the Maybridges and heard her, and asked if he might sit and listen. Rather flustered, she agreed. She favoured Bach, she told him, and the Lutheran hymns, but nothing lugubrious. The vicar's choice of hymns, especially for funerals, was the pits. Really dreadful. She had told him so when he had given her the list for the Bradshaws' funeral, but he hadn't listened. She had been sorry in her heart for their son.

That her sorrow was confined to the son and was in no way extended to his parents became obvious to Cormack in subsequent conversations. To be sorry for the dead, in Cormack's view, was a waste of emotion, but to regret their demise was surely a normal charitable reaction. Her silence on this was surprising. "A dreadful tragedy," he had said, and meant it. Had she responded with something trite about God's will she wouldn't have aroused his curiosity; instead she had smiled enigmatically and asked him what he would like for his evening meal – casseroled steak, or cold chicken as the evening was warm?

It was through Mrs Millington that Cormack met Sergeant Radwell socially. He sang in the church choir and had come to borrow some sheet music so that he could photocopy it, he told Cormack. "I've had to skip a few practices, due to police work, and need to catch up. Dawn understands, luckily."

No trouble about calling her Dawn, Cormack noticed. The young sergeant, monosyllabic when in the company of his superiors, even with the easy-going Maybridge, seemed very relaxed here at the farm. Off duty, he had dressed in a navy blue sweatshirt and jeans, which managed not to look too incongruous in the beautiful little sitting-room which had been made less beautiful by a too-large cherry-coloured three piece suite. The harmonium, the only true antique in the place, glowed softly in the low rays of the setting sun.

"Nice instrument," Radwell said.

Cormack agreed. He listened, rather bored, while Mrs Millington and Radwell had a discussion about one of the arias in the *St Matthew Passion*. Radwell, to make his point, played a few notes on the harmonium with his right hand. Dawn, disagreeing with whatever it was, played it a great deal better with both hands.

Later, when Radwell had left the room to go down to the kennels to have a look at Creggan's dog, Mrs Millington told Cormack about his background. "Graham wanted to be a priest, but hadn't the right temperament. I can't imagine why he became a police-man, he hasn't the right temperament for that, either. Did you know that he was the first to find Susan Martin's body, just two miles across the fields from here? It was a Sunday evening and I'd just got in from church. I shall always remember him running across the yard – well, stumbling – and he could hardly get the words out. I thought he was ill. And then he began to cry . . ." Her voice was without emotion. In the distance someone whistled and a dog barked. She put the lid of the harmonium down very gently. "He needed to use our phone to inform Maybridge, but it was some while before he could dial the number, his hand was shaking so much. When he did get through he kept on saying he was sorry, as if it was all his fault. He's not your cool professional policeman. Never will be."

Susan Martin, Cormack remembered, was Rapunzel Number Five. The only prostitute who hadn't been murdered in the en-virons of a city. It surprised him that Craxton Copse was so close to Macklestone. The name had meant nothing to him when he had read Bradshaw's notes. He wondered if Hixon had been preaching in one of the hamlets nearby. Or had he met the girl in Bristol and enticed her into his car? Bradshaw's notes on all five cases had dealt mainly with inceptive, corroborative and indicative evidence, but had only lightly touched on the non-forensic aspects of direct and circumstantial evidence. As far as Cormack could remember, there had been very little direct evidence. Hixon had been seen in the areas where the murders had been committed, but then so had a great many other suspects. Maybridge and his team had focused on Hixon in the early days of the investigation mainly because Hixon's unstable personality had almost invited them to. The whore of Babylon was a recurring theme in his sermons and he wrote a couple of letters to the *Bristol Evening News* extolling the Liberal statesman, Gladstone, for his mission of mercy in the red light districts of nineteenth-century London. Gladstone, he declared, raised fallen women with the hand of love. Glory hallelu-jah! As prostitutes were being felled, rather than raised, it was an unwise comment at that particular time. But it takes more than unwisdom to nail a murderer. Love in Hixon's case had been carnal lust and the hand lethal. Seminal fluid and human hair eventually obtained and scientifically analysed had put him inside. End of five serial murders. Accolades to Bradshaw. Case closed.

"The body was covered with leaves," Mrs Millington said. "It had been buried a long time. Poor Graham walked over it before he realised what it was. He disturbed the evidence, or whatever his colleagues called it. It makes you wonder how many other bodies might have been disposed of in the same way."

Cormack, imagining Bradshaw's reaction to Radwell's perfidy – for God's sake, walking over a cadaver! – looked at her blankly.

Dawn Millington picked up the sheet music from the top of the harmonium and put it in the music stool. "He called himself the Reverend Hixon," she went on, "and that's what he wanted to be, of course, a pillar of the church. Sad, isn't it?"

Sad? Cormack suppressed an expletive. People were extraordinary. A man commits five murders, is thwarted in his ecclesiastical ambitions, and is put away for life. And this middle-aged, otherwise reasonable woman, who can draw tender music out of an organ and can train people to sing, feels some sympathy for him. How was he supposed to react to that? Politely and non-aggressively seemed the best bet. He told her that he felt he could do with a little fresh air and would take a stroll outside.

Sergeant Radwell liked dogs and it bothered him to see them incarcerated in kennels. Millington's kennels were six wooden sheds, fairly large, erected on concreted areas surrounded with wire netting where the animals could exercise in the open air. The set-up reminded Radwell of a prison yard, but was marginally worse. Cons could mooch around together. These dogs just looked ~~at each other, barked, wagged their tails, let their tails droop,~~ whined, before finally giving up and going to sleep. They were usually there for a holiday period while their owners were away. Today, Creggan's dog was the only occupant and might be there for some time. It looked unutterably sad.

"It isn't right," he said to Cormack, who had joined him. "There's plenty of room at The Mount. It should be there, or Doctor Donaldson should have refused to let Creggan have it." Millington had explained the situation to him. Apparently he had given Creggan a spare key to the kennels so that he could take the

101

dog out whenever he wanted to. Radwell hoped it would be often. Cormack listened sympathetically, more interested in what Radwell had to tell him about The Mount generally than in the doleful little animal.

Private psychiatric hospitals, mostly for short stay patients, were doing a booming business, he'd read somewhere. Over thirty had been built in recent years and took some of the pressure off the N.H.S. The Mount, he guessed, would be limited to about fifty patients. Were all allowed to roam free, he wondered, or was Creggan having preferential treatment? When he had told Maybridge that he would like temporary accommodation in Macklestone, with a view perhaps to buying a property here, he hadn't envisaged anything quite like this. Bradshaw had been working on a murder practically on his doorstep. There was an uncomfortable feeling here of unfinished business. He glanced at the young sergeant's shoes, shabby suede brogues. The corpse of the girl would have been in an advanced state of decomposition. Whatever shoes, boots, green wellies, or worse, from Radwell's sensitive viewpoint, canvas trainers, he'd worn, they would have squelched deeply into human tissue. Had he worn them when he'd run back to the farm, or discarded them in horror by the corpse? They would have been subjected to analysis like everything else at the scene of crime. It couldn't have been an easy case for Bradshaw, but his careful professionalism would have linked the murder with Hixon despite the passage of time and Radwell's unfortunate feet. In this case, identification had taken some while and followed a photograph of the girl after her features had been built up. The forensic expert who had worked on the facial reconstruction had done the best he could with a face that had been savaged, probably by a fox, so that the bone structure was damaged to some extent. The sergeant's feet, a minor irritation or Bradshaw would have mentioned them in his notes, couldn't have done much harm. The girl's name, Susan Martin, could have been her working name; there had been no family to come forward to lay claim to her. Not unusual. Girls took off, assumed a different identity and disappeared. Acquaintances, clients, hadn't been too eager to come forward, either. But someone had. Hixon's third victim had used an alias for her job, too. According to Maybridge she was a

102

twenty-three-year-old woman who worked under the name of Magda, later identified by her shocked and highly respectable family as Gina Gallymore. She had worked for a ponce in the Bath area, wore her long red hair in a plait and smelt strongly of scent.

Maybridge, when imparting information about the dead, was always politely respectful as if they were around, listening. Cormack had responded flippantly about Magda the Magdalene being a more apt description than Rapunzel. Long tresses and pungent perfume. Maybridge had looked at him coldly. "No sobriquet is apt," he'd said quietly. "The Press dreamed up the Rapunzel one. They might have dreamed up something worse. We've gone along with it." Cormack, chastened, had apologised. He tended to forget that Maybridge dealt with both the living and the dead – the transition from one state to the other must quite often have appalled him. Or, at the very least, saddened. Cormack had long stopped thinking of cadavers as people. A reprehensible admission, but necessary for survival in the job. You couldn't pick away at pieces of tissue and wonder if the defunct owner had played bowls on Saturday afternoons, gone in for painting watercolours or beating his wife. Though, of course, if it were necessary to discover if anything like that applied, you channelled your research in that direction. An interesting puzzle.

He asked Radwell if he had worked on all the Rapunzel cases.

Radwell had, with the exception of Jean Storrer, a twenty-eight-year-old unmarried mother found dead near Exeter cathedral. She had worked on her own account. No ponce. And had made enough money to send her five-year-old daughter to a private school. Radwell found it quite easy to be objective about her. "A good-looking woman," he told Cormack. "I saw several photos of her. The other murders he could hardly speak about at all. He had seen them in the flesh and didn't want to remember them. Hixon hadn't been as vehement in his denial of the murder of Jean Storrer as he had been with the others, though he hadn't confessed to it. He had blabbed at some length about the innocent fruit of sinful loins and sent a cheque for twenty pounds to Storrer's child. "Tainted money," Radwell said. "I expect the cheque was torn up."

Cormack tried a little tactful probing about Susan Martin, but got nowhere. Radwell's lips tightened as if he were being offered

103

hemlock and Cormack hastily changed the subject. What had Macklestone to offer in the way of relaxation, he asked, apart from the local pub?

"Professor Bradshaw played golf," Radwell said frostily.

"With you?"

Radwell thawed a little. The Irishman obviously hadn't a clue about the local class system. "No. With Chief Inspector Maybridge, Superintendent Claxby, and with the Chief Constable. And now," he went on bitterly, "presumably he plays with God."

Cormack looked at him, astonished. Strange irony from a failed priest. Bradshaw must have given him hell.

9

Sometime during the night after Simon's visit to The Mount someone slashed all four tyres of his car. The green Lotus Eclat sprawled on the tarmac drive like a huge wounded insect. Simon, scarcely believing what he saw, walked around it, touching the dew-wet metal here and there, before finally and therapeutically losing his temper and kicking it.

Shit, oh shit!

He'd had enough. This and everything else. He'd had a phone call on the bedroom extension just after nine o'clock from Kester-Evans, who wanted to know why he hadn't used the rail ticket the young lady at the church had given him. Muzzy with sleep, Simon had asked what young lady and Kester-Evans had described someone rather like Rhoda. But it couldn't have been Rhoda because Rhoda hadn't given him anything apart from a lot of aggro and pain by going away. He still nursed her nightdress every night though it smelt of washing powder now and not of her. The telephone receiver, on the pillow beside him, had yapped away in his ear. "Simon, are you still there? Are you listening to me?" He'd mumbled that he was. "You're not still in bed, are you?" "No – been up hours." He'd moved a little away from the receiver

105

while Kester-Evans had launched into a long and boring homily about coping in a manly way with his tragic loss, accepting what had to be accepted, and walking wisely into the future as his parents would have wished. "You're a man now, Simon, take on the mantle of a man. When you spoke to me at the time of the funeral about having doubts about your future in medicine, you were in an irrational state. You were grieving. I took little notice of it. Perhaps I should have listened more. Believe me, my dear boy, it is better that you should return for the last few weeks of term. I have been expecting you every day. It is better that you should be here with your peers. If you have problems we will address them together . . ." And so on. Politeness is ingrained, in Simon's case not deeply, but deeply enough not to replace the receiver on the bedside table while Kester-Evans was in full spate. When he had paused for breath Simon had slipped in a "Thank you very much", which was meaningless but the best he could be bothered to do, followed by, "Sorry, there's someone at the door. Must go."

The phone had rung again a couple of times while he was making himself some toast, but he had ignored it. The toast had burnt and he had run out of butter. He would have to do some shopping at the local store, where he would meet people who would be kind and say nice things about his parents and he would smile stiffly back and say thank you very much as he had to Kester-Evans, and tell them that he was managing, and that everything really was quite okay, and he didn't need anyone to come and clean the place for him, or to cook, or perform any other charitable action that probably made them feel awfully good, though of course he wouldn't say that, just smile or sigh as the occasion demanded. The only little glow of light on his horizon was the prospect of taking Sally out for a drive.

And now the car was vandalised.

Vandalism, a twentieth-century British disease.

He wondered if he ought to report it to Maybridge. Probably not. It was a minor crime, the sort the police didn't bother about. Nothing personal about it – no pig's trotter tied to the steering wheel. No threat. Just some yobs who'd got pissed. If he went to see the Maybridges they'd carry on where Kester-Evans left off.

Especially Meg. He was tired of the old refrain: *You are grieving, Simon. Not rational.* He hadn't grieved when Rhoda was here. She would be here still if Meg hadn't upset her.

And he wasn't grieving now. Just bloody furious.

Simon went indoors to phone the garage.

Sally's sunny nature shone most brightly in adversity, like polished brass on a dark day. That this could be extremely irritating to The Mount's depressive patients she had yet to learn. The others, provided they weren't too manic, or schizoid, or stressed, loved her for her cheerfulness. Simon loved Rhoda and wasn't influenced one way or the other. She was sorry that the car couldn't be used for a day or two, she told him with a wide smile, but it was probably a lot healthier to go walking. How about a stroll down to the woods to see the bluebells? Bluebells didn't interest him particularly, but when she found a patch of grass fairly free of them and suggested that they should sit down, he sat. She was wearing a blue tracksuit, a little tight over the hips, but wasn't making any effort to be sexy. That Sally had the knack of oozing sexiness when the occasion seemed right, and appearing coolly virginal when it didn't, he was yet to learn. Street-wise Sally sensed that working on Simon would take time, and there wasn't just the barrier of bereavement to be breached. There was someone else, she guessed, someone absent. Maybe the woman Creggan had told her about, the one who dried her undies on Simon's clothes line and had black hair down to her waist. "Like a Spanish señorita," he had told her, "or señora, not a pretty little bambino like my Sally Loreto." How Creggan could get maudlin on mild beer she didn't know, but he obviously could. She had teased him about being a peeping Tom and he had told her sadly that he wasn't. "If only the occasion would present itself, my lovely child, but it never does. The villagers draw their curtains at night and only the stars smile at me." And then, in a sudden change of mood, he had told her quite sharply never to go out with Simon in his car. "He drives like a lunatic at Brand's Hatch. One of these days he'll be scraped off the road with a shovel."

Sally wondered if Creggan had slashed the tyres. Some of the nurses at The Mount thought he was as sane as they were, which wasn't saying much. The only sane people up at The Mount were herself and the rest of the domestic staff, with the possible exception of the cook, Mrs Mackay. With her it was hard to tell. She didn't socialise. A bit manic, perhaps, the way she washed poultry under the tap as if a whoosh of water would drown listeria, or whatever nasty bug the food people would think of next, and then she would spend ages drying the thing, patting away at it with a paper towel. That the food she produced was so good was surprising, considering how soggy it was at the start. The food was one of the few good things at The Mount – better than the tips. The patients gave her the odd tenner or two when they left, but seldom more. Mrs Bradshaw had given her a brooch shaped like the letter L. "L for Lisa," she said, "my name. And L for Loreto, your surname. Have it. I don't want it." It was made of small enamel flowers and didn't look valuable, though it was pretty if you liked that sort of thing. Sally didn't. Brooches were for elderly ladies, even the word sounded ancient – like corsets. The only jewellery Sally liked was ear-rings, preferably something rather African like large metal hoops, but you couldn't safely wear them at The Mount. Patients on medication did odd things, and even odder things before they were medicated. Doctor Donaldson had warned her but she hadn't taken any notice until a middle-aged bank clerk who looked as harmless as a neutered cat had snatched one of them off and eaten it. Luckily it was small enough and loose enough not to tear her ear lobe – or to stick in his throat and kill him. She hadn't told Donaldson, presumably the patient hadn't either, and she hadn't worn ear-rings on duty again.

She lay back on the grass with her hands behind her head and looked at Simon. He had a pretty awful hair style, short all over but beginning to grow a bit now and straggle on the nape of his neck. If he let the top bit grow and gave it a dollop of mousse it would balance his face better. He had the kind of lips, not too thin, that she wouldn't mind exploring with her tongue, but not yet. She would know when he was ready, probably before he did, but there was no point in rushing it.

A bluebell with a twisted stalk was caressing her forehead. She moved her face from side to side and laughed when it tickled.

Joyous Sally.

108

Oh, God, Simon thought. He didn't know if he liked her or not. When she talked she babbled a lot of nonsense, and when she didn't she lay on her back giggling with her breasts bobbing up and down.

She stopped giggling and her breasts stopped bobbing. He looked away. Too quickly.

She smiled secretly behind his back. "Si . . .mon." Long drawn out like two musical notes.

He kept his eyes fixed ahead of him. They were only just inside the woods and the long grass was a swirl of green all the way down to the perimeter wall. A rabbit, maybe a stoat . . . no, a bird, fluttered through a clump of bracken.

"Si . . . mon." A little crisper.

"What?" He was cross and didn't know why he was cross.

"Present for you, Simon. Look . . ."

He looked round cautiously. She was sitting up now and her hand was extended to him, palm uppermost, holding the brooch which gleamed brightly against her pale skin.

It was a bauble. Cheap. And instantly recognisable. He had been about twelve when he had bought it for his mother's Christmas present. He remembered the day out with his father very clearly. They had gone shopping together in Bristol and his father had told him to choose whatever he liked for his mother and to tell him if he needed more cash. The fifteen quid he'd saved had been ample. Three quid for his mother's brooch, a tenner for a cigarette lighter shaped like a Porsche for his father, together with a couple of quids' worth of cigarettes. His father had been pleased with the lighter, which he had given to him straight away as a pre-Christ-

pre-Christmas present, too, Simon. I've got your Mum a gold bracelet and she might prefer something else – not jewellery – from you." He hadn't said that it was too cheap. And Simon couldn't remember saying that he'd bought it because it was pretty. But his father had looked rather keenly at him and must have guessed. "Okay," he'd said, "let's chance it. Wrap it. Keep it for Christmas." His mother had, in fact, appeared to like the brooch very much, and his father had smiled at her and pinned it on her dress. His gift, the bracelet, had been received with far less

109

enthusiasm. She had made a joke about gilt and gold, and his father had quipped back quite sharply about having a nineteen-carat conscience. None of this had Simon understood at the time. And he didn't want to dwell on it now. Gilt. Guilt. A long time ago. What did it matter?

"It's for you," Sally said. "Your mum's."

It was odd she had been wearing it up at The Mount. He hadn't seen her wearing it around the house. All her other jewellery was good stuff. Perhaps if you wore good jewellery at The Mount it got nicked. This wasn't worth nicking. Or maybe she had genuinely liked it and wore it for that reason. But why give it away?

He asked Sally why his mother had given it to her. Sally explained about the L. "It was just a little pressie, Simon. L for Loreto. She usually gave a cash tip, but she hadn't any cash on her. She didn't have to give me anything, and this was a bit personal, I mean L for her name, too. But she didn't seem too bothered with it – I mean, not sentimentally attached or anything. So I accepted it, but you can have it if you want it, to keep – in memory, sort of – you know what I mean. But if you'd rather I hung on to it, then I will. It's for you to say."

But Simon had nothing to say. He got up and walked down through the tall grass towards the road. His throat was raw as if he were starting a cold and his eyes were burning. He had the same reaction sometimes when he opened the wardrobes in his mother's bedroom and saw all the clothes hanging neatly like brightly coloured shrouds. They had to be got rid of. The lot of them. His father's too. They should all go. Someone from the church might do it. He couldn't do it himself, any more than he could touch that brooch. He wasn't aware that he was clutching the rough stone wall hard enough to flake off pieces of moss and graze the skin of his thumb.

"Simon?" Not the fluting, seductive tone now. Genuine sympathy. He couldn't answer. Not yet. She was wise enough not to mention the brooch again, or to tell him, when she went to stand beside him, that his thumb was bleeding. Instead she suggested that it might be better if they started strolling back. "It's getting chilly."

110

But it will be warmer in time, Simon. And we have all the time in the world.

When you work in a psychiatric hospital you learn some of the jargon. You can't help picking it up. Some of the therapy at The Mount seemed reasonable to Sally. When people were under stress they needed to get away from whatever was bugging them. Her family had bugged her, especially her Da, though, fair play, the old man hadn't done anything he shouldn't. No sin of the flesh. When her Ma had walked out on them he had expected her to get a local job, waitressing or something, and live at home and look after him. If she had she would have landed up in a N.H.S. equivalent to The Mount. As a patient.

To get on in the world you had to look after yourself. *A sense of self* was one of the phrases she'd picked up at The Mount. She had that, all right. She knew who she was. Were there people who didn't, apart from amnesiacs? And she liked who she was. A nice body, kept fit by daily jogging, and a brain that didn't brood or go haywire or cause her or anyone else any aggro. As for sexually induced neurosis – had she got that phrase right? – she hadn't any. And no sexually induced disease. Luck on her side there, of course, though she tended to touch wood when she thought of AIDS. Superstition might be a weakness, but you only became an obsessive if you touched wood or washed your hands all day. She didn't know what category Mrs Bradshaw had been slotted into. Her stay at The Mount had been short and she hadn't spent all the time in bed, though she might have spent some of it in Donaldson's bed. But surely he could have visited her in her home when the professor wasn't there? Cheaper for her. But perhaps she didn't pay any fees at The Mount, got it for free. Donaldson had been looking pretty sick himself since the funeral. And who did he think he was kidding with his vodka and tonic? Was he trying to kill his libido, if that was the word, with ninety percent proof? No more Mrs Bradshaw. No more sex. Oh dear, poor old Doc.

Sally smiled. It was an amusing picture, but it couldn't be true. If you had a good-looking husband like the professor and he didn't fancy you any more you got yourself a toyboy. Or you bunged yourself full of hormones to stop the menopause and had a face

111

lift. Well, you did that if you were normal and had a good 'self image'. If you weren't normal you had it off with Donaldson, or ate too many cream cakes and got disgustingly fat. Mrs Bradshaw had been slim and her jaw hadn't sagged. For her age she had looked pretty remarkable. And she and her husband had both died together, celebrating an anniversary. Nice way to go, if you had to. Unfortunately you had. But when you're twenty-two you don't really believe it. Life is like a long grassy plain that the sun shines on. Somewhere out there, further than you can see, the grass becomes less lush and the sky is darker. You have to start watching where you put your feet. Someone chucks a walking frame at you and it helps for a bit. But not forever. You walk over the edge one day, but you're so old by then you don't much care.

Simon's parents had gone over the edge about thirty years too soon. Fate tended to do that sort of thing sometimes. But only to other people.

If Simon had tried to evaluate his first date with Sally he would have given himself nil for effort and a few pluses to her for trying. Compared with Rhoda she hadn't amounted to very much, a stand-in player on an otherwise empty stage when the star had gone. Even so, she was a warm presence, bonny and bouncy, and thawed the ice of his solitude a little.

She arranged all future dates to slot in with her time off from The Mount, which varied according to her duties. Most of the work was in the kitchen and dictated by the needs of Mrs Mackay: preparing vegetables, loading the dishwasher, and carrying breakfast and tea trays to the patients. It was usually possible to have a couple of hours off in the afternoon, and the evenings, on a duty rota system, were free on alternate days. Mrs Mackay, usually not communicative, had praised her once or twice for doing her job quite well, and then warned her not to get too pally with the patients. "They're not like us, m'dear." A generalisation, Creggan not mentioned, but message received and understood. And ignored.

Sally believed that Mrs Mackay's disapproval of Creggan was due to his spartan diet. His rejection of her gourmet meals must have cut her to the quick. Even the craziest of The Mount's

112

crazies drooled over her culinary art. Creggan's drooling over Sally couldn't be known by Mrs Mackay unless she slunk around his tepee and peeked in now and then, which Sally couldn't imagine, or else Creggan might have said something indiscreet to one of the other domestics and it had been passed on. Sally couldn't believe that, either. Creggan wasn't indiscreet. You said things to Creggan and he talked nonsense back to you. Amusing nonsense. Sexy nonsense. For an old guy he had the hots on pretty often, or seemed to. You couldn't be sure with him. How much was a joke and harmless? How much serious intent? Banter followed by bed, or just banter for the sake of it?

But there wasn't any banter when she spoke to him about Simon. He listened and clammed up. Jealous? Perhaps. It was fun to needle him, but funnier had he snapped back. His earlier warning about Simon's driving wasn't repeated. When she told him that Simon had asked her to sort out his parents' clothes and give them to charity he had looked at her sombrely and, apart from saying it was a miserable task, hadn't commented further.

It wasn't in the least a miserable task, though Simon probably thought it would be. He had to go into Bristol to see his solicitor, he told her, so wouldn't be able to take her out as arranged. And then, looking very embarrassed, he had asked would she mind awfully, not think it too presumptuous (yes, he had said presumptuous, much as Kester-Evans would have done) to get his parents' clothes together while he was out and arrange for any charity she knew about to come and collect? He hadn't said that he couldn't bear to be there while she was doing it, and she hadn't told him that she would be delighted. Her "Of course I don't mind. Anything I can do to help . . ." had sounded suitably sad.

After he had gone she had prowled around the house, as Rhoda had several weeks ago, and imagined herself living there. A very swish, very rich place, Simon's home, though it could do with a few improvements. The fawn-coloured carpets reminded her of wet beaches at twilight. The rooms would look much better with floors of tangy orange and grey or swirls of gold and green, strong gorgeous patterns, big and bold and eye-catching. And the plain velvet curtains had probably cost the earth but the colours were drab and boring, and so were the settees and chairs. She would

113

cover them with a pattern of parakeets on branches or pale pink peonies on a turquoise background. All the rooms, if they were hers, would sing.

Sally, humming with pleasure at the thought of it all, went upstairs, stripped and ran a bath for herself in the larger of the two bathrooms, the one with the corner bath, which was white. As she lay soaking in the steamy water scented with Lisa's bath crystals, she dreamed of improvements here, too. The chrome taps would be changed for gold ones, and the plain white Venetian blinds would be taken down and replaced by black Austrian ones edged with white lace like sexy knickers.

Did Lisa have sexy underwear? she wondered. She had only seen her in her dressing gown, navy blue velvet with white buttons and one button missing at the top which she had pinned with the brooch. The brooch she hadn't wanted.

A woman's undies say a lot about her, Sally believed, even more than the clothes on top. She got out of the bath and dried herself on a chocolate brown towel that matched the chocolate brown carpet tiles – hadn't Lisa had any sense of colour? Then, refreshed, she began turning out the clothes of the dead.

If you have too much of a conscience, Sally told herself, you don't thrive, but if it makes you feel any better about thriving at the expense of others then it's easy to think up an excuse or two. If the Bradshaws' clothes were given to a local charity Simon might meet his mother's grey and cream silk dress emerging from the bingo hall on the back of a slag tall and thin enough to put it on. And his father's tweed suit might be seen adding a bit of class to a wino slurping beer in the local pub. And that was true of all the clothes, which were a mixture of shabby casual (once expens- ive) and restrained smart. Lisa's three evening gowns all had designer labels and she had obviously gone for quality rather than quantity. They didn't look all that much in the hand but the quality of the material was super, one in rich ruby velvet and two in different tones of brocade. Sally, totting it up, scribbled a thousand plus in her notebook.

You get better prices if you don't squash clothes into black bin liners but once you've filled four suitcases and the bed is still piled high with sports clothes, shirts, slips, nighties, briefs, bras, tights, socks, shoes, tuxedos, anoraks, pyjamas, macks, pullovers, etc. etc., then you haven't any option but to use them. By mid-afternoon a dozen bin liners were lined up in the hall, together with a large battered brown leather suitcase which had belonged to Peter and three nearly as large, but lighter in weight and colour, which had been used mainly by Lisa. Sally wondered about the ones that had been incinerated on holiday. They had probably held a couple of thousand quids' worth, too, plus any jewellery they'd had with them.

Sally stopped smiling and sighed.

Being dead was a terrible waste of effort. You gathered up all this stuff and then – wham – you weren't around any more to enjoy it.

But others were. And they'd be fools if they didn't. She'd tell Simon she'd given the lot to Oxfam. Sally, rather tired by now, went back upstairs and had another look through the drawers in case she had missed anything. She hadn't touched any of the jewellery, it might have been listed. And Simon hadn't said anything about toilet things and brushes and combs, or his mother's switch of hair which had been wrapped in tissue in her handkerchief drawer.

Sally had another look at the hair and stroked it gently. It was a bit macabre if you thought of the Rapunzel murders. Lisa had probably bought it a long time ago, before the murders had started. Or it might have been a switch of her own hair. The people in the Nearly New shop wouldn't want it and Simon wouldn't like to see it lying around, any more than he'd like to see the black and gold evening bag that was the only thing of Lisa's that Sally could

On the whole, she thought, it had been a rewarding sort of day. The self-drive van she had ordered to carry her and the loot to Gloucester was due in about twenty minutes. There was just time to hang Simon's present in the empty wardrobe. It had cost her a week's wages, but was probably worth it.

As for the hair, hang on to it? Chuck it?

Chuck it later, perhaps, when she got back to The Mount.

She stuffed it in the pocket of her anorak and went downstairs for a quick g. and t.

Alan Drew, junior partner of the Bristol firm of solicitors Alfringham and Drew, had handled Professor Bradshaw's affairs over the last few years and had known the family well enough to be a bearer of Lisa's coffin at the funeral. One of those onerous tasks you can't politely refuse. He would have politely refused the onerous task his senior partner had landed on him now only for the fact that Alfringham would probably make a worse cock-up of it. A delay in probate wasn't unusual, but the reason for it in this case was rather embarrassing. Everything would be sorted out soon, he hoped. Young Simon was due to inherit a hefty lump sum in due course and there was enough cash in his account in the meantime to see him through. He'd already bought a car with some of it. A talk about cars was as good a lead into the tricky subject of money as anything else. Simon had apologised for being late, he'd had a problem parking the Lotus Eclat he'd said. "New?" Drew had asked. "Almost," Simon had answered. "How new?" Drew had persisted, trying to see the financial background. "Five years," Simon had answered honestly. Drew had relaxed.

It was a hot summer's day, plenty of sunshine streaming into the office, a busy noise of clanging in the distance as Bristol's brave new buildings rose a few inches nearer the sky. Not a day to think about Wills and awkward codicils. Clients tended to have a liking for codicils. They mucked around with them, adding, deleting, so that the Will looked like a musical score of the dance of time. Whoever was in the final *pas de deux* inheriting the lot. In this case, Simon and an elusive lady.

He decided to give Simon the good news first. "Your inheritance, after inheritance tax and including the house and insurance policies, amounts to just under six hundred thousand pounds net. A nice sum."

Simon, who already had an inkling that it would be a fair amount, though not as much as that, nodded happily. Very nice. He would take a holiday in the Far East, perhaps, listen to the Buddhist prayer bells, see the golden temple in Amritsar, trek through the Australian outback, go sailing off Turkey, eat well in Paris, buy a chalet in Austria, climb the Andes and . . . and . . .

Drew, reading his expression correctly, went on briskly. It's a

116

combination of assets. Your mother's inheritance from her family in Norfolk is included. Your father inherited rather less. The rise in property values over the years has been dramatic. Your father's flat in London, which isn't included, is quite small – worth about fifty thousand a few years ago, but double that now."

He waited for the question.

It came. "What flat?"

"Your father's base – his *pied-à-terre* in Islington. His job took him to London frequently. He probably found it convenient to stay overnight."

Simon pointed out that when his father was in London, either lecturing or doing whatever forensic work he was asked to do, he stayed in his club or at the Royal Society of Medicine. "You must have made a mistake."

Drew said he hadn't. He'd liked Bradshaw. And he'd brought a lot of business to the firm. But, at moments such as this one, he wished he'd taken his investments and tax returns elsewhere, or else conducted his extramarital affair with more sense. Not that he blamed him for having a woman on the side. Married to Lisa, it was forgivable.

Simon, coming to the conclusion that his father must have bought the flat recently and had forgotten to mention it, started thinking about the extra hundred thousand pounds. It would buy a Ferrari, a vintage Bentley, or a . . . His conscience suddenly kicked him hard: he was being abominably selfish. He told Drew that he would sell the flat and give the proceeds to Mother Teresa, or to her successor if she wasn't around.

"Commendable," Drew said, slightly surprised. "Unfortunately, it's not yours to sell. Your father has bequeathed it to a Mrs Clare Warwick. Perhaps she was of some service to your father at some time?"

Simon, shaken by what he had been told, mused over the words – 'some service to your father'. What sort of service? *That* sort of service? The kind of service Trudy Morrison might have given his father all those years ago when his mother wasn't there? Or the kind of washing-up and cleaning service she was supposed to give? He hadn't known that his father had other women until he had read his mother's diaries. She had used the word 'screwed' a few

117

times, which had shocked him. The name Clare Warwick hadn't turned up anywhere, and his father had never mentioned her.

"Are you sure you have the right name?" he asked Drew. "It wouldn't be Trudy Morrison, would it?"

Drew, relieved that he seemed to be taking it very well, said he was quite sure he had the right name. It was quite definitely a Mrs Warwick – a Mrs Clare Warwick. (Who, he wondered, was Trudy Morrison?)

The camaraderie of men when discussing the opposite sex has its own lingo, but Bradshaw had spoken of her very protectively. Even tenderly. A serious affair, obviously. She didn't know the flat would be hers, he said. He was just trying to safeguard her future. All this had sounded as if Bradshaw had received a warning of impending heart failure and Drew had wondered if he was physically okay – he'd looked all right – or had merely lost his marbles. Love was an unbalancing disease, cured usually by time and too much proximity. As in his own case. He had been divorced for two happy years. So, apparently, had Mrs Warwick. Bradshaw hadn't been involved in the divorce, he'd told Drew. He'd met her afterwards. Apart from those few details, he hadn't told him anything that might help to trace her now.

And obviously Simon had never heard of her. So no help there.

He wrote the address of the flat and gave it to Simon. "I'm afraid you can't have access. It's hers to sell – or live in – when we eventually make contact with her. She might be out of the country – on holiday. If you should find the keys at home, post them back here. The sooner we get everything tied up, the better."

Before bringing the interview to an end, Drew thought it his duty to fire a few salvoes and sink Simon's yacht in the Caribbean. Well, it was a normal dream for an eighteen-year-old, wasn't it? His inheritance might seem a lot of money, he told him, but he had to consider rising inflation, heavy taxation and other boring things. Tax avoidance was legal, and he'd explain that later. His father had invested safely and that was important, too.

Simon became less euphoric. Money, apparently, was a crafty commodity. If you didn't watch it like a hawk, it became liquid silver oozing away into subterranean passages that led either to the Inland Revenue or the pockets of shady stockbrokers.

He promised to be sensible. A smaller yacht – maybe? A younger vintage car?

When he got home he was relieved that Sally wasn't there. Perhaps she hadn't been. Perhaps the dreaded wardrobes hadn't been emptied. He went upstairs to look. His father's wardrobe had a naked, vulnerable feel to it and smelt of stale tobacco. A red tie, which had escaped her attention, hung like a mute tongue on the tie rail. He touched it and felt a sudden hot rush of tears. Damn, oh damn!

His mother's wardrobe smelt sweeter and was bare, too, apart from a clown-like garment which he identified as a tracksuit in shades of crimson and grey, dangling like a cheerful marionette. A scrawled message on a piece of pink paper was pinned to it:

Just a little pressie.
Love Sally.

He took it out and put it on the bed. So he was supposed to go running, was he? Forget the dead. Life goes on. Well, it did. She was right, of course. But a bright tracksuit wasn't what he wanted just now. He wanted a woman who didn't talk much and never giggled. A woman who brooded over his mother's papers and thought God knew what and lived God knew where. A woman with long black hair that he wanted to stroke. A woman who made his sexuality a glorious and terrible embarrassment, impossible to hide.

10

Rhoda's last contact with Peter had been on the final day of Hixon's trial. He had called at her flat, a five-minute walk from his own, to say that Clare had put on a celebration party – had filled his flat with yobs he didn't know – didn't want to know – mainly journalists – and sleazy creatures who used his lavatory and drank his booze and squeezed any flesh they could get their hands on – and that Clare was revelling in it and wanted Rhoda to go along and revel in it too, and mend the rift between them that had gone on for too long. So he'd come to fetch her – or rather, to tell her. She could go along if she wanted to but he was staying here for a while, with her permission, of course. And had she got a decent drink to give him? No, he wasn't pissed already – apart from being pissed off generally. He wanted to sit somewhere quiet. And listen to silence. Why were Clare's friends so bloody loud?

It was eleven o'clock on a black night of rain. She'd wanted to send him back into it. Instead, she'd asked him in.

It was a similar night tonight, but less dark, and the rain was the warm rain of early summer. The photograph that she'd pinched from Simon and not returned was on the small rickety table she used as a desk. There was a sheet of paper in her typewriter with the heading 'The Games Men Play' – a commissioned piece of nonsense for a magazine. She had chosen to call her contribution 'The Snooker Syndrome' and had attempted to be wryly amusing about balls and phallic cues. Freelance journalism was a penurious occupation, unless you were good at it. Tonight she wasn't good at it.

She was remembering that other night so strongly she could almost smell the wet leather of Peter's shoes and see the hair on the back of his hands. His sexy hands that had probed the cadavers of five strangled prostitutes. She'd asked him what he was celebrating. Nothing, he said. He wasn't celebrating. Clare was. So don't look at him like that. Hixon's conviction hadn't depended on his evidence alone. The bastard would have been convicted without it. It wasn't his fault that the Press had hyped him up - singled him out. He'd just been part of a team.

Modesty wasn't usually one of his strong points. Hixon's last outburst of aggro, widely reported in the evening papers, must have got to him. And Clare's party was just that much too much.

She hadn't gone to it. Parties weren't her scene, either. And the rift with her sister over Peter had seemed more of a chasm than it actually was. But it hadn't been an act of enticement when she had poured him a generous whisky, he'd looked as if he'd needed it, and his hand shook when she handed him the glass. He was cold, he said testily. Why didn't she keep her flat warmer? Because she hadn't paid the last electricity bill yet, she nearly told him. Her money problems had nothing to do with him. She managed.

Clare had been managing rather better, she guessed. A free billet in Peter's flat, and the modelling she had been doing for one of the London stores paid very well. The red outfit she had worn in the photograph had probably been bought at discount – or hired. Hadn't she known that you turn up to that sort of village do wearing tweeds and flat heels? Mrs Maybridge's gear. Why, in God's name, had Peter invited her? If he had.

He had stayed a couple of hours, nursing his whisky and gazing morosely at the two-bar electric fire she'd switched on for him. He was almost fifty – twice Clare's age. And that night he'd looked it. She had sat up with him. Going to bed might have been interpreted as an invitation to join her. They'd had good sex

121

together in the past, but on that last night there had been no sexual pull at all. She'd sensed he had something on his mind. He mentioned Simon once or twice – said he'd had a raw deal – been robbed of a normal upbringing – hoped everything would be better for him in the future. He hadn't mentioned Lisa at all, but by implication everything he said concerned her.

Rhoda picked up the photograph and had another look at it. Lisa appeared so sane, so normal. An attractive middle-aged woman. Had Peter been standing beside her – and Clare absent – it would have been a scene of bucolic bliss. Macklestone on a sunny day – villagers smiling – an enclosed safe little community – hurrah for constancy – married love – no roving husbands – no horror paintings – no hate – no fear – no terrible accident waiting to happen – everything clean and sweet. Macklestone as it never was.

The vicar's grumble about Creggan's dog digging a hole in the cemetery seemed relatively trite to Maybridge until the vicar pointed out that it was natural for a dog to go after bones, but that the bones of *homo sapiens* were sacrosanct. So would he please go along and have a word with Mr Creggan? Maybridge, stifling the retort that it would be better for the vicar to go along and have a word himself, said that he'd mention it to Doctor Donaldson. As medical superintendent, it was up to him to keep his patients and his patients' pets in line.

The vicar, who had been reluctant to broach the subject with Donaldson, was relieved. Several of his parishioners had complained from time to time about Donaldson's so-called progressive methods – with particular reference to letting Creggan creep around in the dark. A psychiatric hospital, especially when housed in a large forbidding building, didn't enhance the village, one of his parishioners had pointed out. It devalued one's property if one wished to sell. Sutton's pious response about being charitable to the afflicted had been greeted with polite derision. "The afflicted, Vicar? Those aren't long-term patients with Downs Syndrome or other incurable genetic disorders, they're victims of their own folly, their way of life, drink, drugs, etc. etc. and Donaldson is reaping a rich harvest." Another parishioner, homing in on the harvest theme, had been equally bitter. "It's all very well singing about ploughing the fields and scattering, but that damned dog of Creggan's has scattered a bedful of tulips at the end of my lawn."

That the dog's holes were, so far, desultory explorations and of more annoyance to Creggan than anyone else, no one knew. Creggan had expected better. The animal had a perverse habit of slipping out of its collar and lead and going in the wrong direction, whereas Creggan knew, or thought he knew, where a hole might produce something of interest – in the copse where the fifth Rapunzel had been found, somewhere just outside the area of the police search.

He guessed when he noticed Maybridge's car in The Mount's drive that a complaint might be about to be made. And wondered how Donaldson would react. Would another bribe pacify him? If so, how much? When money doesn't matter it becomes a bit of a bore. It had bored him for years. How much would bore Donaldson? he wondered. People had different levels of financial boredom. Caviare, for some, descended to the level of baked beans rather fast. He debated whether to go out for a walk and avoid confrontation, or to lie on his bed and feign sleep.

Maybridge had never found Donaldson easy to communicate with, though he had always made an effort to attend any event that Donaldson had put on to give the patients an opportunity to mingle with the villagers. After a period of isolation, stepping back into society is made easier by meeting strangers at an art display or performing, rather amateurishly perhaps, at a musical soirée. Maybridge rather liked Donaldson's old-fashioned use of the word soirée, it had an air of elegance, of peaceful days long gone. That Donaldson's patients were bruised by late twentieth century stresses he could understand, though Victorian stresses had probably been worse. Sherlock Holmes had smoked opium and his doctor creator hadn't condemned him.

Maybridge, rather guiltily, lit a cigarette. Donaldson frowned. "It's not a healthy habit, Chief Inspector. Addictions are easy to acquire and hard to lose. Please put the ash in this." He indicated a crystal inkwell on his desk, a purely decorative item from a patient. He had never been able to call Maybridge Tom, though Maybridge had suggested that he might. Maybridge's attempt to call him Steven had been received coldly and he hadn't tried again. They might live in the same village, drink sometimes in the same pub, but each had his separate professional identity.

"I don't see that this is a police matter," Donaldson commented stiffly when Maybridge told him why he'd come.

Maybridge assured him it wasn't. "The vicar is troubled about the possible disinterring of human remains, though that seems extremely unlikely. The dog could have sniffed out a dead bird, or something. I think it's Creggan's night-time walks that alarm some people and then they complain to the vicar rather than to you. Sutton isn't all that robust when it comes to dealing with criticism. And, candidly, I believe he gets a certain amount of the nimby attitude from his parishioners – you know, not in my back yard – with reference to The Mount."

Donaldson, who knew it only too well and had learnt to ignore it, ignored it again, but it bothered him that the dog had dug a hole in the cemetery. Creggan had promised to keep the animal on a lead.

"Whose grave did it desecrate?"

Desecrate was too strong a word. As far as Maybridge knew, the hole hadn't been near a grave – if it had been, the vicar would have told him. He explained this to Donaldson. "It's probably a lot of fuss about nothing. If the animal worried sheep or cattle there would be cause for complaint. But that could happen and I think your patient should be warned of the consequences."

Donaldson said he had already warned him, but would do so again. Maybridge might consider it a lot of fuss about nothing. He didn't. Matters that at one time he might have dismissed as trivial now tended to loom. Even mildly aggressive attitudes were threatening and difficult to cope with. The professional staff, not normally argumentative, were tending to go more by the book than they used to. And to use bookish words. If you tell a patient he's suffering from cyclothymia you scare him rigid, whereas a few simple words about mood change do no harm at all. He knows that. That's why he's here. One of the psychotherapists, not Sue Raudsley this time, but probably encouraged by her, had argued for the reintroduction of electroconvulsive therapy in place of the monoamine oxidase inhibitor drugs for endogenous depression.

124

The fact that Donaldson used hypnosis from time to time had come in for criticism, too. Lexman, the senior nurse, had referred to it obliquely as "one of the many rather archaic ways of persuading a sick patient he's well". Donaldson could have retorted that a few soothing words that rub out nightmares and make the patient feel better for a while can't be a bad thing. Disinterring memories that are buried deeply and festering can be therapeutic, too, but it's a more painful process and perhaps at times dangerous. Donaldson, suppressing an urge to argue the pros and cons, had said nothing. Lexman depended on him for his salary and if he were wise he would remember it. Or be asked to leave. Creggan, on the other hand, brought the money in.

Which brought his thoughts into sharp focus on him again. Disinterring memories and disinterring bones. Equally hazardous. Only the dog hadn't, which was some consolation. Even so, should he ask Creggan to leave? A confrontation with him might lead to that. It would please the villagers if he went, restore his credibility with his staff, and soothe Mrs Mackay whose dislike of the man was almost paranoid. God knew there was enough paranoia here without her adding to it. Sally, she had told him, might be in some moral danger if she saw too much of him. Moral danger presupposes a degree of innocence in the vulnerable party. Sally might be guilty of active encouragement – or was her relationship with Simon using all her sexual energy? Her physical energy was being expended on the seven o'clock jog around the grounds – she loping ahead of Simon, he looking foolish a few yards behind. A spectacle that amused some of the patients who rose early. He hadn't joined her this morning. Aware of a growing audience, perhaps.

"It's almost two months since the Bradshaws' funeral," Donaldson informed Maybridge abruptly.

Maybridge carefully tapped ash into the crystal inkwell. Peter had been a heavy smoker, too, and then had suddenly given it up and been extremely irritable for a while. One tended to forget the ordinariness of people in the first few weeks after death. They had gone ahead into the great unknown, wafted along to the accompaniment of sonorous church music, and you thought of them with awe. Afterwards you remembered their tetchiness – their fallibility – their kindness – their humanity.

125

"Two difficult months for Simon," he said. "Let's hope everything turns out well for him."

Donaldson agreed. Two very difficult months, he thought bitterly, and not just for Lisa's son.

"Creggan attended the funeral," he said. "I suppose you noticed?" Maybridge had. If allowing him to attend had been part of Donaldson's therapy then who was he to question it? The Mount wasn't a closed institution. Creggan had also been seen by Radwell mooching around the cemetery some weeks later, carrying a bunch of wild flowers. "Rather out of character, wouldn't you say?" Radwell had commented to Maybridge. As no one knew Creggan's character – with the exception of Donaldson and The Mount's psychotherapists – the comment seemed pointless. Radwell hadn't approached him. "He didn't see me," he explained. "It was getting dark. There was no one else around. And he wasn't doing any harm." No pigs' trotters on graves. Nothing nasty. No dog then to dig holes. No point in mentioning it now.

"A great many attended," Maybridge said. "Mostly the media. Some genuine mourners there too, of course; the Bradshaws were well liked."

Speaking well of the dead, or voicing at worst a veiled criticism, is ingrained in most people. Maybridge had valued his friendship with Bradshaw and kept his criticism under wraps. Meg had deplored Lisa's attitude towards Simon but no longer mentioned it. Max Cormack was in a different category – an unbiased stranger. He sensed that the Millingtons hadn't liked Bradshaw and, though deeply curious to know why, he had avoided any conversation that might lead to an explanation. He was, after all, part of the medical brotherhood. His disquiet about Bradshaw's forensic evidence in the case of the last Rapunzel murder had been growing. The professor's reports on the first four murdered prostitutes had been meticulously detailed – the murders had been done by Hixon and proved to have been done. The notes on Rapunzel number five were slipshod – a brief extension of some of the other notes – a postscript that tended to assume too much. Hixon's guilt, had it been based on this evidence alone, couldn't have been proved beyond reasonable doubt. An elastic phrase – reasonable doubt.

126

Where does unreasonable doubt set in, Cormack wondered, and what, if anything, should be done about it?

Creggan's effort to nourish Cormack's doubt was premature. They met by accident a few days after Donaldson had given Creggan an ultimatum – any more complaints from the villagers and the dog had to go. Creggan had promised to be more vigilant. He had bought a new chain-type collar and lead for Perry and taken the dog along to what he thought of as the Rapunzel copse to try it out.

And had come across Cormack who was about to time Radwell's run from the copse to the Millingtons' farm. He had already timed the shorter route to the main road where there was a telephone box. Not vandalised. At a guess there would be about twenty minutes' difference, so why hadn't the sergeant taken the quicker route? Too distressed to think of it? A grassy field easier to run across if you've discarded your shoes? Dawn Millington's bosom soft to weep on while you girded up your strength prior to reporting to your D.C.I. that you've found a corpse . . . and walked on it? Any other reason?

The dog, emerging from the trees and about to leap joyously in Cormack's direction, gave a gargled agonised yelp and arched over on to its back.

"Holy Jesus!" Cormack rushed over to it. "You'll throttle the poor little divil." He snatched the lead from Creggan and loosened it. Creggan, appalled, went down on his knees by his pet. "It's Donaldson's fault. I didn't mean to hurt it." Cormack had met him once before, briefly, in Millington's kitchen where Creggan had been paying for the dog's kennelling fees. Over the odds. In

ack suspended judgment. He asked him why he wasn't using the leather lead and collar.

Creggan explained.

"Even the most reprehensible of grave digging mongrels shouldn't be strangled," Cormack pointed out. "Use its old collar, put an extra hole in it, but make sure it's not too tight." If Creggan hadn't obviously been fond of the dog he would have been worried. A choke chain might be all right used carefully in the right hands, though personally he didn't like them in any hands. Creggan said humbly he would do just that. "And I'll throw this one away."

"Good," said Cormack.

It was the kind of encounter that was difficult to withdraw from. Not casual enough. Where they were standing, in the shadow of the trees, there was the option of walking on together towards the road or taking the longer twisting route peppered with fallen pine cones that emerged eventually on Millington's land. Radwell's route. And, until now, Cormack's. He waited to see which way Creggan intended to go so that he could go in the opposite direction.

Creggan removed the choke chain from Perry. The dog ambled over to Cormack and sat at his feet. A thrush chattered out of sight somewhere and late evening sunlight made gentle amber streaks across a palette of dark green leaves.

"She was naked, wasn't she?" Creggan said.

"What? Who?" Cormack was startled.

"The woman the police called Susan Martin," Creggan gestured vaguely towards the heart of the woods. "The fifth Rapunzel. Poor little lady. Poor little girl. A rose by any other name would smell as . . ." He broke off. "I do beg your pardon. But several weeks underground – a degree of decomposition – and no identifying clothes."

Cormack stiffened. Barriers up. Defences ready. The police should have been more discreet at the Press conference. Everyone knew she had been naked and had long hair.

He told Creggan brusquely that he hadn't been involved in the case at all. Knew nothing about it. "And you can't believe everything you read in newspapers."

Creggan agreed. "I found it very difficult to believe that anyone could identify the woman by a picture of a reconstructed face, especially one that looked much the same as hundreds of other faces."

The reconstruction had been done with considerable skill by Professor Miles Benford, who had done a similar reconstruction in the Edward Carne case a few years previously. The television presenter had been on trial charged with murdering his wife. Apart from the period underground and the reconstruction, there was very little similarity in the two cases. Jocelyn Carne hadn't been a

prostitute, her family background was known, and she had visited
her dentist. Susan Martin either had perfect teeth or her dentist
had burnt all his records and dropped dead. Her teeth hadn't
revealed anything. But as he wasn't supposed to know anything,
Cormack said nothing.

Creggan, after a momentary pause, pressed on. "A little lady,"
he said, "or maybe a floozie, a tart – who's to know? – meets her
end in this wooded glade where the birds sing and the evening sun
is very pleasant and some while later Professor Bradshaw and
Inspector Maybridge, to name but two locals, together with a
professional team which you, Doctor Cormack, have just joined,
have the body presented to them, upthrust to the surface by mother
nature in a quest for justice, perhaps. And you can tell me that
justice has been done – unequivocally?"

It was a carping question. Not accusatory – but almost. Arrows
of misconduct aimed mainly at Bradshaw, and to some extent at
the police generally. A serial murderer gets landed with another
murder – he's carrying the can already, so one more can't make
much difference. Or so Cormack interpreted it. It made him angry.
It was all right for him to harbour suspicions about the validity of
the forensic evidence, but it was a bloody nerve if anyone else did.
Especially this undoubtedly unhinged, unkempt-looking fellow
who was regarding him now with a half smile on his lips. He
wondered how old he was. Not old enough for senile dementia –
early fifties – so what sort of paranoia was it? Police phobia? An
urge to kick the fuzz in the teeth?

"Emphatically," he retorted coldly, "justice has been done. No
need for you to worry about it at all. The verdict on Hixon was
based on sound evidence. Absolutely."

Creggan noticed the over-emphasis. "But no family came forward. If she had been using a different name from her own that
would be understandable – for a while. But when the reconstructed
face was shown in the papers and on television then her family
would have recognised her – had it been a good reconstruction."

It was a point that had bothered Cormack, too. He suggested
irritably that, even in this liberal age, families might prefer not to
lay claim to a tart – especially when the whole wide television-
viewing world was looking on.

"She was identified by her clients," Creggan said, "according to the papers." And then – very abruptly – he changed the subject. "I haven't seen you up here before, Doctor Cormack, but then I usually come later. Moonlight on the black boles of trees is rather splendid. Don't let me detain you from your evening stroll." He clicked his fingers at Perry and the dog followed him obediently down one of the paths.

Cormack watched them go. The encounter had disturbed him. It had come naturally to him to defend his fellow-professionals, but his own suspicions viewed now seemed contaminated by Creggan's paranoia. Why be so concerned with Radwell's delay, a very short delay, in phoning? He hadn't murdered the girl. Just found her, poor sod. A phone call to the police made twenty minutes or so earlier than it had been wouldn't have made a lot of difference. The corpse had to be left unattended for a brief period. Radwell couldn't have mounted guard over it until someone came along. He had acted perfectly naturally. As for identification – Bradshaw's notes might have been sparse but Benford's wouldn't have been. Every step of the reconstruction would have been scrupulously annotated. If Creggan didn't think the corpse was that of Susan Martin, then who did he think it was? Joan of Arc?

It wasn't his case, he reminded himself firmly. And he hadn't full knowledge of it. If he started investigating in the laboratory he would risk the ire of his forensic colleagues. Had anything been amiss they would have reported it at the time. So stop bothering. Bradshaw was probably the genius everyone says he was. It's a comforting thought, so think it.

"Mrs Bradshaw had shoes like those," Mrs Mackay said. Sally, busy spiking small pieces of cheese and sausages and round nutty things on to wooden toothpicks, only they weren't called toothpicks, almost pierced her finger. Bloody hell! A whist drive was going on in the games room and all this fancy stuff had to be carried round in about half an hour. She bled on to a piece of cheese and was about to wipe it off with her handkerchief when she saw Mrs Mackay's sombre eyes watching her. All right, so there were germs. All right, so it wasn't nice. All right, so shove

130

your thumb under the tap, chuck the cheese into the pedal bin and think what to say about the shoes.

Disposing of the Bradshaws' clobber hadn't been a very happy task. Money-wise. The best offer she had had for the lot had been a hundred and twenty-three quid from a second-hand shop called *Pryceless*. Good clobber bought cheap from grieving relatives and sold at about a thousand percent profit. She had told them so and the lady in charge – lady? by God! – had told her to try elsewhere. She had already tried everywhere and other offers had been much the same, but *Pryceless* paid cash. While the owner went to a small room at the back to count it out in tenners, it didn't take long, Sally had removed the green shoes from one of the bin bags. They were Italian, expensive when new, not too middle-aged looking, and in a nice shade of green.

She didn't think Simon would recognise them, but hadn't worn them on any of their dates. That Mrs Mackay should recognise them was amazing. Did the old bat creep around gazing at the patients' feet?

"Really?" Sally said. "Had she really? Shoes like these?"

"Yes," Mrs Mackay said quietly, "just like those."

That Sally might be in moral danger from Paul Creggan worried Mrs Mackay deeply. That she might do a bit of pilfering on the side worried her, too. The shoes, she believed, had been removed from Mrs Bradshaw's wardrobe, either here at The Mount during her last stay or from her home. That Sally had access to the Bradshaws' home, and probably to Simon's bed, worried her even more than Creggan's lechery. But as yet she didn't know what to do about it.

The late Angus Mackay, a pillar of the Lutheran church and as rigid as a block of cement, had seemed a suitable husband when they had married thirty years ago – she had been Sally's age but innocent of the ways of men. He had assailed her virginity like the Black Rod thumping the door of the House of Commons, but had failed to gain entry. Not that there had been anything anatomically wrong with her – just lack of co-operation – and he had stopped short of rape. She would have liked a child, had it been possible to produce one differently. She would have liked one like Sally. But Sally made good. Sally saved.

Sally, neither good nor wanting to be saved, wondered if she could get off the boring task of spiking food and suggested that it would be easier to lay it flat on plates. "Now that I've cut my finger."

Mrs Mackay told her to stir the dip instead, a creamy-looking sauce with a fish flavour, while she did the spiking. "But put a plaster on your finger first. There are some in the cupboard."

The Mount's kitchen was a large utilitarian room with white-painted walls and functional worktops that held an assortment of utensils, mostly in stainless steel, the exception being a set of pretty saucepans given by a grateful patient, together with a note: "For stimulating my tastebuds so wonderfully, may these flowery pans remind you of me and my gratitude." A patient who hadn't been cured, Mrs Mackay had thought dourly, but she had received them politely and put them on a top shelf where they glowed pinkly prettily next to the first-aid cupboard. "If I had my own home," Sally said, selecting a Band Aid, "I'd like saucepans like those."

"What goes into them matters," Mrs Mackay jabbed a piece of cheese, "not how they look." She was reminded of one of Hixon's homilies about empty vessels – or human receptacles, as he'd called them – being filled with a broth of evil and stirred with the hands of sin. Not one of his happier sermons. At his best he'd had the power to soar into the realms of ecstasy and drag his congregation with him. The Welsh called it *hywel*, she believed, the Scots hadn't a word for it, or if they had she didn't know it. Whatever it was, it did one good. She wondered if his talent for words would flourish in the gaol's chapel, or would he be in solitary confinement and gagged for ever?

"Do you think they'll eat all these biscuits?" Sally asked, "or may I have one?" The biscuits were shaped into hearts, diamonds, spades and clubs. She had cut them out earlier from the savoury pastry that Mrs Mackay had made. To ask if she might have one was politic under the circumstances. She had already nicked half a dozen before Mrs Mackay had noticed the shoes.

Mrs Mackay told her she could. "Just one."

Sally chose a heart and ate it. She had tried to persuade Simon to come to the whist drive. It was the monthly one that was open to villagers. The Maybridges would probably come, she had told him. It might have been the wrong thing to say. Mrs Maybridge had put her foot in it, apparently, she wasn't sure how. Something to do with the woman Creggan had nicknamed the señorita – or señora – who had gone away. Creggan had been to one of the bridge parties, patients and guests only, and had pinched her bottom when she had leaned over with the tray of fancies during the interval. He hadn't been to any of the others. It was boring without him. She wasn't even allowed to carry his tea down to his tent, these days. One of the other domestics did it – Mavis Dunoon – but she had managed to slip into his tent now and then when no one was around. "Mavis," he had said bitterly, "a song thrush, how inaptly named – a corn-crake of a woman – a mastodon of a female – an extinct mammalian creature with nipple-shaped prominences on her molar teeth." A bit of an exaggeration. There wasn't much wrong with Mavis, apart from being overweight and over thirty. Her teeth did stick out a bit. Not a lot.

Creggan had asked her if she was still seeing the Bradshaw boy. His name is Simon, she had said. Yes, he knew that, he said. Was she still seeing him? Sometimes, she said. "Has he fucked you yet?" That was a rude question – a rude way of putting a rude question. Old guys shouldn't use words like that. She had glared at him. "I take it," he said gently, "that he has not, and I apologise, my dear child, if I have hurt your susceptibilities by phrasing it in such a gross manner."

"Hm," she had snorted, not appeased. He had been at his weak beer again, she guessed. It filled his mouth up with dictionary words – and rude ones – and he spat them out. "Dear Sally," he had reached out and held her hand, "I'm so sorry." A nice simple apology that time and she had accepted it. "Never get hurt," he had added, "never let anyone destroy you, dear child. There are other places away from here – other places of employment – other boys. Go away, little Sally Loreto, while all is well."

Maybe he *was* a little mad. She had smiled at him doubtfully. He hadn't smiled back.

The seduction of Simon was taking a lot longer than she had expected, and it annoyed her that Creggan might have guessed it. She had lost her virginity at fifteen, a race in those days to see which of her girlfriends could lose it first. She had never had difficulty enticing a boy, just pretended he was enticing her. She had hoped to sleep with Simon on the day she had disposed of the clothes, and had driven the empty van back optimistically and with a handy story ready about Oxfam being awfully pleased. He hadn't been in a good mood. Where were the keys? he wanted to know. Had she emptied the pockets – his father's pockets – and taken out the keys? Rather cross, too, by now (he should have been grateful she'd done the job at all), she'd told him that all she could find in the pockets were handkerchiefs – did his father have a perpetual cold? – and as no one would want those, she had thrown them away. There was no loose change in the pockets, she had added coldly in case he thought she was stealing. He wasn't interested in loose change, he'd said, just keys. Not the house keys, he had those, keys to a place in London his father's solicitor had told him about. They must be somewhere. "Then look," she had said, "but don't look at me. I haven't got them. All I have is a head that's about to split after spending hours doing a charitable job you wouldn't do yourself." The atmosphere hadn't been warm and cosy. He hadn't even mentioned the tracksuit.

On their next date, a few days later, he told her he'd found the keys in his father's travelling case, which seemed an odd place to keep them. And he'd thanked her very much for the tracksuit and was sorry if he'd been pretty rotten to her on the day she'd disposed of the gear, but he got like that sometimes. And where did she want to jog?

It was clear to her that he didn't particularly want to jog anywhere and it took some cajoling to get him to rise at seven and meet her at The Mount on her daily run. They had run together on five mornings, and if he saw that as a penance it wasn't a very long one. He wouldn't mind jogging somewhere else, he said, but he didn't like people watching and he didn't like having to get up so early. What about an evening jog some time – across the fields, perhaps?

It was a reasonable suggestion – with possibilities. She had smiled her happy Sally smile again and said, "Why not?"

Macklestone wasn't brilliant jogging countryside. The main road was lethal and the minor roads had a devious habit of ending up in cul-de-sacs and farmyards. The right of way through part of the Millingtons' farm was one of the few possible options when the weather was dry. To reach it meant passing Mrs Mackay's cottage, which was tucked away like a sullen little toad at the end of a lane. Sally on the whole preferred being spied on by The Mount's patients, who were either madly enthusiastic or insanely jealous (well, she guessed they were), than by Mrs Mackay, who exuded displeasure like a squeezed carbuncle, but as they passed her cottage in less than half a minute of a quick run, and as Mrs Mackay spent most of her off-duty time sewing samplers and making curtains in the room at the back, Sally wasn't too bothered. Mrs Mackay's samplers and curtains were topics of conversation, dry islands of dull talk, when she wasn't busy stirring something or other. The curtain material she had bought cheap at a Bristol market, blue and cream striped cotton. The sampler she was working on showed clasped hands and the words 'To have and to hold'. All this information had been elicited by Sally, who wasn't particularly interested but didn't like silence very much. 'To have and to hold' was part of the marriage service, she had informed Mrs Mackay. There were other meanings, Mrs Mackay had replied. There was virtue in constancy. In having principles and keeping them. To have courage in the face of adversity. To have faith in one's friends. What friends? Sally had wondered. The Millingtons? Mrs Mackay and Mrs Millington met sometimes, she'd heard, and went somewhere to sing. The thought of Mrs Mackay singing made Sally collapse into giggles. It was impossible to imagine. Her mouth was trap shut most of the time. She hoped it would stay trap shut about Simon's mother's shoes.

She wished she would stop looking at them.

Sally, escaping from her gaze, picked up the tray and carried it through to the games room. A bell rang. Half time, or had someone revoked? Revoked – another word she'd learnt. If a psychiatric patient revoked, and thought the accusation unfair, would he fling his cards in his opponent's face, overturn the table, scream? People did scream in The Mount – just now and then – and were taken along to the quiet wing where they could scream in peace and quiet. Or Doctor Donaldson would get them to lie on his couch and say something in a soothing voice until they fell asleep – hypnotism without dangling an object in front of their eyes, some sort of trick. He usually had one of the women psychotherapists with him when he did that. A canny old cove – Donaldson. Very careful. Any accusation of screwing and he'd screw the female patient for damages pretty damn fast.

The games room wasn't as full as usual. Only six tables. It had been a very hot day and the evening light was still strong. Card games were better played in the winter.

Max Cormack, who thought the same but had come out of curiosity, noticed the fair-haired girl standing in the doorway holding a tray. He had seen her jogging past Millington's farm with Bradshaw's son. A happy sort of friendship. She was older than him, he guessed, but not too much older. He had hoped to meet Simon by now, in the pub or somewhere, but the lad seemed to lead a hermitical existence apart from going out with the girl, whatever her name was. Maybridge had told him that the lad was doing all the wrong things, if one viewed life rigidly from a practical angle, but who was to judge? What was wrong for some was right for others, Maybridge had stressed. If a person got knocked down by a car, forcing him to get back on his feet before he was ready wouldn't do him much good. Healing took time. Simon, emotionally stunned, was still groping around. Had he rushed back to school and then on to university in the autumn, his friends might have felt easier about him, applauded his courage, but he had to work things out in his own way.

Maybridge's wife, apparently, would have been one of the applauders. She hadn't handled him very well, she'd explained to Cormack, and felt guilty that she wasn't helping him more, but knew she wouldn't be welcome. "I probably lack sensitivity, or patience, or both. He's an emotional adolescent in need of guidance, but he's so hard to approach."

Cormack had listened without comment. How would Josie settle into this environment, he wondered, when she came back from the States? Would she prefer the wider scope of living in Bristol – the shops – the theatres – above all, the anonymity? Here in this village people carried each other on their backs – or they pushed them away. A normal, not too warm, not too cool mingling seemed to be out. It was a village of extremes. Or maybe it seemed that way because he lodged with the Millingtons. Had

136

he lodged with the family of the bloke who ran the garage and referred to Bradshaw as a good guy, a thoroughly nice chap, he might view it differently. A positive attitude is acceptable. The Millingtons' dislike of Bradshaw, though never openly voiced, was like touching a sweaty hand. This evening he had met Doctor Donaldson for the first time and had deliberately made clear to him that he felt privileged to follow in Bradshaw's footsteps – and then waited for a response. It had been slow to come but, when it had, it had been meticulously phrased, like an obituary. A man of brilliant academic ability. A loss not only to the local community but to the country as a whole. A professorship in forensic science was greatly valued in the teaching hospitals where men of his calibre were badly needed. Was Doctor Cormack interested in lecturing, writing papers and books on the topic, perhaps? Was he planning to follow in his footsteps that far?

A neat steering away from Bradshaw. The sweaty hand again, discreetly gloved?

He would have liked to ask about Mrs Bradshaw but it would have sounded like arrant curiosity, or at the very least, bad form. He had heard she had attended here from time to time as a patient. That made the subject taboo. Mrs Maybridge was the only one who mentioned her, quite naturally during the course of conversation, and had described her as a gifted artist who would have done even better if she had become an illustrator of modern fairy stories. Fresh images seen through her own eyes, as she had put it, and not been so immersed in the past.

Images of the past tended to change with passing time. The murdered girl in the copse would become part of folk-lore one day. In Ireland, Celtic land of ghosts, she would become wraith-like, a gentle creature that had died too young. Here in more prosaic England they might see her differently. A strangled prostitute, labelled with the wrong name, perhaps. Damn Creggan for voicing it. He was relieved he wasn't here this evening. The other patients, most of them good card players, were typical of any social gathering. The only one who got on his wick was a heavily built woman who carried a bag of sweets around from table to table and masticated like a ruminant whilst taking surreptitious peeps at his cards. He didn't discover she was the vicar's wife until later. Her husband, not a card player, had wandered around smiling vaguely and rung the bell from time to time, apparently at the M.C.'s instructions. A bland evening. Rather dull. The kind of affair his parents used to attend in the village hall at home when Father Duffy was the M.C. The Maybridges had the good sense not to come. Perhaps they preferred playing bridge – as he did.

"The pâté is Mrs Mackay's speciality," Sally said, moving over to him with the tray. "And the other bits and bobs are rather nice, too. Try one." She gave him a wide, happy smile.

"Thanks," Cormack smiled back. He felt more cheerful. Not a bad place, The Mount. Donaldson was doing a good job. And he knew how to pick his staff . . . Or maybe he didn't. If sexy signals could be wafted into the air then he was breathing them in alarmingly fast. He stopped smiling. For God's sake, Josie, come home!

"Go on," Sally cajoled, edging closer, "spoil yourself, take two." He was the first presentable male she'd seen in the place since she'd been here. Dark red hair, almost black, probably grew it on his chest, too. Muscles like ropes. Eyes that had seen a lot.

Aware that he was being assessed, mentally stripped naked and approved of, Cormack found himself doing the same in the opposite direction. And stopped. A herculean effort of self-control. If he wanted sex he'd get a tart in the city. Or be celibate.

"I hear you're a Roman Catholic," said a man's voice in his ear.

Transfixed by Sally, he didn't answer.

"A believer in transubstantiation," said the voice.

"The things on sticks are mainly cheese," said Sally.

"A kind of spiritual cannibalism," said the voice.

"And the dip is fish based," said Sally.

"Fish, an early Christian emblem," said the voice. And went away.

Cormack took two biscuits with pâté on them. And waited for Sally to go, too. "One of the nutters," she whispered, between giggles, and moved on to the next table.

The air, neutered once more, became breathable. Cormack ate his biscuits and resisted glancing after her. No wonder the Bradshaw boy was happy to stay put. Grief? Emotionally stunned? Hadn't Maybridge eyes in his head?

Happy is a weak word. Simon's emotions tended to swirl together like clouds in a dark sky, edged here and there with flashes of light. He was reasonably happy lying in a field with Sally after they'd jogged. Happy because the exercise was over and that his body had calmed down. Hers probably hadn't, but that was her problem. Girls were lucky they had nothing to get an erection with. They were never embarrassed. Rhoda had put him into a state of almost perpetual embarrassment. And he couldn't forget her. That Sally wanted sex with him was perfectly obvious. But he wanted it with Rhoda. His body might not mind one way or the other, but he minded inside his head. There's nothing beautiful about love – it's a torment – a pain – it's full of anger. He wanted to hurt Rhoda because she wasn't there. He wanted to hurt Sally because she was there. Most of all he wanted to hurt himself. He envied his parents for being dead. He wished he were dead. Peaceful. Done with. Finished. Or he wished he were alive – properly alive – blazingly – marvellously alive. In bed with Rhoda.

Sally bored him.

It was the ultimate insult. No boy had ever been bored by her before. She toyed with the idea of dumping him. He bored her, too. Doctor Cormack wouldn't bore her. Max Cormack was a man, not a smooth skinned boy who still had traces of acne. And Cormack, unlike most older men, was free – no wife. And he had a good job. No house of his own yet, but he'd get one. When she had come to work at The Mount she had assessed the male potential. Patients as possible prey were dismissed: they would be more trouble than they were worth. The medical and domestic staff were married, about to be, living with someone, or so unattractive they'd stay single for ever. Cormack was in a class of his own. Hard to hunt down, though. He had no reason to visit The Mount. The whist drive had been a one-off. His forensic work took him out every day into places where she couldn't follow him. If he went to the pub, he didn't go when she did. Getting Simon to go with her wasn't easy, so she didn't go often. People kept bothering him, he said, asked how he was getting on, that sort of thing. She knew that. So they drank in his home. His *nice* home. In a few years he would be properly grown up. And besieged by women – like his father had been, according to gossip. He was at his worst now. Raw. Bereaved. He would improve. Simon, a few years in the future, might be a prize, and she'd be a prize idiot now if she ditched him. So hang on. Keep an eye on Cormack and play the game, whichever way the dice fell.

"There are times," she said dreamily to Simon, "when I feel like turning Catholic."

This was so extraordinary he stopped being bored. They were sitting in the summerhouse because it was too hot to sit outside. The sun seemed to sizzle the gnats that were jumping up and down like tiny creatures from hell. Hell. Heaven. Religion. "Why Catholic?"

Because church might be a handy place to meet Cormack.

"Why not?"

He asked her if she was anything now. Did she believe in anything? She said she believed in transubstantiation and hoped she'd got the word right. She didn't know what it meant. Something to do with fish?

The conversation reminded him of his recent visit to the cemetery. He had gone along to look at his parents' grave, the first time since the funeral, and just couldn't believe in it. A mound of earth with a temporary headstone. It meant nothing. The vicar had suggested that he should get a permanent headstone soon. Apparently you could get a catalogue from a monumental mason and choose what you liked. It had all seemed too gruesome. And final. He had asked where the strangled prostitute had been buried. Over by the wall, the vicar had told him. No. No. No. Not *over* the wall. In consecrated ground. Even suicides were buried in consecrated ground these days. "The church is charitable, Simon." And particularly charitable in the case of the prostitute, apparently. Money had been raised locally for the burial as no one had come forward to claim the body and she had died in the environs of the village. Simon wondered how much his father had contributed – a hundred quid for Rapunzel number five? He cringed, deeply ashamed. It was a disgusting thing to think.

After the vicar had left him, he strolled along by the perimeter wall to see if he could find the grave. The headstones in this part of the cemetery were very old – seventy or eighty years in some cases – and were mainly slabs of slate with mossed-over lettering that was difficult to read. There were a few flowers on some of them, which was odd. Did great-great-grandchildren bother with their ancestors? Apparently some of them did. He didn't at first recognise the Rapunzel grave because he had forgotten the name. It came back to him when he saw the small neat headstone of pale grey granite with the lettering in black:

IN SAD MEMORY OF SUSAN MARTIN

According to the date, she had been twenty-six. To date accurately wasn't always possible, his father had told him once, but his father had dated this one. Or someone had. *In sad memory*. Whose memory? The words were very troubling. No epitaph might have been better than one made up by strangers for a stranger. He imagined the church council gathering together in the vestry and jotting down their ideas on scraps of paper. They had paid for the headstone: they could say what they liked. They had no memory of her. Hadn't even seen her. Blank pieces of paper. Blank minds.

While he had stood looking down at the grave a squadron of Red Arrow aircraft had flown low overhead – banking – weaving – screaming their way up into the clouds. Watching them made him feel better. It wasn't all death and doom around here. Maybe he would be a pilot one day, or a racing driver. Juvenile ambitions that he was supposed to have grown out of. The aircraft became silent in the distance, crimson sparks of light where the sun caught them, and then nothing.

That night he had dreamed of them, but in the dream they had merged and become the threatening bird of Grimm's story. It had come swooping down at him in the dark, crushing his nostrils with its heavy wings so that, gasping for breath, he had torn at it in panic, breaking the thin sinews of the feathers, thinner than a child's fingers, and scattering them over the bed.

Sitting here with Sally now he thought of the nightmare again and shivered despite the heat. The almond tree was just a few yards away and he could smell its sap, or maybe its leaves. Why had his mother been so obsessed with the horror stories of long ago? Shouldn't Grimm's fairy tale about the murdered child buried under the tree, and the appalling bird perched on one of its branches, have revolted her?

"All the blossom," he said, "has gone."

Sally was still thinking about Cormack. The Irish had big families. Or they used to. Perhaps not any more. "Birth control," she said, "is important."

Simon looked at her, puzzled. The almond tree – the birds and the bees – pollination – the Durex in his pocket. The world was more than a little mad, but not at this moment threatening.

11

Drew recognised Rhoda immediately she walked into the office. It took her a few minutes to remember him. He had been sombrely dressed for the funeral in a dark grey suit and had exuded dark grey disapproval at her, along with everyone else, when she'd dropped the camera. Today, casually dressed in light grey cords and a white short-sleeved shirt, he seemed benign, though obviously very surprised.

She had phoned the office after reading the firm's announcement in the personal column of the *Daily Telegraph* requesting Mrs Clare Warwick to get in touch with them. She was Clare's sister, she explained, and wanted to know what it was all about. She would have to be told personally, and not over the phone, Drew said. Very well, she agreed, she would travel to Bristol to see him this afternoon. No 'ifs' or 'buts' or 'Is it all right with you?' She was coming. His curiosity was titillated and he didn't argue.

Anticipating that the solicitor would need proof of identity, she had brought her birth certificate. She had earlier searched Peter's flat for Clare's, and for Clare's divorce papers, but hadn't found them or anything relevant to her at all, apart from her clothes in the wardrobe, which hadn't included the red dress or hat.

143

And there hadn't been any letters piling up in the hall. Just a lot of junk mail which she got rid of on her weekly clandestine visits. The firm's recorded delivery letters hadn't been delivered as they hadn't been signed for, Drew explained. It was fortunate that the personal announcement had drawn a response. "A valid one," he added, "and so far the only one."

He glanced at her birth certificate, noticed that her father had been a colonel in the Royal Engineers and that she was thirty-two years old. He handed it back. "No documents relevant to your sister?"

"Sorry, no. She has them with her. Wherever she is." *If she's anywhere.* Three words thrumming in her head. Not to be expressed yet. "Why are you trying to trace her?"

Drew told her, sketching in the background, about Professor Bradshaw's visit to the office just a few months ago. The drawing-up of the codicil according to his wishes.

Her mind, focused until now wholly on Clare, began focusing on Peter. That he should bequeath the flat to Clare didn't touch her at all emotionally, though it surprised her, but his presence here in this room, not so long ago, became suddenly very real. Tears were alien to her, but they were burning in her eyes now and, ashamed of them, she turned her head away and forced her attention on her surroundings. The certificates on the wall were a blur of black words on white vellum with crimson seals like blobs of blood. Certificates of competence. Of know-how. A room where Wills were made. Where Peter had made his. Imagining Peter here, perhaps seated on this chair, was like imagining him clothed in black crêpe. Virile, lying, bloody-minded, hot-tempered, faithless and, God help her, tenderly loving Peter. The funeral service had frightened and appalled her but this was going deeper like the careful slow probing of his scalpel on an already open wound. His hand was on this. It affirmed his death. She believed it, not just intellectually as she had before, but physically. In the tips of her fingers, her breasts, her gut. She hadn't realised she'd loved him or could remember him with so much pain.

She wiped the tears with the back of her hand. Grimaced. "Sorry . . . it's just that . . ." Just that. Nothing. She shrugged, not knowing what to say.

Her tears had surprised him. Her face, with its heavy dark wings of hair, had seemed emotionless as if sculpted in marble. He asked her if she would like a cup of tea – and hoped his secretary was still there to make it. It had gone five o'clock.

The question was so trite that it nearly rocked her over into laughter. Listen to that, Peter. What kind of silly scenario have you landed me in? And what, for Christ's sake, have you done to Clare? Nudged her back into the land of the living, perhaps? Affirmed that she is still alive? A legatee – a recipient of your gift? Or about to be?

A few moments of optimism calmed her. She declined the tea.

It was time to get down to business. Drew told her it was necessary to get more background information. He had a scribble pad on his desk and unscrewed his fountain pen, ready to make notes.

For Rhoda it was like someone taking her hand in a foggy landscape with the promise of guiding her through it. She told him she had reported her sister's disappearance to the police at the local station near where she lived. Details had been taken but she had sensed that the young Met. officer who had interviewed her hadn't taken her very seriously. Apparently, when adults took off the police saw no pressing need to go looking for them. And she had probably reported her missing too soon – a few weeks after she'd last heard from her.

Drew pointed out that the sibling relationship, though close, wasn't as close as the marital relationship. A husband reporting the disappearance of his wife is taken seriously and the information is acted on at once. The same applied to children. And people living together. Brothers and sisters tended to make their own separate lives and often drifted away from each other. Rhoda reminded him that Clare was divorced and her ex-husband had seen no reason to get involved. And no, there was no sinister implication there. An amicable divorce. No maintenance. Clare hadn't asked for it, didn't believe in it. So no hassle over money. Her ex-husband – totally unreliable, pea-brained, currently working as a ski instructor and flexing his sun bronzed muscles to the delight of pea-brained females on dry ski slopes – well, it was summer – was as harmless as that kind of beautiful muscular hunk usually was. But no – to answer the question, not asked but implied, he had no motive to murder her.

A sparky lady, Drew thought, amused. If she were always this outspoken, a rift with her sister was easy to understand. But why should she think her sister might have been murdered? It was an intriguing situation and he was beginning to enjoy it. Which was reprehensibile.

He asked her if she thought the obvious relationship between Bradshaw and Mrs Warwick might have some bearing on her sister's disappearance. Had there been a row, for instance, when Mrs Bradshaw had learnt of the liaison?

Rhoda thought about the photograph and the anger that had shown in the sketch, but didn't mention the latter. How could she? She had trespassed on Lisa's territory, stolen her diaries and broken all rules of reasonable behaviour by moving in on Simon. In many ways her behaviour had been worse than Clare's. She needed this man's professional respect and goodwill. She answered that it would be natural for Mrs Bradshaw to be angry, though she might not have known that Peter was so seriously involved with Clare, involved enough to bequeath her the flat. Which, incidentally, seemed an extraordinary thing to do. In the normal way she wouldn't stand to inherit for another twenty years or so. "She's twenty-four. I don't think the relationship would have lasted that long. And there's no child to provide for. Bequeath is an old man's word."

It wasn't, but he didn't argue. He needed more details and pressed on. "Names and addresses of your sister's friends would be useful." She had already contacted them, she told him, but he noted them down just the same. And then he asked for details of the places where she had worked. Her first job had been as a chalet maid in an Austrian ski resort, where she had met her husband, and she had helped out with that sort of thing until the marriage broke up. Afterwards she had done some modelling, which had paid better than anything else and was the reason why she hadn't reverted to her maiden name after the divorce. She was known as Clare Warwick, not well known, but her future had seemed promising.

Rhoda broke off. Until that point it had been easy to state all the facts calmly. The past tense was like a dark presence in a sleazy room. Waiting.

"The future is probably still very promising," Drew said, a little too heartily. "Have you a photograph of her?"

"Nothing very clear. Only a snapshot." Rhoda had brought it with her and passed it to him. It had seemed sensible to combine the visit to Bristol with a brief call on Simon at nearby Macklestone and return it.

Drew recognised Bradshaw and Lisa, but no one else. "Which one is your sister?" But he had guessed before she pointed her out that it was the girl standing next to Bradshaw. The colour red made a strong statement. It was a 'look at me' colour. He could imagine her on a cat-walk, wiggling her hips and doing those fancy steps they did on cat-walks. An attention grabber, Rhoda's sister. He wasn't impressed. He handed the snap back. It was no good for identification purposes. "She doesn't look like you."

"No. Younger. Prettier. Dresses better."

He didn't pay her the obvious compliment. Rhoda at any age, and dressed as tattily as she was now in a dark green cotton summer skirt and a top in a shade of sludge, would still be remarkable to look at. He asked her what she did for a living.

"Freelance journalism." But she wasn't here to talk about herself. "What about Simon? Does he know about the flat?"

"Yes, I told him a little time ago. He seemed to accept the situation."

A healthy anger against Peter flared. If anyone should have the flat, he should have it. "If it were in my power to hand it back to Simon – on Clare's behalf – then I would."

Drew didn't deal in ifs and buts, or in sudden surprising senti-
mentality. He glanced at his notepad. There was a lot on it, but not much a firm of solicitors was capable of handling. A private detective agency was better suited to tracking her down, but would be extremely expensive. Advice from Detective Chief Inspector Maybridge would cost nothing and he knew him well enough to approach him. As the Metropolitan Police had the matter in hand, though they might not have done much about it so far apart from adding her name to the Missing Persons Bureau computer, it might be better to see Maybridge privately. He

could liaise with his London colleagues officially if he thought it necessary, or he could advise Rhoda to go back to them and make her own enquiries.

He asked her if she knew Maybridge. "You might have met at the Bradshaws' funeral?"

"I was *persona non grata*," she reminded him drily. "He'd hardly come and shake my hand."

"Well, he could have ticked you off for creating a disturbance," Drew teased. "If you'd like me to try to arrange a meeting with him during his off-duty time – this evening, if possible – I'll go along with you, if you don't mind my divulging that Bradshaw has bequeathed the flat to your sister. It adds some urgency. He'll know the best procedure. If he is available, it might mean your getting back to London rather late. Would it matter?"

It wouldn't, of course. An interview with Maybridge, especially if his wife was there, might be difficult and embarrassing, but it would be made easier and more productive if she had a solicitor with her.

"Nothing matters," she said, "except finding Clare."

Maybridge's availability was always unpredictable. He told Drew, in response to his phone call to headquarters, that he had a meeting with Superintendent Claxby scheduled for the early evening and didn't expect to be home much before nine – followed by a later commitment to drive over to Clifton by ten thirty to pick up his wife, whose car was in for a service. "Another evening," he suggested, "or a brief meeting tonight?"

Drew, after consulting Rhoda, settled for the brief meeting. He would take her for a meal somewhere in the Macklestone area beforehand. There wouldn't be time afterwards if she was to catch her London train.

The Avon Arms did pub lunches and evening snacks. Most of the food was frozen and bought in large quantities from a nearby supermarket. On Fridays, it was supplemented by three dozen savoury flans baked by Mrs Mackay and delivered by her in her fifteen-year-old Ford Cortina. Her friend, Dawn Millington, received them and carried them into the pub kitchen. To step across the threshold of a public house was something Mrs Mackay wouldn't do. Feeding the drinkers, however, didn't blot her moral code and it blotted up the beer. She was doing nothing wrong. All the ingredients, imaginatively put together and not necessarily expensive, were strictly recorded in an account book. The money she made on the flans was money for her skill, she wasn't stealing from The Mount's store cupboard. This she made very clear to Doctor Donaldson. He was extremely embarrassed and wished she wouldn't do it. Didn't he pay her enough? Was it a subtle, or maybe not so subtle, way of asking for a rise? He had put the question to her as tactfully as he could. She had assured him that she was perfectly contented with the salary, but there might come a time in the future, when she reached retirement age, when part-time cooking would make life a little easier for her financially – and be an interest. She was building up for the future now. That was why she had bought her cottage and was furnishing it with the flan money. As she rarely spoke very much, Donaldson had felt he was being assailed with information. Had she pointed to the mixing bowl on the kitchen table and said briefly: "Look, I'm doing it. You're not losing out, so stop interfering," it would have embarrassed him less. He could have told her to stop – or leave. Not that he would have done. He needed her and she knew it.

Mrs Mackay's building for the future was being erected to a smaller degree socially. She and Dawn Millington shared a liking for choral music. And she and Dawn Millington's husband attended the Nonconformist chapel and sat in the same pew. Dawn Millington's once-a-week stint as a barmaid was attributable to the shortcomings of the Common Agricultural Policy, according to her husband. A lowering of standards, deplored but financially

Cormack, hearing most of this from Mrs Millington, was amused. On Friday evenings, she had explained to him, there would be a cold supper laid out for him on the dining-room table, or a slow cooking casserole in the kitchen which she could safely leave for him to help himself. Alternatively, if he wanted some decent pub grub, all the locals in the know went to the Avon Arms and ordered a flan. The other food was rubbish. What her husband did on her absent evenings was a mystery. Probably grabbed some bread and cheese and ate it seated on his tractor. Cormack's attempts to socialise with him had been abortive and he had stopped trying. Some people are born taciturn.

And some – like Cormack – need human contact that is warm, cheerful and undemanding. And preferably female. He was missing Josie. Letters and phone calls made matters worse. Her letters spoke of love – her breathy voice on the telephone spoke of it, too – but letters are just pieces of paper and a telephone is a piece of metal and sweet Mother of God he wanted more than that.

He had taken his secretary, Sofia, out a few times, but it was a relationship that had to be handled with some delicacy. He wasn't sure what her background was: of mixed Eastern and Western parentage, he guessed. The Western attitude to a casual sexual relationship might be accepted by her as a fact of life but, without being overtly prudish, she didn't approve of it. In other words, he couldn't take her to bed. He liked her, respected her, and if his body occasionally lusted for her, he controlled it severely. Talking shop, now and then, helped to prevent over-heating. Cadavers are cold.

Going early to the Avon Arms to eat a flan on a Friday evening might not be the acme of gourmet delight – as far as he knew – but it would make a change. He invited Sofia and she accepted. Her boyfriend was away for a few days, she told him, so she was free that evening. That Josie was away – far away – she knew. At times Cormack wondered if the boyfriend – nameless – existed. He seemed to be away a lot of the time, too. She was a good old-fashioned girl, and would have made a good old-fashioned nun if she hadn't been a Muslim, or whatever. She controlled her sexuality and helped him to control his, which was no bad thing. Josie would be home in eight months.

Sally, who couldn't control her sexuality even if it were just she and an octogenarian eskimo in an igloo in the frozen wastes of Greenland, was becoming progressively more irked by Simon. He wouldn't *respond*. She had bought herself a mini skirt in thin black leather, rather too hot just now. The sun must be finding holes in the ozone layer and blasting through. When it missed the holes, it was cold. It had been chilly when she had bought the skirt in Bristol a few days ago. It had cost her the equivalent of what she'd made on Mrs Bradshaw's three evening dresses and the professor's tweed jacket, she'd worked out. She had spent some more of the loot money at a Redolence Salon – rather posh and expensive. Ten quid for a facial. The Patchouli Parlours were run by the same company, the girl who was steam cleaning her face told her. Patchouli was an Indian scent. Some of the men clients preferred citronella, which was more lemony. The Redolence company marketed it under the name of Citre, which didn't mean anything but sounded macho. Would she like a sample for her boyfriend? It had been the kind of sales talk she usually ignored, but she felt she owed it to Simon to get him something and bought him a small bottle. Her sexy skirt and the pressie might help matters along, she hoped.

Simon, not impressed with either, had thanked her politely for the body lotion – would his father have used this sort of stuff? – and put it on the shelf in the bathroom. He wasn't just bored with Sally these days. He was bored with himself – his aimless existence – mooching around – or driving around – not fast – he was even getting bored with speed. All his dreams of exploring the world seemed to be disappearing. He'd probably end up sitting with a lot of geriatrics on Brighton promenade. Donaldson would have told him that he was suffering from exogenous depression – natural a few months after a bereavement – had he gone along and asked him. But Simon's last contact with Donaldson was the last contact he wanted with him. It had produced Sally, which had been helpful for a while. But the only lasting help that would do him any good would be Rhoda.

"This house is getting disgustingly dirty," Sally grumbled as they sat together in the kitchen, wondering what to have for supper. He agreed. Rhoda had kept the place looking reasonable when she hadn't been upstairs, working. Not that he had wanted her to dirty her hands with housework.

"You could try washing up," Sally said tartly, "some men do. Try it sometime. It won't shorten your willie."

Oh, sparkling, happy, nice Sally. What's happening?

She looked in his fridge and didn't fancy what she saw in it. The sort of frozen stuff the Avon Arms gave its customers late on Fridays, and all the time on other days. She glanced at the kitchen clock. It was getting on for seven thirty.

"If we move," she said, "we'll be in time for a flan."

"A what?"

She explained. "And please don't say you don't want to come, Simon. There won't be many there this early. Nobody's going to bother you. It will be just a pleasant normal evening out down at the local. And what's wrong with that?"

Charles Hixon, in one of his sermons, had described taverns as ampitheatres of sin. Which proved he hadn't been in one. The Avon Arms, like most pubs, was cosy. There wasn't a large gladiatorial area in the middle. Sin, if it occurred, might be in the eye of the beholder, but usually the scene was pleasantly convivial. Marital combat, or combat of any other kind, wasn't overt.

The bar was shaped like a horseshoe and made from a large hunk of ancient oak. It took up a lot of space. The restaurant area had been the original kitchen and was approached through a low archway with a sign over it: Pub Grub – Mind Your Head. Having the eating area separate made it legally acceptable for children to be on the premises. The serious drinkers stayed in the main bar and had their pub grub, if they wanted it, at small tables.

Cormack, as serious a drinker as most of his compatriots, could take it or leave it. When driving, or out with Sofia, he left it. A pint of beer didn't count. Sofia always had orange juice made from fresh fruit and cooled with ice. A small fleck of pulped orange was on her lower lip and Cormack wondered if she would leap back with dismay if he wiped it off. Her pale pink lips were a gentle contrast to her pale brown skin and her dark blue linen dress completed the picture. Well, he could look. It had been a day of combined business and pleasure – business at the forensic science laboratory at Chepstow – and the pleasure of driving there and back with her through pleasant countryside. He was still house hunting in a fairly desultory way. If Josie didn't want to settle here, there were other attractive areas not too far from base. Thinking about Josie and looking at Sofia's lips was a kind of balancing exercise in restraint. Damn restraint! He leaned across the table and gently removed the fleck of orange with his little finger. She didn't leap back. Just smiled and said thanks.

Sally, seated with Simon at an alcove table and with a good

view of Cormack's back and Sofia's front, swore quietly into her gin and tonic. She wasn't too alarmed, just mildly upset. Simon asked her what was the matter. Nothing, she told him. He thought she might be annoyed because they had arrived too late for a flan and were making do with chicken in a basket. The couple she had been watching had a flan. It wasn't his fault, he pointed out to her, he couldn't help being waylaid by someone he didn't know but who knew his parents and kept on sympathising. "Anyway, this chicken isn't bad."

"There are birds and birds," Sally said enigmatically. "Would you mind changing places, Simon? I'm not comfortable sitting here."

He didn't think she would be comfortable sitting anywhere in that skirt. It looked like black rubber and probably stuck to her chair. The evening was very humid. He agreed to change places and offered to freshen her drink. Freshen. A stupid word. He wished he could freshen his mind – dunk it into a bucket of cold water. A double gin, she told him, and a small bottle of orange. Yes, orange, not tonic.

While Simon was fetching her drink, Sally made eye contact with Cormack. It wasn't easy, but Sally was skilled. Once aware of her, Cormack was startled into a quick grimace of recognition, an alarmed smile. A fair had come to his Irish village a long time ago and the girl he had been with had taken pot shots at a row of cardboard squirrels moving with erratic jerks in front of a cardboard rural scene. If you potted a squirrel you won a bag of peanuts. She had potted nearly all of them and loaded him with nuts. They had eaten them lying on straw in her father's barn, mouth to mouth like salty French kisses. Afterwards they had made love. He sensed that the blonde waitress from The Mount would have an aim just as deadly. But his nuts were for Josie.

He picked up the menu card and asked Sofia what she would like to follow. The choice wasn't large. Ice-cream. Gateaux. Coffee. She settled for a strawberry ice-cream and wondered why Max seemed suddenly *distrait*.

Simon, returning with the drinks, wondered why Sally was suddenly sunny. Her warmth, her cheeriness were back. She thanked him for the drinks. Touched his hand. Drew her chair nearer to his. Pressed her thigh so close that he could feel the slither of the leather against his jeans. Her conversation, that had become a long grey drool, was now a long bright drool. She laughed a lot and he felt rotten about not finding what she said particularly funny.

"I think you should be introduced," Sally said at last.

"What? Introduced to whom?" The room was full of people, most of them villagers who had been tactful enough to leave him and Sally alone.

"Come along, Simon. Your father would wish it."

"Wish what?"

She linked her arm through his and almost frogmarched him to the table where the red-headed chap and his girlfriend were sitting.

"This is Professor Bradshaw's son, Simon," Sally said, "and this, Simon, is Doctor Cormack, who has your father's old job."

Cormack, very annoyed, stood up politely. What a calculating little bitch. What he had been witnessing out of the corner of his eye had been a cold-blooded charade. She'd been using the lad. An idyllic picture of young love? Rats! Bloody squirrels!

He introduced Sofia.

"Charmed," Sally said, her eyes little glints of steel, "absolutely delighted." Sofia smiled weakly.

Sally asked if they might join them for a few minutes. "Would you fetch a couple of chairs, Simon?"

Simon was looking at the man who had taken his father's place. It was at moments like these that the severance pain hurt again and reversed the healing process. When his father had been this man's age he, Simon, had been a child, about nine or so. They had done things together. Gone on outings. During the period of his mother's absence, when Trudy Morrison, the housekeeper who couldn't cook but was very pretty, was looking after the house, they had made up a threesome once at tennis. He and Trudy at one side of the net, lobbing balls at his father, and his father, who wasn't much good at it, missing most of them. It was when Trudy was reaching for a ball that she had slipped and fallen. His father had picked her up very gently and sworn at a lot of people who seemed to think she was making a fuss about nothing. She had been hurt enough to need to have her arm in plaster. Another time

154

he remembered was when Trudy had found the birds' nest in the apple tree and had made a joke about a cuckoo. His father, overhearing, had shaken his head warningly. It hadn't occurred to him then that they might have been lovers. And he didn't want to think of it now, but the girl sitting at the table would be about the same age as Trudy was then, and the man – Cormack – was looking at her and . . . and . . . time was vicious . . . it kept moving on . . . killing . . . replacing . . .

"The chairs, Simon," Sally said.

He looked at her dully. Chairs? What chairs? The two from the table they'd just left? But why? He didn't want to sit with this man and this woman.

Cormack felt compassion and wondered what the right words were to express it – were any words right? His own father was still alive, thank God, and he couldn't get under this lad's skin and feel what he was feeling, but he could sense it to some extent. He put his hand on Simon's shoulder very briefly. "Sorry." The other words stayed inside his head, the usual clichés of commiseration. He wished he could take a walk outside with the lad – just walk – there's sympathy in companionship and silence. A foursome was the last thing the boy needed and if the bloody girl mentioned chairs again he'd bloody brain her. Any sexual attraction he'd felt for her earlier was killed stone dead.

It was necessary to withdraw and with as much good manners as he could muster. Not easy. Sofia hadn't finished her ice-cream and was too shy to get on with it now that the blonde bosomy girl was standing over her.

Cormack launched into a leaving speech. "I'm sorry, but we have to be on our way almost immediately." He smiled at Sofia. "As soon as you're ready." Surprised, she picked up her spoon and began eating, too fast, and giving up on the wafer, put it at the side of her plate. "It was a successful whist drive up at The Mount the other evening, very enjoyable Miss . . . er . . . ?"

"Loreto. Sally Loreto. Call me Sally."

"And the refreshments you carried around on your tray and tempted us with were superb."

Sally wondered if this was a social put-down and decided it wasn't. This man wouldn't give a damn what she did for a living.

155

He had been receiving her signals like bursts of electricity up to the last few minutes. It was something to do with Simon's standing there. If only he'd fetched the chairs when asked and not looked so po-faced – if he had just co-operated – not thrown a spanner in the works and fused everything back into gloom.

"Well," Sally said lightly, "I'm glad you enjoyed it. You might come to The Mount again for the next one – it's quite soon – or for bridge."

Cormack said he might, but his work kept him rather busy. "Congratulate your cook on the flan this evening. It was quite excellent."

"Was it?" said Sally, smiling valiantly.

At his home, a few minutes down the road from the Avon Arms, Maybridge was apologising to Alan Drew and his client that he couldn't give them more time and more hospitality. It seemed churlish not to offer them a meal. Had Meg been there, she would have got something together while he'd given the problem all the time and attention it deserved. Instant coffee or a soft drink for whoever was driving and a choice of something stronger for the passenger was the best he could do. They'd had an early dinner at a pub near Stroud, Drew explained. They were fine, honestly, didn't want anything. Except advice.

Maybridge's first impression of Rhoda didn't tally with Meg's, possibly because she wasn't putting on any kind of act. He listened to what she had to say – truth slightly edited, he guessed – and did a little reading between the lines. Her connection with Peter, through her sister, put her activities at Simon's home into a different light. Her unofficial sleuthing was unwise, but worry about her sister might have unbalanced her judgment, and Simon hadn't complained. It was obvious that she wished him no harm, her concern for the boy was genuine. It was wrong, she said, that he should be done out of any part of his inheritance.

And it *was* wrong, if you viewed it from the strictly moralistic angle, but the chances of its being put right were remote and depended on the goodwill of the missing sister. She would probably hang on to what she had.

If she were still alive, and there was no reason to fear that she

156

wasn't. Hixon had been safely locked away when the photo was taken, and there weren't any other serial murderers roaming around – as far as he knew.

He asked Rhoda if they had parted on good terms last time they had met. She admitted they had had an argument. "About her relationship with Peter. I thought the situation could be dangerous."

"Dangerous?"

"Well – unwise."

Unwise. A watered-down word, but surely nearer the mark. There had been sibling rivalry over a shared lover, perhaps. She hadn't spoken Bradshaw's name with cool indifference, though she had tried to, and she had avoided looking directly at him. Peter had a lot to answer for. Clare Warwick was by no means the first of his extramarital adventures. If there was an after-life, his hell would be celibacy.

It seemed safe to assume that the sisters had quarrelled and the younger one had taken off in a huff. A simple explanation. If that were so she would return in her own good time and wonder what all the fuss was about. Only there hadn't been any fuss – yet – the only one who seemed to be worried was Rhoda. More than worried. Extremely anxious.

Drew had brought a typed résumé of everything that Rhoda had told him earlier in the office. He passed it to Maybridge. "If you think this might be of any use, keep it. I have a copy." It looked business-like, he hoped, and took the emphasis off the social side of the evening which had started quite delightfully with an alfresco meal of freshly caught salmon washed down with a good quality Chablis. He and Rhoda had taken a walk afterwards by the river which ran along the bottom of the inn's garden and the evening had been golden and very promising – or perhaps he had been a touch optimistic about the promise.

Maybridge, scanning the notes, realised that most of the information could have been imparted over the phone, though he was glad it hadn't been. It was interesting meeting her. That it was rather more than interesting for Drew was obvious. He tried to remember his marital background and had a hazy recollection of Meg's mentioning that he'd married the daughter of one of her university colleagues, a law graduate, and that it hadn't worked. Two professionals getting scratchy in the domestic cage – happier apart. Maybe it wasn't Drew – another solicitor – but the words had stuck. He and Meg had been scratchy at that particular time, too – job pressure, but no wounds of any consequence. Meg and Rhoda would be glad to have missed each other, he guessed: antipathy between women doesn't dissipate very easily.

He smiled at her. "Telling someone not to worry is about as much use as telling a tooth to stop aching – but – well, for what it's worth – try to be positive. People, even sisters, can behave with crass stupidity. Forget to write. Not bother to get in touch. Lack the imagination to guess you might be anxious. I'll find out what's happening at the London end and keep Alan informed."

She felt reassured. He had a quality of kindly honesty and would do all he could. She thanked him briefly. "It's good of you to bother."

He responded by wishing her a safe journey back to London. She stood a far greater chance of being mugged on the train, he thought, than of anything dire having happened to her sister. It was unfortunate they couldn't have met earlier in the evening.

It was unfortunate for Simon, too. The timing couldn't have been worse. He and Sally were walking out of the Avon Arms when Drew and Rhoda were driving past. "Looks as if the lad's got himself fixed up," Drew pointed them out. "Young love." He slowed down. "Do you want a word with him?"

Rhoda, speechless with relief, shook her head. If she were a praying woman she would have thanked whatever god had been wise and wonderful enough to fix such a neat and natural solution. The busty little blonde girl had her arm around his waist. She was perfect for him. Just what he needed. The crush he'd had on her was over. The burden had gone.

12

Rhoda had turned towards Drew and was smiling at him when Simon saw her. He watched the car moving slowly down the road and then gradually picking up speed. He couldn't believe what he was seeing. Rhoda and Alan Drew. Alan Drew who knew his father. Alan Drew who had carried his mother's coffin. He wanted to run after the car, hammer on the bonnet, yell at Drew to stop. And then look at her. To make sure. She wouldn't come and go. Ignore him. Not come near him. Just like that.

Would she?

He found it difficult to move. Sally's arm was like a warm snake around his waist. He took her hand in his cold one and thrust her aside.

And stood looking after the car until it had gone.

"A woman of that age shouldn't have long hair," Sally said nastily. She only had Creggan's description to go on – the black-haired señora – but looking at Simon's face now told her who it was. He was pale apart from blobs of colour on his cheekbones and on his forehead. Was that what love did to you – bring you out in a rash? It was funny, in a way, but she didn't dare smile. The bloke the woman had with her wasn't anything special. Not

159

like Cormack. Cormack's brush-off had hurt a bit, but she'd get over it and try again.

She asked Simon what he wanted to do. They couldn't keep standing here like a couple of zombies. A walk up into the woods, while it was still light? "I don't have to get back to The Mount yet."

He told her he was going home. It was a dismissal she wouldn't accept. The evening, she hoped, might have a few plus points. It couldn't be minus all the time. Black clouds with silver linings – that sort of thing. Anyway, she could do with a few more drinks and the professor's cupboard still had a reasonable stock left. She walked a few paces behind him because she couldn't keep up. After moving off in a sort of daze he seemed to have got himself into gear and was going at a pretty fast clip. People in a temper were like that sometimes. They walked off their rage.

But you can't walk off pain. You can walk until your heart thumps and your breath comes too fast, but it's inside you all the time. You can't out-walk it. Out-breathe it. It's in the air – on the Macklestone road – in the cool of the darkening house. Simon, aware of Sally's presence, but in a peripheral way as if she were part of the furniture, ignored her and went upstairs.

Sally, listening in the hall, heard the bathroom door close. Yes – well – upsets took her that way too. He might be there some time so she made for the drinks cupboard in the sitting-room and poured herself a gin. He had a fixation on that woman – or was obsession the word? – so there could be a bit of passion in him somewhere. A relief, really, to know that. He wasn't a poofter, though she'd begun to wonder. She went to sit on the sofa and removed a pair of his trainers which had been slung on it. This was a nice house. An expensive house. Not the kind of place you gave up on. Perhaps the señora, whatever her name was, had a house of her own. An even better one. Or the bloke she was with had. She hadn't even waved to Simon. Just ducked her head and pretended she hadn't seen him. An uncaring sort of bitch, really.

Sally sipped her gin, listened to the toilet being flushed, and heard the sound of Simon's footsteps as he climbed to the top floor. She had been up there only once, on the day she had packed the Bradshaws' clobber. The place had the look of a rich kid's playroom, she'd thought then. Not that she'd liked the mural much. It hadn't seemed the sort of thing to make a kid happy. Young boys usually liked bug-eyed monsters. Bug-eyed monsters were cheerfully hideous. The creatures in the wall painting seemed to be suffering from anorexia nervosa, or one of the other daft dieting diseases Donaldson catered for, and they had twined poisonous ivy in their hair. Simon had probably been brought up looking at the wrong things. Which explained a lot.

If he had any sense he would paint it out. It would be therapy to do something like that. Sitting brooding wouldn't do him any good, if that was what he was doing. He could, of course, be hanging himself from the hook behind the door. She considered the possibility with equanimity, not believing it. Gin was a calming drink; her mind was untroubled.

She went upstairs after a while to see what he was up to and found him tearing up sheets of foolscap paper, closely written on, and cramming the torn paper into a wicker wastepaper basket. He didn't glance at her when she came in. It would do him good, she told him approvingly, to do just that. Some of The Mount patients got rid of their aggro by sticking pins in themselves, before they were stopped: tearing up paper was a better way. Would he like her to help – to tear it up with him? It sounded deeply sarcastic but wasn't intended that way.

His voice was small and tight. "Go away."

"A little painting, then?" she suggested. "I can get rid of some of that for you. You're too old to have kids' pictures on a wall."

She looked in the cupboard over the sink and found a glass jar of powder paint that had been mixed several months ago and gone solid with age. She half-filled the jar with water but it wouldn't absorb the paint and there was nothing to stir it with. Shaking the jar wasn't any use, either, and it slipped out of her hands and broke, depositing a small damp mound like a cow pat on the floor.

"Sorry, Simon. I'm a little whoozy. Didn't mean to make a mess."

She hadn't meant to cut her finger, either. She asked him if he would mind very much if she wiped the blood off with a corner of the quilt. And wiped it off before he could answer.

161

Simon stopped tearing up Rhoda's notes. She wouldn't need them. She would never come here again. Doing this to her wouldn't hurt her. There was nothing he could do to her that would hurt her.

And there was nothing he could do to himself that would make him feel halfway alive again. Unless . . .

He looked at Sally. "All right," he said.

She understood him immediately. Gin didn't turn her on, but it didn't turn her off, either. Had she been sober she would have undressed more seductively and not got her feet tangled up in her knickers. She would have taken better charge of him, too, not let him fumble around so much. He was a male virgin, whatever that was called, and she should have helped rather than giggled. But he got there in the end and she held his head against her breasts and kissed his hair, which was damp with effort.

Sated, surprised, wanting to weep, to laugh, but mainly wanting to sleep, Simon rolled away from her and fell off the narrow couch on to the floor. The thump crashed him back into the reality of the here and now. Sleep fled. Rhoda's sacrosanct couch. He had made love on it. His pre-sex gloom returned, tinged with guilt. Sally's laughter tinkled like lute strings plucked by demon fingers. He wished to God she'd shut up.

"You've got to go," he told her.

She thought he was being extremely ungrateful. Why did she have to go? She had been very nice to him. He had enjoyed it. And it hadn't been at all bad for her, either. All he needed was practice.

"I've got to wash the quilt," he said.

Wash it? Was he daft? Okay, so there should have been a towel or something, but it wasn't a clinical exercise, damn it. It just happened. Didn't he know that? How would it have been for him if she had been the other woman? Would he have cuddled up with her all night? Was he being deliberately rude because she wasn't the other one?

"What's her name?" Her voice was sullen.

Simon was tugging at the quilt. "Whose?"

"The black haired witch's."

"I don't know who you're talking about." He kept on tugging

162

and she grabbed the other end and tugged back. She needed it to cover her, to keep her warm.

He was the stronger and pulled her off the couch, forcing her around the room towards the door, both of them treading on small slivers of glass and not noticing, lips compressed with effort, eyes slits of anger. He inched her out on to the landing and on to the top step of the stairs. Not cautious, not caring if the other fell, they slithered precariously, each step down his victory, reversed when she gained a step up. And then her hands wouldn't take the strain any more and she slackened her grip, but didn't let go. The last three steps were taken fast, the quilt softening the impact. Battle scarred – he had a cut lip and she had bumped her forehead on the banister – they sat together on the bottom step, naked, breathless and momentarily at peace. It had been a passionate few minutes, rather fun in its way, she thought. Had they made love now, they would have made it better – after a rest. He told her he was sorry and asked if she were all right. Her head throbbed, but not too badly, but there was blood on the quilt – from their feet, which were resting on it. "Your blood is bleeding into mine," she told him, "like a gypsy love ritual."

It hadn't seemed to him like an act of love – his act of love with Sally. And he had forgotten to wear his sheath. He was more sober than she was, but even less rational. Rhoda's desertion, her rejection, couldn't be viewed coolly by him. And the last thing he wanted was to have Sally's plump foot resting on his. He limped into the bathroom and came back with a wet towel for both of them. And he wiped her feet and she wiped his. And the glass, as small as sugar crystals, was picked out carefully by both of them.

Like monkeys picking fleas, she giggled.

Not a Rhoda remark.

He told her he was cold and was going to get dressed – in the clothes in his bedroom. He wasn't going up to the studio to walk on glass, and if she went up she had better be careful.

Cormack, she thought, would have treated her with more charm. He would have fetched her knickers, her tights, her skirt and T-shirt. Oh, and her shoes. A charming man would walk on razors for the woman he loved. She told Simon he was a boor and it sounded like a bore. He told her she bored him too and left her sitting there.

Some while later, in retrospect, Simon realised he should have played the scene very differently. Failing to push the quilt into the washing machine – it was too bulky – he should have parcelled it and taken it to the dry cleaners the next day. Not try to burn it. And he should have made sure that Sally had got herself dressed properly so that she could have walked back to The Mount looking decent. Or he should have driven her. And she could have helped by behaving differently, too. If she had needed bandages for her feet she should have asked him, not left blood in her shoes after trying to force them on, and then nicking his trainers.

And if she had wanted to stay the night she might have talked him round into letting her, but she had got into his bed when he'd been downstairs and she'd put on Rhoda's nightdress, which she'd found under the pillow. And she had laughed her silly laugh that made her boobs go up and down when he'd told her to take it off. And she'd called him a transvestite, which he bloody wasn't. But he shouldn't have hit her. Not that he'd hit her hard. He didn't think he had. He hadn't meant to hurt her.

Sally would have returned to The Mount if Simon's trainers hadn't been two sizes too big. She had torn her knickers into strips and stuffed them into the trainers to make them smaller and to ooze blood into, though the cuts on her feet weren't oozing so much now. They were oozing very little, in fact, but hurt like hell. So did her forehead where she had bumped it. And Simon's open handed slap across her nose had drawn some blood, too. She told herself that she was in a state of collapse and wept a little as she walked. Or tried to walk. It was like being on stilts, one trainer lifted up like a clod, put down again a few inches further forward, ditto with the other trainer. Left, right, slow, slow, slow.

She decided against going along the main road, which was smoother and not much longer, in case someone in a car stopped and finished her off. The lane was rough and brambly and frighteningly dark. She might get finished off here by a lurker in the bushes, but by the time she reached Mrs Mackay's cottage she didn't much care. There were no lights on and she nearly walked into the back of the Ford Cortina which was parked with its boot jutting out.

Cars, in the past, had formed makeshift beds. A mixture of discomfort and delight. Disappointment, too, depending on who she was with. She could adapt herself without too much trouble to the back seat of almost any car, but not this one. Mrs Mackay's car was adapted to transporting flans and the wooden trays on the back seat were a permanent fixture. You can't rest on trays and Sally needed to rest. The front seat wasn't comfortable unless she sat up straight. The only advantage the car had were doors that locked on the inside. It was while she was trying to arrange her body into a foetal position, with her knees just missing the gear lever, that she set off the horn with her elbow. It bellowed into the night like a cow in labour.

"You should have rung the bell, m'dear," Mrs Mackay told her placidly, a little later.

Sally had never admired Mrs Mackay, apart from her ability to cook, but that she could be so placid in the middle of the night, under these circumstances, was amazing. She had appeared at the car door wrapped in a dark green dressing gown and wearing matching slippers edged with fur. The large torch she was carrying might have been an implement of defence, if necessary, but at least she hadn't brandished it. When she had realised who it was, her eyes had widened slightly in surprise and she had smiled a bitter hurt little smile as if Sally's pain and blood and general despair were, for a few minutes, hers. She had looked at her with love.

Which was alarming.

as the night wore on, as kind.

The cottage had a musty smell of wood smoke and old clothes and was heavily raftered. The grate, put in by a previous owner, was of black iron with insets of tiles down the sides depicting flowers the colour of faded puce. It was the kind of grate that appeared in yuppy conversions and cost a lot. Sally, hazy with gin but not too hazy to bother, valued it at three to four hundred quid and wondered why Mrs Mackay hadn't sold it. Apart from the cash, which could be used to buy something else, it looked awful.

165

An oak sideboard taking up a lot of space looked awful, too. Junk or antique? Sally didn't know. Probably junk. Why hadn't she bought herself a decent three-piece suite? The only bright thing in the room was a large home-made circular rug on the stone floor – a picture in wool of a cat and a dog sitting amicably together in front of a cottage which was prettier than this one.

She had been put to sit on a beige moquette chair near an oil heater with the heat turned low and given a tumbler of warm milk.

Mrs Mackay gently probed. "What happened, m'dear?"

Sally said she had been raped and battered and nearly killed.

Mrs Mackay, flinching, asked who had done those terrible things.

Sally told her that Simon had.

The next twenty minutes were fraught with indecision. Should the police be called? The pros and cons of professional interference, and retribution, were gone into. Mrs Mackay was astute enough to guess that the Bradshaw boy, scum though he undoubtedly was, hadn't raped a virgin. And rape in a court of law might be difficult to prove. Assault and battery, including doing something dreadful to the poor girl's feet, wouldn't be difficult. She suggested making a phone call to the local police station. "Now, m'dear, while your wounds are visible."

It was tempting. Sally thought about it. She had been roughed up by others in the past, worse than this. In Simon's case, it had been a slapped face and slapped pride. And some of what she felt now was the result of drinking too much. And this milk was making her feel sicker. She asked if she might visit the toilet.

The narrow little bathroom on the first floor had a new suite in pale blue and the tiny window was draped with nets. Sally got sick into the toilet bowl, bringing up the milk. She needed a drink of something sharp, even tea would have been better than milk. She looked doubtfully at the tooth mug, but it might have held the old girl's teeth so she didn't risk drinking from it. Instead, she cupped water from the tap into her hands and drank as much as she could and then washed her face and dried it on the towel, which smelt of cheap soap.

The soap in Simon's bathroom – his mother's soap – had been deliciously perfumed. Yves Saint Laurent. And the towels were thick and warm and expensive. Nicer if they hadn't been brown, but that was a minor point to quibble over. And the loo in Simon's mother's bathroom had a seat of real wood and had been warm to sit on. And the corner bath – well – when you thought of that bath and this bath and looked at the taps. And thought. Not just about the bathroom, but about everything else. Well, you didn't let a stupid row over a stupid nightdress with a stupid boy who had thousands of quids in the bank spoil the future you might get if you had any sense.

You didn't call the police.

Mrs Mackay took a little dissuading. The lout, she declared, should be punished. "He might have lost you your job, m'dear."

This was an aspect that Sally hadn't considered. Mrs Mackay's view of her was clearer than Sally's reflection in the mirror over the fireplace, which was restricted to her face. Mrs Mackay saw all of her. The zip on her scanty leather skirt had stuck halfway up and it clung precariously around her knickerless hips. Her white T-shirt, no longer white, had some graffiti on it which Mrs Mackay didn't understand but was probably rude – something about chasing a dragon with angel dust. Her plump pretty legs, ending in those grotesque shoes of Professor Bradshaw's unsavoury son, completed the picture of a girl on the downward path to ruin. She looked like a woman of the streets. And she smelt of drink. If she returned to The Mount looking like that and crept along very quietly to her room in the staff's quarters, she might get away with it, there were no rules about returning at a given time, but if Donaldson happened to be around and saw her, and if he scolded her and she was insolent, he would have the chance he had been looking for. He would sack her. Sally sacked would be Sally doomed to a life of depravity.

Sally, sitting here in Mrs Mackay's living-room in the middle of the night, was Sally delivered into caring hands. Mrs Mackay looked up at the sampler recently completed and hanging on the wall. To Have And To Hold.

Crazy schemes evolve in the hours of darkness when they seem clear and sane. Sally, she suggested, might stay here a day or two. It would give her a chance to heal. The bruises on her face would fade and the cuts on her feet could be attended to. Also she could have the chance to be better clad in more suitable clothes. Mrs Mackay could fetch them. She would tell Doctor Donaldson that Sally had been called away suddenly to attend a sick relative, or deal with a crisis at home, and then when she was ready she would return looking sober and clean and respectable and her job would be waiting for her.

Sally considered this without much enthusiasm. She didn't want to stay here, but she didn't want to be chucked out of The Mount, either. She needed to be at The Mount to be near Simon. You don't abandon a battle because you've been shot full of shrapnel, but she didn't see why he shouldn't receive some of the flak. At this moment she'd like to gouge holes in him. So let him start worrying.

"To say I'm with relatives would be a lie. It's better to say nothing." She touched the bruise that was forming on her forehead. "Patients who are concussed lose their memories sometimes. I'll disappear for a few days then go back and say I can't remember where I've been. If you don't mind putting me up then I'll stay."

Mrs Mackay, aware of a mind more devious than her own, looked at her with carefully concealed pleasure.

"The son," she said, "will suffer."

Sun? Sally wondered. The dark moonless sky, framed like a black rectangle in the cottage window, showed no sign of dawn.

And then she understood. Simon son of Peter. If he hadn't been such a shit they'd be cuddled up together now in the bed where he'd gone off his rocker and her nose had bled into that silly twee-looking nightdress which she'd scrunched up into a ball and stuffed under the mattress. He'd probably found it by now and washed it.

"He's an obsessive," she told Mrs Mackay, "he washes everything. His dad would be ashamed of him."

Sally's hangover the following morning was like being visited by a malevolent enemy who would go away eventually. Incapable of clear thought, she made no effort to rationalise anything. She was here in this rather lumpy bed in a dark little bedroom across the passage from Mrs Mackay's bedroom and next door to the loo.

168

She didn't like being here but her body in its present state wouldn't like being anywhere. Sleep was an escape. It came and went. When it came it wasn't comfortable. She dreamed of a story her infants' school teacher had read to the class about Alice drinking a poisoned potion and growing huge – head squashed against the ceiling, foot up a chimney, arm through a small window like this one a few feet from the floor. After waking from that, she dreamed the cottage was on fire and she couldn't get out.

But she had got out and gone to the loo.

Downstairs in the narrow little hall Mrs Mackay heard her moving about and replaced the telephone receiver. She had intended making a call to her mentor, as she thought of Mrs Hixon, but it would have to wait. She needed advice. This situation might grow into something too difficult to handle. She wanted to be told not to do it. She needed a few wise words from the Scriptures to guide her.

The practical side of her nature told her to fetch Sally's clothes, get her tidied up, then drive her back to The Mount. Today. Sally could tell Doctor Donaldson she had fallen, or anything else she chose to tell him. Sally wasn't her responsibility.

The loving, lonely, emotional side counselled her differently. She couldn't help being fond of the girl. Being fond of someone is as natural as being hungry. She assuaged hunger, her own and the hunger of others, with food of the flesh and went to infinite trouble with it. Obesity, according to Donaldson, was the result of compensating for a lack of some kind. Mrs Mackay was verging on being obese. Had she been lazy she would have been – nervous activity kept her weight controlled within reasonable limits. The pyjamas she had given Sally last night had been size twenty. The jacket had reached the girl's knees. She had refused to wear the trousers. When she had peeped into the bedroom at dawn she had noticed that the girl's shoulders were bare. Either the jacket had slipped off or she had taken it off. Sally's nudity worried her. Not that she had any guilty thoughts about it in relation to herself, her fondness for her wasn't carnal, but Sally semi-nude and asleep seemed infant-innocent and vulnerable. She had gently, quietly tucked the sheet around her and folded the blanket back a little as she seemed to be very hot. Cheeks flushed. Forehead moist and creased into a frown. The bruise just above her left temple was a greenish purple. A cold compress might help later.

She felt a surge of anger against the Bradshaw boy again as she went into the kitchen to prepare two trays. The smaller one held medicaments – lint, cotton wool, antiseptic, a bowl of ice-cubes from the fridge. The larger was set with cereal, fruit juice, milk and a flask of tea. Tomorrow, Sunday, the assistant cook took over and she would be home all the morning and would have time to make Sally the kind of breakfast that would nourish her – freshly baked croissants, the best cut of bacon carefully grilled, toast with her own brand of marmalade that smelt of orange groves in the hot sun.

She would *care* for her.

She went upstairs and knocked at her door. "May I come in, m'dear?"

Sally, back in bed after being to the loo and feeling lousy, grunted.

Mrs Mackay, taking this as assent, opened the door and smiled at her anxiously. "Are you better, m'love?"

Sally didn't mind m'dear, but she thought m'love was overdoing it a bit. She said she wasn't feeling better and wanted to go to sleep. "Have you an aspirin, or a tranquilliser?" Mrs Mackay said she'd get some from The Mount's pharmacy. She would have to tell the pharmacist that she needed them for herself. Lying didn't come easily to her, but for Sally's sake she would have to lie, these were mitigating circumstances.

She fetched the trays and put them on the bedside table. The tea in the flask should stay hot for some while, she told Sally, but it would be wise to make the cold compress for her forehead straight away before the ice melted. Should she do it for her? Sally said she'd do it herself thanks and added without much hope that medicinal brandy was better than tea when you didn't feel well. To follow strong drink with strong drink seemed to Mrs Mackay the height of folly. The inebriates at The Mount who had come to dry out should have been looked at more closely by the girl. Look, learn and inwardly digest. There was no such thing as medicinal brandy, she told her, any more than there was medicinal gin. Her stomach would settle in time and she would return as soon as she could with some tablets for her head.

What seemed to be Sally's incipient alcoholism was upsetting. She had guessed she might take a glass or two of lager now and then, but if she drank more heavily in her spare time then she had kept it well concealed. It was young Bradshaw's fault, of course. He was the one who took her to the Avon Arms, according to Dawn Millington who had seen them there together. His was the bad influence. The sins of the fathers, her mentor had quoted to her once, using her husband's words, are branded on the souls of their progeny.

The friendship between Mrs Mackay and Hixon's wife had formed slowly over the years. They had first met at an orchestral concert in Bristol where by chance they had been seated next to each other. A casual reference to charismatic church music had resulted in an invitation to attend a meeting in Bath where Mrs Hixon's husband, Charlie, was to speak a few words. The few words, over the years and in other places, had grown into a spate. His own charisma was powerful, if you liked that sort of thing. Mrs Mackay, inarticulate, tightly buttoned up emotionally, felt a great release as she listened to him. He was a good man, she informed her friend, Dawn Millington, a sincere man and an asset to any church of any denomination with his lay-preaching. Mrs Millington, confirmed in the C. of E. which didn't encourage lay-preachers, nevertheless went along with her a few times and understood her enthusiasm. It might be something to do with the vocal chords, she said, with what seemed to Mrs Mackay unseemly humour, none of the famous lay-preachers, present or past, had ever croaked their sermons, they had delivered them full-throatedly. Songs of redemption bursting forth in great paeons of praise.

Mrs Hixon, quiet, mouse-like, walked in her husband's shadow in the days when all was well. She was a forgettable woman who wore cotton gloves at all times, summer and winter, due to a mild skin disease. Her eyes had a dark imploring quality as if she begged for kindness and understanding. And she apologised a lot. Hixon called her Mrs Hixon, as if she weren't an individual in her own right, and in those good pre-prostitute days she had been happy to let it be that way.

In the bad days, when the devil and all his hordes descended on them and there was no more tranquillity, her nature changed.

She believed him innocent.

Her voice, still quiet, was no longer meek but incisive with rage. The mouse-like creature had become a sabre-toothed tigress who stood up for her man. Journalists hoping for a wronged-wife article to print in the tabloids after the trial approached her brashly with large sums of money and were shown the door. And, uncharacteristically, retreated through it. Fast. Some saw her as a martyr burning at the stake and hurling blazing faggots at her tormentors if they came too near. Even the hardest-boiled recognised pain, but this was pain plus. They respected it.

She visited him in prison in the segregated area where he spent his time with other sex offenders – not all murderers – and in her eyes he shone like a light in the blackest of wildernesses. He told her to pray for his persecutors and she did, with her fingers crossed not meaning a word of it, and just loud enough to embarrass other prisoners and warders close enough to hear. She uncrossed them when he began his litany of hate against those he said had framed him – particularly Bradshaw. Bradshaw was the epitome of evil. He mocked God. He fornicated. He concocted evidence. God had taken his life – hallelujah – but his sins lived on. The hatred spilling over on to his son might seem to some unfair, but the Good Book wasn't unfair, the Good Book condoned it. That the Bible might be interpreted differently occurred to her, but she dismissed it as heresy. Sins of the flesh, of the spirit, it was all the same. It passed on. She agreed that retribution was necessary and did everything he suggested. It was a war of attrition fought with zeal. And her conscience was as clear as a pale blue sky on a summer's day. Hixon's conscience she never questioned. The secret chambers of his mind were locked as securely as his cell door.

Mrs Mackay, relieved to find Sally's door unlocked and that there was no one in the corridor to observe her, went in to fetch her some clothes. Sally's jogging suit, which was respectable, had been splashed with mud and left lying on the wardrobe floor. Unlike the leather skirt which might not wash, this could be, but was rather bulky and too hot to wear around the house. She had brought a Tesco's carrier bag upstairs to the domestic wing – no

172

one would query its contents if they happened to see it. It was just large enough to hold a lightweight dress and cardigan plus underwear. But she didn't seem to have a lightweight dress and cardigan. She had jeans and T-shirts and one cotton skirt that looked as if it might fit a child of twelve. As for underwear, it consisted of elasticated scraps that weren't halfway decent. And no nightwear. The Mount wasn't all that warm in the winter. Maybe she kept warmer, more suitable clothes in the brown plastic suitcase on top of the wardrobe, but there was no time to look in it now. Someone might come. A quick glance in the dressing-table drawer showed an untidy assortment of toiletries and a black and gold evening bag, the kind that elegant middle-aged ladies such as Mrs Bradshaw might have owned. Perturbed, Mrs Mackay took it out and opened it. Inside was a plait of hair, as soft as a fox's pelt and with great tensile strength.

13

Donaldson reported Sally missing at seven thirty on Monday morning – two days later than he should have done. She had been seen with Bradshaw's son on Friday evening, he informed Maybridge over the phone. They could have spent the night together and gone off somewhere on Saturday. A weekend taken without leave was an annoyance but he hadn't been unduly concerned until she had failed to turn up last night.

Maybridge, who had just finished his breakfast, asked him why he hadn't contacted Simon before contacting him. "Because it might be an embarrassing intrusion," Donaldson said with surprising illogicality. "I wanted to avoid that. It's in your hands now, Chief Inspector. You must do what you think best."

There were times when Maybridge wondered if the stresses at The Mount were making the fabric crack. Donaldson should have made the preliminary enquiries immediately: embarrassment as an excuse for being lax wasn't acceptable. He thought fleetingly of Rhoda's sister, but couldn't equate the two. This girl had been expected back, her absence noted. He and Radwell were due to continue an investigation into a series of car thefts in the area but this should take priority. He told Donaldson that he and his sergeant would call on Simon within the next half hour and report back. "In the meantime, find the girl's home address, she may be there, but don't alarm her family until you hear from me."

It was a delicately silver-toned morning. Drifts of mist laced the bushes and made soft patterns on the lawn. Later the day would be very hot. Simon's car, hazed over with dew, was parked in the drive.

"Good weather for fishing," Radwell commented as they parked behind it. He felt very cheerful. His summer holiday in the Lake District was due in three weeks. Twenty-one days of duty were bearable when there was a break at the end of them, and recently he'd felt better able to cope. Superintendent Claxby hadn't been harassing him so much.

Maybridge suggested that fish might rise more readily to the bait in the rain. Making polite, often dull conversation with Radwell had become a habit. When he wasn't defending him from Claxby's barbs he was encouraging him for work well done. Police officers need to grow a tough protective layer of indifference. Radwell hadn't.

"There's a peculiar smell here," Radwell sniffed, "something burning."

Maybridge had noticed it too but was more concerned about getting into the house. He pressed the front door bell and kept his finger on it for a couple of minutes before giving up and leading the way round to the back. The kitchen door was closed but not locked. He rapped on it and went in. The smell here was the fresh clean smell of washing-up liquid. Everything had been washed and put away, with the exception of a mug which held dregs of coffee. Maybridge touched the electric kettle. It was warm.

"He's outside, sir," Radwell pointed down the garden. "In the orchard."

Simon, who was rarely up this early, had forgotten how dew-wet the grass could be. His sandals were sodden. Early morning privacy might be desirable for what he had to do, but not if it made everything impossibly wet. He wanted to dispose of Sally's bloodstained shoes, which were still up in the studio. Either burn them or bury them. It didn't seem right to parcel them up and post them back to her. And if he put them in the bin the refuse

175

collectors might wonder about the blood. And a half-burnt quilt which had blood on it too would make them wonder more. Trying to get a decent fire going was difficult. He hadn't been able to find any cans of petrol or turps in the shed, and the fire-lighters he'd used on Friday night must have been damp and weren't much use. It had rained all day Saturday and yesterday so he had cleaned the house. He couldn't think why, except that it needed to be cleaned. When he had been putting the crockery away he had found a box of green scented candles which he had pushed into what remained of the quilt (too much) and had left smouldering. Later today he'd get petrol and make a proper job of it. If it didn't rain. It didn't look as if it would. In the meantime he had to rake out the candles, which were making a disgusting smell. He hadn't realised they smelt like that. People would wonder what he was up to.

"Hello, Simon," said Maybridge.

Simon, startled, dropped the rake and nearly pronged his foot. There was a burst of bird songs somewhere up in the branches behind him. It sounded derisive, as if all nature were laughing at him. Christ! What was Maybridge doing here? And he had his sergeant with him. Had someone – the neighbours perhaps – complained about the smell?

Maybridge had been in a great many confrontational situations in the course of his work. Guilt and embarrassment weren't always distinguishable. And in this case friendship and professional caution married uncomfortably. He asked Simon if he was doing some gardening.

Simon picked up the rake and propped it against a tree. "I meant to tidy up the grass. Just came to see if it is dry enough to put the mower on. It isn't."

"So what's the rake for? Don't you have a box on your ma-chine?"

"Yes, but it will need raking too."

Maybridge made a few casual comments about the garden and then suggested that they should walk back to the house. He hoped Sally would be in it. The boy's demeanour was sending out alarm signals and he seemed reluctant to lead the way past the bizarre compost heap. Gardeners tended to throw peculiar combustibles

176

on to their tips, but he had never smelt one quite like this. There was a green oily trickle of something pungent that was burning slowly amongst the stiff dirty folds of what looked like an old blanket. A brown and yellow one.

"Why?" he asked Simon bluntly, pointing.

Simon blushed. He hadn't blushed for a long time, but the familiar hot rush of blood to his cheeks seemed worse than ever. What could he tell him? I had sex on it. With Sally. It should have been with Rhoda.

Maybridge, not getting an answer and peering more closely at it, suggested that he might have been using candles to set whatever it was alight. An odd method.

Simon agreed huskily that yes they were candles. He had been doing a bit of clearing and had chucked them out. He added that his mother had bought them one Christmas together with a perfumed cone – the sort of thing they had in India – to make a nice smell in the hall.

Radwell, contributing to the conversation at the wrong time, said that an aunt of his had something similar once – a small brass Buddha which was placed over the cone on a brass tray. It smelt like incense.

Maybridge gave him a Claxby look before turning back to Simon. The boy was as nervous as a trapeze artist on a slack rope. He was trained to spot a weakness – move in – cause pain if necessary – get the truth.

"Simon, where's Sally?"

"What?" Simon's blush faded. "What do you mean – where's Sally?"

Maybridge's own pain – yes, it was there, he didn't like what he was doing – eased. The boy would need to be a very good actor to simulate that sort of surprise.

He told him that Sally hadn't returned to The Mount and had been missing for two days. "And now, let's go inside. You can make coffee for us and we'll talk it over."

Strong sweet tea is good for shock but Simon had been asked for coffee, so he made it. He asked if he should put it on a tray, with some biscuits, and carry it through to the dining-room. There was more room in there for them to sit. Maybridge said that the kitchen would do and commented that it was very clean. "Did Sally tidy it for you, Simon?"

"No, I did it. After she'd gone."

"So it was a social visit. Tell us about it."

Us. Radwell was leaning against the sink, cup in hand. Simon hardly knew him. He was a lot nearer his age than May-bridge was. Telling the sergeant on his own might be remotely possible. Telling Maybridge would be like telling his father. Only his father might have had more sympathy – certainly more experience.

Simon said that he and Sally had come back here, after a pub meal at the Avon Arms, just to have a drink.

Maybridge didn't point out that they could have had it there. It was an odd reversal of procedure. "Go on."

"Well, that's it. We had a drink. Talked. Looked at the telly."

"Oh, yes? What did you see?"

Simon invented. "The usual rubbish. Car chases to music."

Maybridge hadn't been looking at the television at all, but it sounded a likely answer. He glanced at Radwell. Radwell nodded.

"So you were together all of Friday evening. In the Avon Arms, then here. Did you go out together again later?"

"No, we stayed in."

And went to bed, Maybridge guessed. And probably had an argument at some stage. "How did you cut your lip, Simon?"

Simon licked the tender area, which he had forgotten about until now. The truth was easy. "I fell downstairs."

It made a change from walking into a door. Had he been kissing her too ardently? Maybridge wondered. She might have bitten him.

"Were you and Sally upstairs together – before you fell?" He couldn't put it more tactfully.

"Yes, for a while."

"All night?"

"No."

"What time did Sally leave you?"

Simon didn't know, so said nothing. Coffee was a bitter drink and it was getting cold. He could have done with something stronger. Whisky. He tried to protect himself from memories by

178

blanking his mind. The kitchen walls were painted shit yellow. He felt nauseous.

"What time, Simon?"

"Late. It was dark." He hadn't seen her go.

"Before or after midnight?"

He couldn't guess. It was impossible to try. He had been afraid of what he might do to her – hitting her had been bad enough – and had gone outside. He had been in the summerhouse – sitting there in the dark, shaking. He might have been there a long time. It had felt like half the night.

Maybridge repeated the question. There was an edge to his voice now.

"Probably at about eleven." He could have said three o'clock – one – four – any time. Why were police so obsessed with time?

"What was she wearing when she left you?"

Last time he had seen her she had been crouched on his bed – naked – and clutching Rhoda's nightdress – taunting him with it. But she would have left wearing everything she had arrived in, apart from her shoes.

"I think she was wearing my trainers. I can't find them. And she had a black skirt and a white top."

Maybridge had noticed the plaster on Simon's left foot. One of the straps had been slackened to make room for it.

"Why would she be wearing your trainers?"

"We'd cut our feet. Walked on glass."

It sounded like a bizarre masochistic ritual. An accident, of course. He asked Simon how it had happened.

Simon tried to draw a credible picture. "Sally went up to the studio. She wanted to paint something. She dropped a glass jar of powder paint. It broke. We both walked on the pieces. They were hard to see. We weren't wearing shoes."

"Then – what?"

"We were carrying the quilt downstairs. And fell."

"What was the point of removing the quilt?"

Simon looked away. "There was blood on it – from our feet."

Maybridge wondered fleetingly if Simon had deflowered a virgin. Unlikely.

"Did you have sexual intercourse with her?"

179

Simon didn't answer.

"For goodness sake boy, grow up! I'm not being prurient. If you raped her she would have left in some distress. I'm trying to understand the mood she was in when she left you."

Simon passed his tongue once more over his swollen lip. "I didn't rape her."

"So she agreed to your . . . making love?"

"Yes."

"Did you make love – on the quilt – after you'd cut your feet?"

Silence for a moment. "Yes."

In a court of law that would be a leading question by a defence lawyer, Maybridge thought ruefully. He had been a fool to ask it. He wished this boy were a stranger, not Bradshaw's son. It was difficult to distance himself.

"The quilt . . . is that what you're burning outside?"

"Yes."

"Why?"

"Because of the blood."

It sounded like a scene of carnage. The girl might be lying upstairs with her throat cut.

"Simon . . . did you hurt Sally . . . in any way?"

Simon was beginning to understand what Maybridge was getting at. She had gone off – walked away – not gone back to The Mount. He might have wished her dead when he hit her, but was appalled now to think she might be. Someone might have murdered her. Maybridge, quite obviously, thought he had.

"Take a walk around the house," he invited him. "Look in all the rooms – in all the cupboards – under the beds. I didn't strangle her. She isn't Rapunzel Number Six." And then he began to giggle, as Sally had. But his eyes, Maybridge noticed, were brimming with tears.

Superintendent Claxby had known Professor Bradshaw a long time, but he didn't know his son at all. And his contact with Macklestone village was practically nil, apart from an occasional game of golf on the nearby links. Maybridge's professionalism was sharp edged – usually – but could perhaps be blunted in this sort of situation. He didn't see much point, at this stage, he had just told Claxby, in sending in the forensic team. There had been a bit of a mess up in the studio – some paint dropped – which tallied with what the lad had told him. And a pair of green shoes had blood on them. But Simon had explained that, too, and there were shards of glass on the floor which had confirmed what he'd said. "As I see it," Maybridge stressed, "it was a couple of youngsters having it off. Getting a bit rough. Had a row, probably. Why test for blood and semen when he admits she was with him?"

Claxby, who would test that the sun was in the sky if it seemed in the remotest degree relevant, said that if she had still been with him – had walked out of the studio or whatever place coitus had occurred – and assured him that all was well – then tests wouldn't be necessary. Until she was found – or her body was found – there would be an intensive search – door to door – garden to garden – field to field. Statements would be taken. And blood – any blood – especially blood on a quilt that was being burned – would be investigated, analysed, and recorded.

"You've been remiss. You should have brought the lad in to make a statement. He's probably building a huge bonfire in his garden right now."

Maybridge, who had believed that possible too, had brought Simon in and had left him in Radwell's care in the police canteen. A reassuring area where he could have a bite to eat if he wanted it. The superintendent might want to have a word with him, he'd told him. Claxby's reaction was more or less what he had expected, but he had hoped to do a little softening up first.

He said mildly that Simon was on the premises. "I anticipated you might want to interview him yourself, sir, but don't expect him to be lucid. Sally's disappearance has shocked him. I don't believe he had anything to do with it."

"That's the trouble," Claxby observed drily, "your belief. What has that to do with anything? His father dealt in facts. If his father were here now – and it was your lad – he wouldn't make a fuss about a normal routine procedure. He'd get on with it." He held his hand up as Maybridge was about to respond. "All right, don't say it – you're not biased. The fact that you've known him since he was an infant has nothing to do with it. Just remember it has nothing to do with it. And keep on remembering it. When I've heard what he has to tell me I'll send him back home, but when

181

he gets there he'll find that the blanket, quilt, whatever it was he was burning, is no longer there. Make sure it isn't. Is it too much to hope you might have the shoes?"

Maybridge said it wasn't. He had removed them with Simon's permission.

"Good," said Claxby, jovially sarcastic. "Good. Hope you said 'please'."

Simon had hoped that Maybridge would sit in on the interview with him but he had things to do, he told him, and would look in on him later at home. He might have good news for him by then. "In the meantime, try not to worry. Superintendent Claxby played a lot of golf with your father. If your own handicap is less than ten, don't tell him." Joke. Simon smiled wanly.

That Simon was emotionally tender and not in the least like his father was immediately obvious to Claxby. He became less aggressive. "Thank you for coming to help us."

Simon nodded mutely and took the chair that the superintendent indicated. It had been rowdy down in the canteen, a restrained rowdiness, young policemen off duty enjoying a break. It was very quiet up here. His father had described Claxby to him as a dapper sort of chap – wears stiff white collars with studs in them. Why that memory should come to him now, in the middle of all this angst about Sally, he didn't know. The brain was like a giant computer with an odd retrieval system. He tried to remember why his father had mentioned him at all. Something to do with wiping mud off his golfball with a handful of grass. That was it. His father had told him not to be so bloody fastidious. "Or you'll grow up like Claxby – terribly clean." Simon's dislike of his father's job – his obvious dislike – must have rankled.

"What are your thoughts on the young lady's disappearance?" Claxby asked. He glanced at his notepad whilst waiting for an answer. Loreto – odd name. Sally Loreto.

Simon said the first word that came into his head – a Kester-Evans word, but it was accurate. "Dismay. I shouldn't have let her walk back on her own."

"So why did you?"

"She went while I was out in the garden. I didn't know she was going."

"Did she walk out on you because you'd quarrelled?"

"You could say that."

Claxby's smile was a tired parting of the lips. "I could say a great many things, Simon, but that wouldn't get us very far, would it? I want to hear what you have to say. Did you quarrel?"

"Yes."

"What about?"

Simon gritted his teeth. No way was he going to tell this man what they'd quarrelled about. He said he couldn't remember. "We'd both been drinking." Well, she had been boozed up. He hadn't been. He didn't think he could have done 'it' if he had been. Though perhaps he could have, he didn't know.

"So you were under the influence of alcohol?" Claxby observed.

"Not exactly. Just a bit . . . sozzled . . . sort of."

"Did she allow you to take advantage of her when she was a . . . bit sozzled?"

That anyone could take advantage of Sally, sozzled or sober, was hard for Simon to imagine.

"I didn't take advantage of her. We agreed."

"So you had coitus?"

The last time Simon had heard the word had been in a biology lecture and was linked to the word 'interruptus'. It hadn't been interrupted. He didn't think he would have been capable of interrupting it – or that Sally would have let him. She'd had him clasped firmly to her and was making moaning, happy sounds. Oh God, what if she'd got pregnant?

Claxby noticed his look of alarm. If violence had occurred, it must have occurred then.

"Tell me about the blood," he invited pleasantly.

"What blood?" Simon re-focused his thoughts to a different part of his anatomy. "Oh, that blood. We'd cut our feet. I expect Chief Inspector Maybridge told you."

Claxby admitted that he had. "Forgive me, but I need to hear it from you, too."

Simon told him.

Claxby decided to accept the explanation – for the time being. It sounded silly enough to be true.

"Was there an element of jealousy when you quarrelled? Another boyfriend, for instance?"

Simon shook his head. "If she had anyone else, she didn't say. But I did notice when we went to the Avon Arms that she . . . well . . ." He broke off.

"She what!"

"Seemed rather interested in . . . well, wanted to talk to . . ."

"Talk to? Talk to whom?"

"Well, actually, he had a girlfriend with him, and I don't think he . . . I mean it was Sally who . . ."

Claxby poised his pen over his notepad. "Name him," he ordered brusquely.

"Doctor Cormack."

Claxby replaced his pen unused. He wasn't a swearing man. 'Good heavens' was his strongest expletive. He refrained from using it. This lad's father had created emotional mayhem, and was perhaps linked to that other woman whose disappearance they had just started to investigate in liaison with the Metropolitan Police and her Bristol lawyers. Now Cormack, who had digs in the village, had entered the scene – and another woman had gone missing. What was wrong with the air of Macklestone that it should pollute the morals of forensic pathologists?

It was difficult to believe that Cormack might be involved – but by finding it difficult he was falling into what he thought of as the village trap – the trap that Maybridge might fall into. City crime was anonymous. Usually. Village crime was like that poisonous plant that opened wide its petals and engulfed everyone, innocent or guilty. Perjury and protection, dissimulation and – what had the lad said – dismay? – coloured the scene. Villagers tended to clan up. Form a mafia. Had Hixon been a villager, not a member of a hard-nosed city community, he would probably still be roaming free, self-righteously murdering the 'fallen'. It was re-assuring to know that Miss Loreto wouldn't walk into him.

Claxby asked Simon to fill in her background for him. "Tell me about her parents."

He couldn't. She had never spoken of them. "But she knew my mother."

"Ah," Claxby said, politely non-committal. "And your father?"

184

"No. She'd never met him."

"Did she ever speak of anyone – friend or relative – that she might have gone to?"

"No one I can remember."

"Was she happy in her employment at The Mount?"

"She didn't say she wasn't."

It was a line of questioning that Maybridge would pursue with the medical superintendent but sometimes an outsider's viewpoint was useful. In this case, apparently not.

"How would you describe Miss Loreto's personality? Happy? Sad? Well-balanced? Moody?" This was the medical superintendent's territory too, but he wanted the boy's response.

Simon said she was jolly. He couldn't think of any other way of describing her. Most of the time she had been. Most of the time she had been all right. He had always felt he should be grateful to her and couldn't quite manage to be, though he had tried to laugh at her jokes. Had she been different in some indefinable way, he might even have learnt to be fond of her. That he couldn't feel any tenderness towards her made him feel an absolute heel. When they'd had sex she'd been a mindless body beneath him. He'd closed his eyes. Had she spoken, he couldn't have done it. Moaning was the kind of noise anyone might make. Even Rhoda.

Claxby pondered over the word jolly. If this lad had killed the girl, jolly would be the last word to come into his mind. She wouldn't have died laughing, heaven help her.

So give him the benefit of the doubt.

He explained about the house to house search procedure. "We're not singling you out. It's routine. I want you to write a brief statement of what you've told me. It's fresh in your mind now. Later, if she's not found, we may have to go into it again – unless someone saw her after she'd been with you."

Writing a brief statement was extremely difficult. Simon hadn't the remotest idea how to do it. After several attempts, during which Superintendent Claxby absented himself, Simon wrote in what he hoped was Claxby's style:

Miss Loreto and I ate a meal at the Avon Arms, leaving the premises at approximately nine o'clock. We returned to my home where we watched television. Later Miss Loreto dropped a jar of paint in the studio. We had coitus and inadvertently walked on glass. The blood on the quilt was from our feet. The blood on Miss Loreto's shoes was from her feet. I believe she borrowed my trainers to walk to The Mount. I didn't see her go. I was in the garden. She didn't say goodbye.

Claxby, returning, read it through and wasn't pleased. He told Simon to do it again. "And put in the dates. Friday was the twenty-third, in case you've forgotten. She may have left you in the early hours of the twenty-fourth. If you're not sure, then say so. Today's date is the twenty-sixth. Put it in, then sign it." He wondered if it was a deliberate parody, but decided the boy hadn't the wit for it. He was as odd as his mother, but she was reputed to be highly intelligent when normal. Admittedly, when your girlfriend is missing you're not normal.

He told Simon that Sergeant Radwell would drive him back. Then asked him a final question. "Where do you think the search should begin . . . if she doesn't return?"

Simon looked at him blankly. What was he supposed to say? Craxley Copse, where Rapunzel Number Five had been found? In the grounds of The Mount? In Millington's farm? In Paul Creggan's tepee? He said stiffly that he had no idea. It sounded off-hand, as if he didn't care.

Sally's father certainly didn't care. He wasn't in the least alarmed, he told the local police officer when he was eventually traced to a new address in the Birmingham suburbs. His daughter had a habit of going away and not getting in touch. He hadn't had a penny piece from her since she had walked out of the house when she was seventeen, all of five years ago. He could have been dead and buried for all she cared. She wasn't dead and buried, was she? Just gone. So what was all the fuss about? She'd spend all her life going – here – there – anywhere. But not coming back. Oh, no. Never coming back. Not to him.

The old man had become suspicious then. What had she done? Why were the police after her? If there was bad blood in her she didn't get it from him. He was as straight as a die – always had been.

Assured that she wasn't on the run, he lost interest. Some made their beds, he said, and lay on them. Others picked them up and walked. And kept on walking. Like Felix, the cat. Her mother had walked off, too. And there was no use the police thinking Sally might be with her. She'd emigrated. Yes, emigrated. No, he didn't know where. Somewhere far off. She'd gone with a coloured bloke. A waiter. Could be in North Africa. Could be dead, of course. Smoked fifty fags a day. Or used to.

Some families, the police officer commented over the phone to Maybridge, deserve to be left. Her father was a miserable old whinge-bag.

Not a very professional remark, but heart-felt.

Maybridge told Donaldson they'd drawn a blank and that a full-scale search would be put into operation immediately.

"And I want to have another look at her room. Is there a woman member of staff who might know her well enough to notice if any of her clothes are missing?" Donaldson had accompanied him the first time and had let him into the bedroom with the staff key – he had locked the room that morning – but he hadn't been of much use. Maybridge had noticed the suitcase on the wardrobe and a pink plastic mug holding a toothbrush and a tube of toothpaste on the shelf over the washbasin. Most civilised people departed with their toothbrushes, he believed, even if they left everything else behind.

Though Sally had been liked well enough by the staff, Donaldson said, she hadn't developed a close friendship with any of them. Her working relationship with Mrs Mackay had been affable despite, or perhaps because of, the older woman's maternalism. "She tends to be concerned about her moral welfare as her own mother should have been when Sally was considerably younger. She's almost obsessive about this. It was at her request that I stopped Sally taking Paul Creggan his morning tea."

A deliberate aspersion? Maybridge wondered. Was Creggan more libidinous than the other male patients? A necessary question, perhaps. He asked it.

Donaldson shrugged. "As far as I know, he's never stepped out of line."

187

As far as Donaldson knew might not be far enough. "I need to speak to him."

Creggan had left the premises on Saturday morning. "He's gone on one of his business trips and might be away some while. His attendance for therapy at The Mount usually covers three or four weeks at a time, but follows no definite pattern. He comes when he feels the need."

Maybridge said that he would return – and pronto – for questioning, whether he felt the need or not. "And in the meantime I want to speak to your cook. Up in Sally's room. When I've finished talking to her I'll come down to your office for details of Creggan's background – all relevant information – home address – type of business he's involved in – business address and so on. And I want a list of all the patients – with comments – type of illness – behavioural problems – and don't start talking about ethics, they'll be interviewed in your presence, but I and my colleagues might need some guidance from you as regards credibility – approach – and so on. And the professional staff will be interviewed, too – and I want them listed as well – but the psychological aspect won't pertain and you won't sit in on the interviews."

Maybridge noticed with a touch of amusement that Donaldson looked startled. All right, so he was revving up. Into the job now, not your friendly neighbourhood cop any more. Just as well they'd never been on Christian name terms. Not his fault though. He hadn't started questioning Donaldson yet. Not at any depth. Claxby might want to do it. Claxby's fear of personal bias was understandable. He hoped he hadn't been too fierce with Simon this morning.

Mrs Mackay was preparing orange sauce for the roast duck which was on the dinner menu when Donaldson told her to leave it and accompany the Detective Chief Superintendent to Sally's room. The command gave her a bit of a turn. Her common sense had told her that the police would be involved at some stage but, now that they were, she hoped she could cope. She could be accused of harbouring the girl. And asked why. Or Sally could be accused of filling the suitcase in her bedroom with stolen property. If she had. Which would make her an accessory. She had placed the black and gold bag on the bedside table. An unspoken accusation, and Sally had looked at it and yawned. She was yawning a lot – when she wasn't being difficult.

Mrs Mackay's obvious reluctance to accompany Maybridge was attributable, Donaldson thought, to having to delegate the sauce-making to her assistant who rarely achieved her culinary brilliance. Maybridge, who had only seen her at a distance before, attributed it to the natural lethargy of an ageing woman. She reminded him of an anaconda. Her cheeks were plump and dew-lapped and her eyes, which were of a pale watery blue, were hooded. He apologised for the inconvenience.

Up in the bedroom she noticed that the suitcase was still on the wardrobe and relaxed a little. She relaxed more when Maybridge explained what he wanted of her. It was easy to supply. If a girl intended going away she wouldn't leave her clothes behind – and her washing gear. She risked mentioning the suitcase – "And that." He nodded. Gaining confidence, she found a nylon weekend bag which she had seen earlier on a peg in the wardrobe and pointed that out, too. "Take my word for it," she said truthfully, "the poor girl never came back."

Maybridge asked about her family. "Did she ever mention her mother?"

"Sally had no family, Chief Inspector. The poor girl was a waif. No one cared."

A waif? What was she getting at? She hadn't been brought up in an orphanage. On a desert island. In total isolation. Her father might be a totally unsatisfactory parent, but he existed. She had lived with him for seventeen years. Maybridge asked her what she meant.

Mrs Mackay was looking past him at a poster picture of a pop group cavorting themselves in unseemly sexual attitudes. She had thought it disgusting last time she had been here and had been tempted to take it down.

"She never had any love – or guidance. She was a waif of the spirit, a target of lascivious men."

Maybridge was startled into silence. What was she trying to tell him – that Sally was a tart? Lascivious. What an odd word to trip off her tongue. Or rather, fall off it with a clang.

"Oh," he said, and then after a moment or two, "can you enlarge on that?"

If she could, she wouldn't. She shook her head sadly.

Maybridge moved in briskly from a different angle. "I believe you provide the Avon Arms with pizzas on a Friday?"

She winced. "Flans," she corrected him.

"I beg your pardon, flans. As you probably know, along with everyone else in the village, Sally was in the Avon Arms on Friday evening with Simon Bradshaw. Did you see her that evening – on her own – or with anyone else?"

"I don't attend public houses."

"You haven't answered my question. You could have seen her anywhere."

She was becoming tense again. "If I had seen her, do you suppose I could have persuaded her not to embroil herself with him?"

Embroil. Lascivious. What an extraordinary vocabulary this woman had.

"Simon Bradshaw is a perfectly ordinary young man, Mrs Mackay. Why should her association with him be harmful?"

"If it was harmless why didn't she return to The Mount? Why is everyone looking for her?"

A natural response, of course. A great many would ask it, including his police colleagues. Simon was in one hell of a mess. He tried to take the focus off him. "I appreciate your concern for her, but she'll be found more quickly if we don't hypothesise, so let's concentrate on what we know. She has been missing since some time on Friday night or Saturday morning. It was assumed that she walked back to The Mount in the dark, but didn't arrive. To get here she could either go along the main road or take the short cut past your cottage. You might have seen her – not necessarily in Simon's company but on other daylight occasions, perhaps, with someone else?"

"She jogged with him."

"With who?" It was a faint hope that she might come up with the name of another lad.

She didn't. "The one we're talking about. He's of bad stock. Of bad blood. She tried to be kind to him. More fool she. He's his father's son. And his mother was mentally afflicted. He should have left the village after the funeral. She would have been safe."

Maybridge came across prejudice from time to time, but it rarely

190

bordered on hatred. This did and was difficult to understand.

"Have you ever met the lad?"

"No."

"Then don't you think you're being rather unfair to pre-judge him?"

She didn't answer. This policeman hadn't seen Sally's wounds.

Maybridge had been aware for some years that though the villagers as a whole admired and, in most cases, liked Bradshaw, there was a small coterie who disapproved of him. For one thing, he lacked discretion. He womanised too openly. His relationship with the au-pair, Trudy something or other, during Lisa's absence a few years ago, had been blatant. The rumble of criticism had grown apace at the time of the Hixon trial. He had called Hixon a Bible freak and used similar language that offended the suscepti- bilities of the religious and quasi-religious. Hixon's murdering hands had ranked second in villainy to Bradshaw's sardonic tongue in the view of the less well balanced in the community. Claxby's idea of a village mafia was true only insofar as a mafia is loyal to its own, but it didn't encompass all the local population. Hixon had his followers here who believed an innocent man might have been convicted on flawed forensic evidence – especially in the case of Susan Martin. They had never dared whisper this to Maybridge, but you don't need words to tell you the way the odd breeze is blowing. You smell it. Feel it. It ruffles you up the wrong way. It makes you mildly angry.

Maybridge was mildly angry now that the prejudice of this woman should be extended to Peter's son. He hoped she would keep her mouth shut. Prejudice is a lingering malaise, the virus air-borne by gossip, but he doubted he could talk her out of it and didn't try. He thanked her rather curtly for her help. "And if you can think of anything that might give us a lead to wherever Sally is, then get in touch."

She nodded and watched in silence as he locked the bedroom door. As from now she would have a truthful excuse not to bring Sally the clothes she had been demanding. As from now she would buy her garments that were suitable – or make them. The clothes she had arrived in had been destroyed in the washing machine, she had told her, and were beyond repair.

14

An investigation into the whereabouts of a missing person is carried out quickly and thoroughly when there is disturbing evidence pointing to murder. Holes dug by Creggan's dog that had been filled in and re-planted were dug again by squads of police officers looking for Sally's body. Barns and outhouses were searched. House to house enquiries were made and a few entered for a cursory look around. Simon's house was ransacked and the bloodied nightdress held aloft like a flag of doom. Simon, standing at the bedroom door, looked at it, appalled. If she'd had to bleed on anything why did she bleed on that? He had wondered what had happened to it. He hadn't realised that her nose had bled that much – and he was frightfully sorry he had caused it to bleed – but the scruffy-looking plain clothes detective constable didn't seem to want to hear what he had to say, just looked contemptuously at him before putting it into a plastic bag. Maybridge had taken possession of the shoes in a civilised manner, and the quilt had been quietly removed, but the nightdress had been flaunted. Exhibit number one: Rhoda's nightdress, but Sally's blood.

Simon went downstairs to the living-room and sat upright on the sofa opposite the window. Some of the squad were poking around outside but he was barely aware of them or of the room he was sitting in. His mind was busy trying to understand what was happening. And why. Horror builds up slowly. In the morning he had been shocked that Sally had gone and he had been treated with some concern. And the interview with Claxby hadn't been too difficult to cope with. The superintendent had been calm and polite. But this locust visit that invaded his home was something else. It stripped him to his nerve endings so that he physically ached.

He was still sitting, dazed, when the squad took their leave an hour later. They had tidied the place up and explained that they were taking the nightdress, the bedding and some items from the studio floor, and that he would be contacted again in due course. Not by them, he hoped. He wished Maybridge would come. He needed someone here beside him. Someone like his father.

When Meg Maybridge rang his bell shortly before nine o'clock she was breaking every unwritten rule in the book. A police officer's wife shouldn't succour a suspect: Thou shalt not give him bed or board or sympathy. But when the storm breaks around the head of a boy you've known most of his life, and you knew his mum and dad, and you can't believe he'd hurt anybody, then you don't stand back and do nothing. "Come on home with me," she ordered him briskly. "I've made David's bed up for you – at least for tonight. Tom's at headquarters and won't be back until late. There's no point your staying here on your own and worrying."

The discussion at headquarters had been going on for some while and with a degree of intensity. Rendcome, the Chief Constable, the nuances of the word 'sir'. When it sounded like chipped ice it registered disapproval not quite bordering on insubordination. Maybridge, on the other hand, just sat and looked miserable. Three items with blood on them were enough evidence for Simon to be brought in tonight, Claxby kept repeating. That the nightdress had been hidden under the mattress was a sure sign of guilt. His statement about the blood on the shoes and the quilt had been a cock and bull yarn, pastiche Chandler – well, the last sentence had been. Claxby quoted from the statement which he had on his desk: "'She didn't say goodbye'. Obviously not, she wouldn't be capable of it."

That the superintendent had been human enough at one time to read Chandler's *Farewell My Lovely* and *The Long Goodbye* was surprising, but that he should make a comment like that and remain bitterly serious was in character. Claxby was an upholder of the law, as they all were, but to him it was engraved on tablets of stone. Had Claxby been on Mount Sinai he would have struggled down the mountain in record time with the commandments strapped to his back. And got on with the job of implementing them. Fast.

Simon Bradshaw should be brought in again for questioning – now – and detained overnight and for as long as the law allowed before being charged, he insisted. "The girl disappears after leaving blood all over the place. He admits the blood is hers. How much more evidence do we need, sir? Her severed head?"

Rendcome turned to Maybridge. "You know the lad better than I do. What's your opinion?"

Maybridge, shocked by the discovery of the nightdress, would have agreed with Claxby had Simon not been involved. He didn't seem to have the temperament for it. You can't talk about gut feelings in this kind of situation, and he wasn't sure what his gut feelings were. He hoped Simon was innocent, but hope is optimistic doubt, which isn't a professional state of mind. As a professional policeman he thought Simon should be brought in. He guessed that Rendcome, as a professional policeman, thought the same. Both he and Rendcome had memories of Simon's father, as had Claxby, but Claxby's memories didn't count. Nothing would colour his judgment. Maybridge looked for reasons that might delay the inevitable. "So far," he said cautiously, "the evidence is circumstantial. I've never known the lad to be violent. I think we should wait a few days sir, and make further enquiries. The Mount is a psychiatric hospital. One of the patients, Paul Creggan, is due to be brought back from London tomorrow for questioning. He left the premises at the weekend."

Rendcome, relieved, agreed that this seemed the best course. "Meanwhile, young Bradshaw should be kept under surveillance. Unobtrusively."

194

Claxby, slightly mollified by the proviso, said he'd see to it. Had Simon Bradshaw been the son of Joe Bloggs, he thought, he would be spending the night minus his shoelaces and tie as a guest of Her Majesty in a small room with bars on the window.

Simon, in David's large airy bedroom in Maybridge's home, replete after a substantial supper of roast lamb which he thought he wouldn't be able to eat but had surprised himself by being hungry (he hadn't, after all, eaten much all day), tossed and turned under the duvet and kept up a running conversation with himself inside his head. He should be out there looking for Sally. He had been told to stay put by the plain clothes policeman, the boss of the squad who had taken the nightdress away. But did he have to listen and take orders? Yes, obviously he had. But he'd come here. Organised searches by the villagers would be made; he might be able to join one of them. But that was leaving it late. The sky was starless tonight and there was a drizzle of rain on the window. If she were out there – under a bush – in a field – the rain falling on her – hurt – dying perhaps – and he was lying here – doing nothing – cold with guilt one minute, burning with shame the next – and he failed to stay awake and stopped thinking of her . . .

Meg, looking in on him quietly just before her husband returned, saw that he was deeply asleep and she was reminded of David at the same age. Her son had had his traumas, too, but nothing this bad. She hoped to God the girl was all right.

Sally, drugged to her eyeballs, was having the most appalling dreams. In her last coherent state of mind she had threatened the old bag that if she didn't fetch her clothes soon she would walk back to The Mount naked. Mrs Mackay, not sure how Sally would take the news that the police were out looking for her, had been evasive when Sally had asked her what was happening. It took time before people began worrying, she soothed. In a few days Sally's feet would be healed and she would return to The Mount and carry on as usual. A meeting with Mrs Hixon in a café near Horfield Gaol in Bristol had convinced Mrs Mackay that she was doing the right thing. The suffering of Bradshaw's son would be nothing compared to the suffering of her husband, she had pointed out. Her husband was in for life. Simon Bradshaw was just getting a small taste of misery. When he had suffered enough it would end. As for Mrs Mackay's worry about the illegality of the situation – laws were man made. Nemesis, the goddess of retributive justice, was above human law. "And you care for the girl, don't you?" she had asked, smiling coyly. "Who better could look after her until she is well? Do you suppose it was by chance that she found her way to you on Friday night? Believe me, she was guided to you by the Divine Will. A precious being has been placed in your charge. Mould her. Pray for her. Then send her forth when she's beautiful in flesh and mind and spirit."

A tall order.

Mrs Mackay bought Dettol for Sally's feet (her nose and forehead had healed). Her mind and spirit she couldn't do much about apart from keeping her quiet with a cocktail of barbiturates dissolved in the most tasty of soups. When the squad of police failed to do a spot check inside the cottage and satisfied themselves with a routine enquiry at the door followed by a look inside the coalhouse in the back yard, she became convinced that Mrs Hixon was right. Had it been part of the Great Scheme of Things for Sally to be found, she would have been then. "You'll soon be better, m'love," she told her when Sally tried to get downstairs on legs that felt like nerveless pieces of plastic, and the floor and ceiling splintered into hard black squares and triangles that tended to come up and hit her. She guided her gently back to bed and arranged a couple of bolsters on either side of her. "To make you comfy, m'dear." As going to the lavatory didn't seem safe unless she was there to help her, she left a commode and toilet paper in the bedroom, and locked the door.

Sally, not drugged, would have broken the window. And yelled. And kept on yelling until someone came. She would have saved herself eventually.

But Sally slept.

Having a row with Meg and making Simon get up at dawn and go home were two emotionally bruising experiences for Maybridge – especially the latter.

He had tried to point out calmly to the boy that as a policeman

196

he had to observe certain rules of professional behaviour and having him there put him in an invidious position. He couldn't tell him he was under surveillance. "If I'm seen to be helping you too openly, then I can't help you at all. Superintendent Claxby will be taking over from me in all further interviews with you – on the orders of the Chief Constable. I'm sorry about this, but I haven't any say in the matter." Later, he had broken a few rules of confidentiality by telling Meg about the build-up of evidence against Simon. She had listened in silence, deeply perturbed, and her anger with him abated. "The happiest day of my life," she said sadly, "will be the day of your retirement." His, too, on occasions such as this. There were times when he wondered why he had chosen the profession.

Paul Creggan's moods of dark disillusionment with his job came and went, but he ran his multi-million-pound business with considerable skill. He attributed his success to his acumen in choosing the right female staff. It was, after all, a feminine product that was on sale – apart from Citre – and Citre was bought by women for men, according to a survey he'd had done. Very few men bought the product for themselves. The full range of perfumes sold under the Redolence logo were to be found in salons within the large better class stores up and down the country. His senior executives, all women and London based, were well paid, well educated, well groomed and well motivated. The perfume industry rolled along on well oiled wheels, gathering momentum, and caused him no hassle. It was one hundred percent legitimate.

The aromatic oiling of the wheels of the Patchouli Parlours, however, needed watching. It tended at times to clog. It had clogged badly when Hixon had murdered one of his girls. She had broken all the rules and might have broken his business if the police had probed a little deeper. The ponce, a nasty little geezer who ran a similar establishment in Bath, had lured her. And she had moon-lighted.

The Patchouli Parlours might not be as white as driven snow but they were elegant places to work in and the girls, carefully chosen, weren't coerced into doing anything they didn't want to do. If they showed particular aptitude in attracting male customers for aromatherapy plus extras they were rewarded with a flat above the premises – free. If intake fell, they lost the flat. While the flat was theirs they were promoted to managerial status and wore a brooch in the shape of the letter M. That M might also stand for Madam amused some of the livelier ones. The French version – Madame – one of them suggested had a ring of class about it – so why not use it? When Hixon had started his lethal campaign the jokes had stopped. The business had slumped, too. Understandably. The incumbents had kept their flats – and status – it wasn't their fault. Business, now that Hixon was safely locked away, was booming again.

There were times when Creggan saw himself blackly as King Rat and wished he could chuck it all in, but it would take someone with the funds and ability of an emperor rat to buy it. Such men existed but to find them you had to trawl in deep waters and perhaps finish up drowned. In his darkest moments he imagined himself at the bottom of a tarn in a quiet dun coloured landscape where sheep safely grazed and only entrepreneurs perished. These moods tended to come upon him when he was undergoing massage with aromatic oils in his regular Gestapo surveillance visits to the Parlours outside London. He hated the smell. He could smell the bloody stuff for hours. It clogged his pores. Got into his clothes. Clung.

He had suggested to his wife, the blonde bitch on his back, that the Parlours should be closed – not sold – closed. Finished with. But she had pointed out that a move as unbusiness-like as that would invite investigation and she didn't see why she should suffer financially for his unpredictable conscience. "Take your holiday," she had urged, "wear your sackcloth and ashes for a while, and come back when you're normal."

He was normal when he lived in the tepee.

He was grass-roots normal there.

He wished he would live in it for ever.

To be peremptorily summoned back to it by the police, however, was a bit of a shock.

Maybridge conducted the interview in Donaldson's office, and as Paul Creggan was, or had been, a patient, Donaldson was sitting in on it. It looked like a role reversal situation. It was Donaldson

198

who seemed sick with nerves. He couldn't keep his hands still and seemed to be having an intense psychotic relationship with a carafe of what looked like water. It mesmerised him. If it contained what Maybridge thought it contained, then he wished he'd take a swig of it and calm down. It was understandable that he should worry that one of his staff was missing, but surely he shouldn't be this worried.

Creggan's leaving Macklestone at the vital time had placed the focus on him temporarily. Creggan under the spotlight wasn't blinking. He was extremely bland. And extremely well groomed. The erstwhile tramp-like individual wore a Savile Row suit, Gucci shoes, and smelt of roses.

Maybridge offered him a cigarette.

Creggan declined. He indulged in the occasional cigar and wished he had one with him now. Cigars had a good strong smell. So had carbolic soap. He had arrived without having had time to bathe or change his underwear. His Daimler in the car park made the kind of statement he usually tried to avoid and stank with exotic fragrance. He had told his chauffeur to open all the windows and take a stroll around the grounds and if the damned car was stolen then so be it. He might not be going back. He didn't know why he was here.

Maybridge told him.

Creggan was surprised but not immediately perturbed. He had expected this to be a business investigation, though on reflection that would have been conducted in his head office in Regent Street. He had half-hoped that it might have something to do with Susan Martin, the fifth Rapunzel, that her true identity might have been discovered. That his little Sally Loreto had skipped off somewhere didn't alarm him. His alarm might grow as time went on, but he'd had no close link with her. Not like the other one.

"Tell me more," he said suavely, "and how you think I might help you."

Maybridge gave him the outline but Creggan's section must be mapped in by him. "She was seen at the Avon Arms on Friday evening. She didn't come back to The Mount. You were in your tent here on Friday evening and left on Saturday morning. Tell me about your movements up to today."

Creggan's movements were as innocent as Simon's. He had walked his dog at around midnight before clouds obscured the moon, but under the circumstances it might be unwise to admit it. He said he'd slept all night. He had phoned his wife on Saturday morning and decided to go home for a while. He felt rested enough to carry on with his business affairs again. If this were the kind of enquiry in which alibis were necessary then he could write Maybridge a list of people he'd been with so that Maybridge could check.

Maybridge suggested he should do so. "But Mr Millington told me that you collected your dog and walked it on Friday night. Please explain that first."

Creggan apologised. He said he'd forgotten. "Doctor Donaldson will vouch that my memory isn't all it should be."

Maybridge looked at Donaldson. Donaldson looked at his carafe. Silence. "Well?" Maybridge prompted.

Donaldson said vaguely that Mr Creggan's medication might have blurred his memory a little. And then remembered belatedly that Creggan had no medication whatsoever. A lapse of concentration. He had more important things to worry about. Someone somewhere was having access to a lethal dose of tranquillisers. A recent check in the pharmacy showed that the pilfering had been done at random by someone with no medical knowledge and probably in a hurry — a few pills of this and that — not all benzodiazpines, some a lot stronger. A patient could have stolen the key. His own investigation was being hampered by this one. It should be reported to the police now. If someone was poisoned he would be held responsible.

He forced his attention back to the interview. Creggan was saying that Millington had been perfectly correct to state that he had walked his dog on the night in question. He remembered it now very clearly. He also remembered meeting Millington late one night in Craxley Copse a few weeks ago. Millington had been blocking badger holes so that foxes couldn't escape the hounds by hiding in them. He was presumably being paid for this by the Master of Fox Hounds. Dwindling farm profits had bizarre consequences.

Maybridge, not sure if Creggan was devious or just uncaring

about Sally, knew that in this instance he was deflecting attention from himself. Millington took night walks, too. Okay, point made. Bradshaw had had a stand up row with Millington about messing up the badger setts, or something equally unlikely for a man who liked to hunt. Past history. Maybridge had forgotten the episode until now. He brought Creggan back to the present. "Have you ever seen Sally – off the premises – walking on her own or with someone else? In the copse, maybe? Anywhere?" He wasn't loading the question against Creggan. He didn't think he would be sufficiently indiscreet to carry on with the girl openly, or admit to it if he had. But he might have seen her with someone else. Not Simon. He had questioned Mrs Mackay along the same lines, with no luck.

Craxley Copse was very evocative for Creggan – an area of some beauty and of great gloom. He could smell the place – damp leaves – fir cones. In no way ever did he associate it with Sally, but it was a place of death and Sally was missing. He began to feel more concern for her. His natural caution nudged him to be careful but he had been careful a long time, disassociating himself when he should have come forward and told the police what he knew. The two cases were very different, the odds against Sally's demise were high, even so one could never be sure. He had seen her with Bradshaw's son.

"Tell me," Maybridge urged, aware instinctively that Creggan might be holding something back, but hesitant.

Creggan let the words come – slowly and carefully. He didn't look at either Maybridge or Donaldson as he spoke, he saw a wider audience in his mind's eye. And he saw her. Not Sally. "She worked under a different name from her own," he said, "most do. I knew her background – most don't. She was one of my employees – a good one. She had a flat on the premises. Her parents were Canadian, she told me, but she was born over here. Her parents went back to Vancouver. She stayed. When she got tired of the aromatherapy business she worked for an escort agency – no, not the kind you think – she escorted children to and from boarding school when the parents were abroad. In between she took jobs as a temporary nanny or housekeeper. Ask Simon Bradshaw about her. She fell and broke her wrist when she was playing tennis one day with him and his father when his mother was away. She played other games with the professor, too, on and off over the years. If the corpse in Craxley Copse had a damaged hand then you can call her Susan Martin if you want to. But it wouldn't please her. She had stopped being Susan Martin a long time. She was christened Trudy Morrison and she's a lot older than the date on the gravestone. How the professor could get away with that sort of deception I don't know, but he did. If you don't believe me, disinter the body and let Cormack look at her hands."

Maybridge drew deeply on his cigarette and the silence grew. He had been pushed back in time and all the niggling anxieties he had managed to subdue were painfully present again. Both of the skeleton's hands had been severed. Too neatly, according to Radwell, who had been the first to discover her, to have been done by an animal.

He looked over at Donaldson but Donaldson was intent on pouring a stiff drink of vodka into a glass. Some of it spilled.

Creggan, master of the situation, temporarily and perhaps perilously, felt a surge of pure relief. Potent as champagne. His unpredictable conscience had probably smashed his empire if Maybridge took what he said seriously and began probing. Either way he felt less of a King Rat. Trudy had been a warm, loving member of the human race. A pretty long-haired Rapunzel that he guessed Hixon had never met. He had handed her identity back to her. A small gift too long delayed.

"Bull shit!" Donaldson stood up. He had been badly shaken and controlling his anger was difficult, but it was necessary to assume the therapist role and take command. "This is an investigation into the disappearance of Sally Loreto, Mr Creggan. We don't want to hear a fanciful farrago of nonsense about a dead prostitute." He addressed Maybridge. "I think it would be better if you deferred your talk with my patient until he's in a more rational frame of mind."

Or you are, Maybridge thought, or both of us. He didn't know what to say or do and was grateful for a respite. He would report it to Claxby and Claxby would tell Rendcome who might let the matter lie. It was up to him. For Simon's sake he hoped that Creggan was truly out of his mind. He looked at him thoughtfully. Creggan, genuinely amused, smiled. He seemed alarmingly sane.

15

Anger makes you strong, Simon discovered, and he was getting very angry indeed. When Maybridge had made him get up and go home at a time in the morning he had never seen before, he had felt like weeping. Maybridge hadn't looked happy either. To be deserted by the one person you thought was okay, even though that person came out with what sounded like reasonable excuses, was wounding. To be thought capable of killing Sally and burying her in the garden was worse. It was bloody insulting.

And everyone seemed to think it – even Meg. She kept visiting and she brought him food so that he always had something in the fridge, but she looked at him as if she wasn't quite sure about him and hated herself for not being sure. He told her rather truculently that he wasn't in the habit of doing people in, and if Sally turned up dead it wasn't his fault. It sounded brutal, as if he really were capable of killing her. But he did care what happened to her. He was sick with worry about her. Not selfishly sick – though he was that, too – probably a mixture of both. Meg had tried to soothe him, and even put her arm around his shoulder and given him a swift kiss. "Don't worry, kiddo – everything will work out okay, you'll see." The brief show of affection had cooled his anger and brought tears – not shed, luckily. She had gone quickly, perhaps aware that they might be.

People tended to go quickly, the few who came at all. The vicar had arrived, carrying a small black leather-bound Bible as if it were a talisman against evil. He didn't seem to know what to say, so Simon had taken him into the living-room and offered him sherry. It was all he had to offer. He and Sally had drunk pretty well everything else. He said, "No, thank you very much, Simon. I just called to see if I could be of any assistance." To help the police dig up his garden? Simon wondered. "The last time I was here," the Reverend Sutton had gone on, rather tactlessly, when Simon hadn't responded, "it was the funeral of your poor dear parents." It sounded accusatory, as if his poor dear parents would be forgiven if they threw celestial bricks at him.

An unexpected visitor who annoyed him even more was Kester-Evans. Sally's disappearance was reported in most of the tabloids, accompanied by a rather blurred photo of her taken by one of The Mount's patients. Sally in her jogging gear looking very busty and dishevelled, the kind of snap she'd hate. Simon had barely recognised her. *The missing girlfriend of Professor Bradshaw's son*, was the caption.

Kester-Evans had brought the local paper with him. He marched straight in with it and put it on the hall table. "There are innuendoes in the journalese," he said, "that I don't like. When I stopped for a meal at the local hostelry I heard gossip I liked even less. Where, as your headmaster, have I gone wrong? Where have I failed you?" A difficult question to answer. Simon, still angry, no longer cowed, was tempted to try. Instead he offered him sherry.

"Don't be ridiculous, boy!"

Kester-Evans strode ahead of him and, as he didn't know the geography of the house, finished up in the kitchen which was getting stacked high with unwashed dishes again. He spun around on his heel. "Where do we sit? I want to talk to you."

Simon took him to his father's study. The activity in the garden couldn't be seen from here.

It was an appropriate setting. Kester-Evans sat at his father's desk, which was slightly dusty, and pointed to the leather chair by the bookcase. "Sit there and listen to this," he said peremptorily, "and listen well: *'Justitia erga Deum religio dicitur; erga parentes pietas.'* Now translate."

Habit dies hard. You might be eighteen, falsely accused, or about to be, and very annoyed, but when your former headmaster speaks in that tone and points a bony finger at you, you do as you're told. *"The discharge of our duty towards God is called religion; towards our parents, piety,"* Simon intoned.

"Quite. And the source of the quotation?"

Simon didn't know.

"Cicero – who was slain. And your parents met a sad and violent end. Their deaths were a terrible shock for you and I've tried to be tolerant, but your actions over these last few months have been stupid in the extreme." Kester-Evans went on to enumerate the many ways in which Simon had been lacking in duty – to God and his parents – but mainly to his *alma mater*. "Your father placed you in my care. We, at the school, did all we could for you. We guided you towards the career your father had planned. You threw it all away. Had you acted dutifully and honourably you would be taking your place in medical school this autumn. You've rejected a golden opportunity, boy. In a few years' time you could have been in a position of authority, carrying on the work of your father, earning respect. Instead, what do you do?"

The question hung in the air like a balloon filled with nitrous oxide. To answer honestly would be to puncture it. Simon, edging on hysteria, didn't dare. Laughter and pain were a dangerous mixture. He tried looking at Kester-Evans objectively as if he were a wax-work with nothing coming out of his mouth. The old boy was wearing a university tie and a cream jacket. He was a thinner, taller, older version of Superintendent Claxby. Claxby, Simon sensed, had never been a real buddy of his father's. Not like Maybridge and the Chief Constable. And he couldn't imagine his father getting on with Kester-Evans. Kester-Evans was a pompous twit. His father was rational about most things, he wouldn't have gone overboard had Simon told him he didn't want to go in for medicine, he would have suggested something else. He kept thinking of the last time he'd seen him – by the car at the school gates. His father's hug, uncharacteristic and very affectionate. He'd said something about life being a survival course – arriving where you wanted to in the end. And just before they'd left home he'd sent him down the garden to say goodbye properly to his mother. These memories were precious. He needed them now. He wished Kester-Evans would go away.

He did eventually, but took a walk down to the orchard first to see what the police were doing. When he returned to his car where Simon was waiting to see him off, he shook his head sadly. "My dear boy, what can I say?"

"Goodbye," Simon suggested. It sounded ruder than he had intended. He apologised and thanked him for coming. "It was good of you to bother. I know I've made a mess of everything, but not as much of a mess as you might think – and if I could tell you all that in Latin and make it sound good then I would, but I can't."

Kester-Evans, about to get into the car, stopped. "Latin has its limitations," he observed drily, "and so, I fear, have I. You have my phone number, Simon – use it if you need me."

The vicar and Kester-Evans had been a pain but the Press were a torment. They had behaved well at the funeral, looking suitably doleful and keeping in the background. That had been the end of a story. This was the beginning of one. They roistered. Simon disconnected his telephone and the doorbell, but couldn't prevent them thumping on the door. He drew the curtains on the down-stairs windows and when an intrepid reporter from one of the tabloids found a ladder in the shed and climbed up to Simon's bedroom window, Simon threatened to push the casement open and knock him off. Maybridge could have told him that you don't treat the Press like that. That they had a job to do. You needn't go to the other extreme, however, and offer them sherry, though a few cans of bitter were in order – or even tea.

Beleaguered, Simon retired to the studio at the top of the house. Up here the anger bled out of him. Without it he was weak.

Sally was weaker, and getting weaker every day.

While Simon sat on the couch and gazed blankly and with deep depression at the mural his mother had painted all those years ago, Sally in her bed at Mrs Mackay's not only saw it, she lived it. The bedroom, with its low ceiling and tiny window, seemed caught in a grey web that dragged it silently out of her vision and the other land crept in. The trees were oppressive: too tall, too rough, too close. Their boles were gummy and the resin smelt of sweat. Forest pools as white as milk, where she tried to bathe, fumed with bubbles of antiseptic and hands kept reaching for her when she tried to move away. There were beautiful people here and horrific creatures and they changed their skins and one became the other. A boy was being fattened so that a witch might eat him. He poked animal bones through his cage to deceive her. Rabbit bones streaked with blood. She kept hearing a voice like a low drone of bees in the distance: You'll be better soon, m'dear . . . drink this, m'love . . . just a few more days, Sally . . . a few more days of rest . . .

It was becoming impossible for Mrs Mackay to look after Sally and do her job at The Mount. She had a good supply of tranquillisers to last a while so she had no need to return for a week or so. She phoned Doctor Donaldson and told him that she was unwell and needed a few days off.

Like Sally, Mrs Mackay had picked up scraps of information about medical matters. Sleep therapy helped healing – both mentally and physically. Sally's feet, which didn't have a chance to walk, were already getting better. And Sally had stopped being obstreperous. During the first couple of days she had been very cross and used four-letter words a lot. Why the fuck, she wanted to know, was Mrs Mackay refusing to fetch her clothes? And why the bloody hell had she put a perfectly good leather skirt in a washing machine when all it needed was to have the zip sewn? She

preached at, and given Mrs Mackay's revolting pyjamas to wear. And Simon hadn't raped her, if she wanted to know, she had raped him, or shown him how because he didn't know much about it, and if being here was supposed to be getting back at him, then she'd got back at him enough, and if it lasted any longer he might forget all about her and find somebody else.

Mrs Mackay had repeated most of this to Mrs Hixon and Mrs Hixon had suggested that Sally was protecting the lout and that at heart, despite her bad language, she was essentially very sensitive and kind. "Persuade her to stay a few more days," she urged, "she'll thank you for it in the end. You're her salvation."

Getting Sally to sit up and take nourishment was becoming more and more difficult. All Mrs Mackay's culinary skills came into use in an effort to tempt her, and the cottage smelled like a gourmet's dream. Without food she would become poorly, without drugs she would become obstreperous. Sometimes the nourishing liquid wouldn't stay down and the barbiturates came up, too. There were brief moments of consciousness when Sally became aware that Mrs Mackay was sitting at her bedside, sewing. "A dress for you, m'love," Mrs Mackay crooned. "A pretty dress for when you're well." It was pale blue with sprigs of daisies on it and when it was finished it would have a white lace collar. Sally, too weak to say fuck it, looked at it bleary eyed. And she looked at Mrs Mackay's hands that were like the rabbit bones in the forest. She didn't want to be touched by them and tried to move her head away when they stroked her hair – which seemed to have grown very fast. It was in long blond curls reaching below her breasts.

Mrs Mackay looked at her lovingly. She was beautiful with the switch of hair combed out of its plait and attached carefully with hairpins to her own short tresses. At night she removed it and put it in the black and gold evening bag that Sally had stolen from Mrs Bradshaw. "Thou shalt not steal," she whispered. "Thou shalt not commit adultery."

Claxby didn't believe in tempering the wind to the shorn lamb if a short sharp gale did the trick. When dealing with a psychiatric patient, however, he proceeded with more caution. If Donaldson had asked if he might sit in on the interview he wouldn't have argued, but he didn't invite him. Maybridge had prepared him for what Creggan had to say and Claxby, at first very sceptical, heard him out. When he finally dismissed him with the request that he should make himself available if called upon for another 'talk', he had come to the conclusion that there might be some truth in it. Creggan had grown rich on immoral earnings, though that might take some time to prove; he had chosen his words carefully. The fifth Rapunzel was probably Susan Martin, alias Trudy Morrison, one of his madams. Creggan wouldn't gain anything by saying she was if she wasn't. On the contrary. He had laid his business open to investigation by coming forward now – perhaps prodded into action by the disappearance of Sally Loreto. Assuming that he was of reasonably sound mind – he appeared lucid – and could be believed, then Professor Bradshaw had done a cover-up. Why? He threw the question at Maybridge, who tried to field it.

"I can't think of any reason why he should."

"Can't or prefer not to?" Claxby suggested. "We both knew Peter, Tom. And you knew him better. Did he have a liaison with the woman, as Creggan said? Was there village gossip?"

There had been and Maybridge couldn't deny it. "There wasn't necessarily any truth in it."

Claxby agreed. "But let's assume it was true, and explore a few possibilities." He enumerated them on his fingers. "One – she disrupts the marriage. Lisa, mentally unstable as we all know, kills her. Peter disposes of the body. Two – Peter, perhaps because he is being blackmailed by her, disposes of her. Thirdly, and keeping it in the family, Simon, aged about sixteen at the time and perfectly capable of murder, gets rid of her, out of loyalty to his mother, perhaps. It's the old scenario, played many times before, but in this case the forensic pathologist is in an extremely good position to cover his family's backs – and his own."

It is particularly sickening to try and make out a case against a former colleague, now dead, and Claxby wasn't enjoying it, but he had seen the professor's reports on the fifth Rapunzel murder and had they been made by anyone more junior they wouldn't have been acceptable. The forensic expert called by the defence had lacked Bradshaw's forceful personality and hadn't impressed the jury. Deference to Peter's skill was all very well, but in this case the skill could have been misapplied. Hands torn off by an animal – Bradshaw's evidence – and hands chopped off by a knife were two distinctively different pictures. Hixon had never mutilated his victims.

He went on: "The fox, or whatever animal was around, conveniently ravaged her face, too. And as I remember it, Hixon tended to leave his prostitutes decorously clothed, after arranging their hair. The only link that the Fifth Rapunzel had with the other four was the long hair. Has the missing Sally Loreto got long hair,

209

too? Not that it makes any difference unless young Simon has a predilection for it."

"You're biased against the lad," Maybridge tried to stay cool and failed.

"Well, there has been rather a lot of blood," Claxby said mildly, "and you're biased in the other direction. I'm just keeping the balance."

Claxby's interview with Donaldson was bland. Temperamentally they were in many ways akin. Had they found themselves in an uncongenial social gathering they would have gravitated towards each other and discussed matters of no great consequence very peaceably. Claxby sussed out that the medical superintendent wasn't happy in his job, but who would be? Running a psychiatric hospital must be at least as stressful as being a senior police officer, only the pay was better. He made a note about the stolen drugs which Donaldson reported and promised to send one of his officers to liaise with him. A conversation that had started with routine questions about Sally Loreto became a discussion on safety precautions when you had a large number of psychiatric patients in your care. This led, as Claxby intended, to Lisa Bradshaw. "Was she very emotionally disturbed?" Donaldson, expecting the question, spoke of mild neurosis. "A danger to herself and perhaps to others?" Claxby persisted. Donaldson looked at his carafe. "The lady is dead, Superintendent. She was a very gentle person." Claxby sensed evasion. "Have you ever had occasion to treat her son?"

"No." Donaldson could have added that he had no reason to believe that Simon was capable of violence towards Sally. But everyone was capable of it. Patients, under hypnosis, had spoken of murderous acts contemplated but never done, and had come round looking dazed, emptied of emotion, even relieved. Lisa's question on waking was usually, "How was it – was it okay?" or "By God, I trust you, don't I!" But sometimes she had awakened and wept in his arms. Her weeks away from home, when Trudy Morrison had taken over her house and her bed, had been spent in a small beach house on the Yorkshire coast. Bleak. Bare. Lonely. He had spent a few days with her and driven her back here before taking her home. She hadn't wanted to walk in on Peter's Dianeme, as she called her, a reference to a woman in a poem by Herrick, she explained. "So phone the house for me, Steven, and ask Peter if the bitch has gone." A bizarre order and he'd done it. His role as Lisa's crutch, and very occasional lover, had been difficult to sustain, but without her he was bereft. Trying to preserve an acceptable picture of the past was the best he could do for her now. He answered the question that Claxby hadn't asked. "Paul Creggan is schizoid. Disregard anything he might have told you." It was the first time he had made a professional diagnosis of the man. He hoped the superintendent would believe it. Claxby, aware of possible emotional involvement, kept an open mind.

Claxby's careful picking and choosing as regards who should be interviewed by Maybridge and who shouldn't took some thinking about. Surveillance of Simon had begun almost immediately and he had been told that Maybridge's wife had taken him home for the night and Maybridge had returned him first thing in the morning. He had been amused. No harm done. He hadn't mentioned it to Maybridge. Having met Donaldson he knew that his D.C.I. could have conducted the interview with him without bias. Whether he would be biased towards or against Doctor Cormack was difficult to guess. He was a neighbour – Maybridge and his wife would have been hospitable – the newcomer would have been made welcome. But he had taken over the job of a dead colleague and might have criticised him. If Simon hadn't mentioned that Sally had spoken to Cormack in the pub, it wouldn't have been necessary to interview him at all. In his professional capacity Cormack had done the usual analyses connected with the case. All blood samples found on the premises were Group O, the most common group and shared by both of them. As yet Cormack hadn't had direct contact with Simon. Both he and the boy had been spared that embarrassment. Claxby told Maybridge they would visit him together that evening up at his digs and have a word with the Millingtons at the same time.

Cormack had spent the afternoon making a corpse pretty after degutting it – or pretty enough to be taken to a chapel of rest. When he arrived back at his digs he wasn't in the mood to be quizzed about Sally. His feelings about her were ambivalent. Simon shouldn't have battered her – if he had. But if any girl had cried out to be battered, then she had. Her sexual charade with Simon, put on for his benefit, had repelled him. He had passed Simon's home on the drive to the Millingtons and noticed that the garden was still being dug – about another quarter of an acre to go, he reckoned. And the Press were hanging around looking like a right lot of bastards. That Simon might be the prime bastard, and deserved everything that was coming to him, he couldn't believe. He had liked the lad on that brief encounter at the pub – a quiet youngster – naive – easily put upon. So what should he say to Maybridge and the superintendent, who had come to ask about Sally? Tell them she was a nice girl – obviously not a candidate for murder – so the lad wouldn't have done it? Or, more truthfully, that she was the kind of girl to drive any lad berserk? He compromised by saying he hardly knew her, she was a waitress at The Mount, they hadn't socialised. For a non-class-conscious Irishman it sounded snooty. Claxby thought his attitude perfectly natural. Maybridge didn't. He sensed a degree of sympathy for Simon. It was reprehensible, perhaps, but he felt the same.

Cormack outlined his movements over the weekend. It had been spent with Sofia in London. They had gone to see a musical on Saturday evening and had stayed at a hotel in separate rooms. Very pure. She would alibi him, of course, he suggested stiffly. Claxby said it wasn't necessary. He hadn't thought for a moment, etcetera, etcetera . . .

Maybridge, mildly embarrassed, said he'd go and have a few words with the Millingtons. The Millingtons were having more than a few words, *sotto voce*, in the kitchen. Dawn wanted to complain to Maybridge about the way the squad of policemen had dug up her asparagus bed just because Creggan's dog had dug a hole in it earlier. She had lost the whole crop. Millington, usually cantankerous and pleased to complain about anything, wouldn't. "Let it be," he muttered, "let it be." As Creggan had removed his dog after walking it last Friday night, information already passed on to Maybridge, and as there weren't any other dogs on the premises, Dawn had suggested crossly that the squad should be invited back to break their shovels on the cemented area of the kennels. She was tired of hearing the animals bark and of cleaning up their mess; she would turn it into a herb garden. Maybridge, walking in on the last sentence, wondered why a proposed herb garden should provoke such angst. He asked them if they'd thought of anything since his last visit – or heard of anything – that might throw some light on Sally's disappearance. A question that might be rather annoying if seen as persistent probing, in this instance soothed. They knew nothing useful – sorry – and hoped she would be found soon. Claxby walked into the kitchen a few minutes later, asked the same questions, and was given the same answer and a cup of tea. A wasted evening, he thought, but necessary. It was when they were leaving that Dawn began praising Radwell. The sergeant had a beautiful tenor voice, she told Claxby. He was an asset to the choir. "But I shall always remember the poor young man's distress when he came here to phone after finding the body of the woman in the copse. He was almost in tears. He said she was in a dreadful state."

Claxby tut-tutted, a sharp little rat-tat through clenched teeth that sounded more like gunshot. He hadn't been aware that the sergeant had come here to phone. He had imparted information to these people before he had contacted the police. He'd skin him!

The Chief Constable instructed the Press Officer to call a Press conference for eight o'clock on Wednesday evening. The area of search was to be extended to Craxley Copse. If Simon had been involved in the murder of the fifth Rapunzel then Sally might be buried in the vicinity, Superintendent Claxby had pointed out. She hadn't been found in his garden – yet – so look in the copse. Rendcome thought it an appalling notion, based on Creggan's scurrilous aspersions on Bradshaw's integrity. Nevertheless he agreed that the search should be widened. He warned the Press Officer to say as little as possible. "State that there is no new evidence – there isn't. If anyone should mention the Susan Martin murder then say there is no link. Tell them we are just covering as much ground as possible in the vicinity of the village." A Save the Badger group, incensed that the setts might be tampered with, were a temporary diversion, not anticipated but welcome, and gave the Press something to write about.

Simon saw his garden emptying of the enemy like water down a plug hole. He went outside and breathed in great gulps of evening

213

air. For the first time for days, after self-imposed house-arrest, he felt uninhibited, free. He imagined himself jogging with Sally – and liking it – more than liking it, being ecstatically happy about it because she was alive and here. He wanted to run – run – run – and hear her feet clipping along ahead of him – she had always been ahead of him. Had she run off under a pale evening sky, like this one, or better still in the bright light of morning, he wouldn't have this feeling that something awful might have happened to her. But she had gone in the dark. And there was nothing he could do. For her. Or for himself.

Except go away while he had the chance. He still had the keys of his father's flat.

A relay of unmarked police cars followed Simon on his drive to London. His route to Islington was circuitous. He didn't know the way. Eventually abandoning his car down a side street, he took a taxi and arrived at eleven thirty-six. The information was passed to headquarters by the officer on surveillance duty. He was told to wait, watch, and do nothing until further orders.

The flat was smaller than Simon had expected. For a hundred thousand quid it wasn't impressive. He hadn't brought a torch and groped around in the narrow hall before finding the light switch. The electricity hadn't been turned off. The steep stairs led up to accommodation over a shop and consisted of two bedrooms, a sitting-room, kitchen and bathroom. It was basic. Unaware of London prices, he thought his father might have done better. The furniture was a mixture of antique, mostly too big, and modern. In the larger bedroom a melamine wardrobe and a double bed took up most of the space. The smaller one was unfurnished apart from a two-tiered metal bookcase holding an assortment of paperbacks including some early Penguin editions in orange and white and green and white covers. His father had probably bought them in a job lot, he wasn't much of a reader. His mother would have approved of some and been contemptuous of others. "The way you furnish your mind is of more importance than the way you furnish your home," she had told him in one of those rare moments when she had spoken to him as an equal, if not in intelligence, then in maturity. His father had chipped in that other people's bookshelves were as revealing as their laundry baskets, but you could look without being rude. Simon's choice, he had teased him, had been like rather smelly socks.

Simon went into the larger bedroom again and looked in the wardrobe. A woman's clothes, a blur of colours, very bright some of them, and a few city suits of his father's were squashed untidily together like two people sharing a small bed. He felt a pang of sympathy for his mother and for the first time ever was on her side. His father might have needed the love and warmth of somebody normal, but understanding that wasn't quite the same as looking at the evidence. His mother had needed someone, too.

The living-room, which looked over the street – a rather sleazy street, not well lit this hour of the night – was nondescript, mostly done up in different shades of green and cream as if no one cared a great deal. It wasn't evocative of his father, no personal imprint of any kind.

He went into the kitchen and noticed that the fridge was connected but empty. He was hungry and couldn't do much about it. Some fish and chips would have been marvellous. There weren't any drinks on the premises apart from tea and coffee. No milk. He made himself some milkless tea, then went into the bedroom again and drew the curtains.

He slept in his underpants and socks, he had packed nothing, and woke a little after midnight when the light was switched on.

"So you've done a runner, Simon," Rhoda said quietly. "I thought perhaps you might."

The owners of the shop downstairs had noticed the drawn curtains and had phoned her. They were a couple of brothers originally from the West Country who had sold the flat to Peter, and had become friends over the years. They knew the background and thought Clare might have returned.

Disappointment that it was Simon and not Clare was difficult to suppress. His eyes were half closed against the light. He looked pale, very tired, very young.

He mumbled, "I'm dreaming you."

"Yes," she said, "you're dreaming me," and put out the light. Dream on, she thought. Get what rest you can. She would return in the morning with some food for him.

215

His dramatic rupturing of what had seemed an idyllic relation-ship with the missing blonde had shocked her. He was the type to be hurt. Not to hurt. He would need all the help she could give him.

Simon woke to the smell of bacon grilling and, ravenously hungry by now, went to see who was in the kitchen. So it *had* been Rhoda in the night. He'd had too much buffeting by a malignant fate in the last week or so to feel much about anything. Including her. He remembered being angry with her a long time ago – it felt like years. Seeing her now didn't jolt him into a state of emotional turmoil, but he was glad she was there. It didn't occur to him to wonder why she should be. It seemed natural for her to turn up. She always had.

Relieved that he was accepting her presence so casually, she asked him if he had slept well. He said he had, thanks.

"You're looking scruffy," she observed. "There's plenty of hot water for you to freshen up, but you'd better eat first."

It was like the old days at home. Rhoda cooking for him, caring for him, being critical. No intervening days of trauma.

She had breakfasted earlier and went through to the bathroom while he ate. She set out Peter's toiletries where he could see them, and put Clare's where he couldn't. A couple of toothbrushes sharing a mug had a raffish air of propinquity. She took the pink one out. Now what? she wondered. The situation was bizarre. His calm unnatural. When would he be ready to talk? She wanted to hear the facts, not the guesses of journalists. He had the dazed look of someone recovering from an accident, not clearly aware of anything yet.

She returned to the kitchen and poured his tea for him.

He asked her what day it was, not that it mattered, but time seemed to have got out of sequence.

"Thursday."

"It's raining?"

"Yes." She had hung her wet anorak on the hook on the back of the kitchen door. He was looking at it, and at her hair which gleamed with moisture.

"You've been out somewhere."

"Yes – to my own flat. And yes – before you ask it – I have a

216

key to this one. Your father gave it to me. I look in now and again. And let's leave it at that, shall we? At least for now. Do you want more toast?"

He didn't. She had overdone the last piece and the smell of it reminded him of the burning quilt. And that evoked other memories.

"You forgot to take it with you," he told her.

"What?"

"Your nightdress. The police have it."

She knew nothing of the background: details of the investigation had been kept from the Press. All she knew was that the search was on and his garden was being dug. And the inference was strong enough that though Simon wasn't charged with murdering the girl yet, he soon would be. She asked him why the police had her nightdress. He said he didn't want to talk about it.

"If you don't tell me I can't help you."

He was grateful she wanted to help him, but he didn't see how she possibly could. To escape further questioning he told her he was going to have a bath.

He took his time over it, lying in the cooling water and trying to think things through. He would probably have to have a lawyer at some stage and wondered about Alan Drew. Perhaps he didn't do criminal work – just divorces, petty ordinary stuff. He explored his feelings about Rhoda sleeping with Drew. If she had. It was like sticking a pin in himself, a light cautious prod followed by a deeper one. Yes, it could draw blood, but at least he wasn't haemorrhaging over it.

Rhoda washed up then went to wait for him in the sitting-room.

When he joined her she asked him what his immediate plans were. "How long do you intend staying here?"

He had no idea. "A woman called Clare Warwick owns the flat. She might come any time. When she comes, I'll go. Or before she comes, if the police arrest me. I wish my father had left the flat to you."

She looked stricken. "Simon . . ." She couldn't tell him. She went over to the window and stood with her face averted. He was puzzled by her reaction to a perfectly ordinary remark. If his father

217

had given her the key to the place, then it might have been more than a casual friendship.

If it was, he didn't want to know.

The room was feeling stuffy. He told her he wanted to go out. The rain had eased and there were patches of blue in the sky.

She turned to face him. "Where do you want to go?"

He remembered he'd left his car somewhere, but he had no idea where. It had probably been stolen by now or impounded by the police. It didn't matter. He couldn't drive anywhere – there was no place to drive to. He would be arrested eventually, but for the next few hours he was free. "Anywhere – just walk around."

"Do you want me to come with you?"

"Of course." What did she expect him to do – go out and leave her? But she had left him and he had made a big thing of it. Met Sally and . . . "We bled," he said, "both of us. There's blood on your nightdress. Hers."

"Oh God, Simon, what have you done?"

"Nothing. She just walked out. We had a row. I hit her. She had a nosebleed. That's all." He didn't expect her to believe him. Nobody did. People had been convicted of murder in the past without the body being produced. They were put away on circumstantial evidence. Hixon had killed five women and had raised hell about the last one. He should have shut up, he'd had nothing to complain about. All five bodies on the mortuary slab, examined by his father, guilt positively proved.

"I wouldn't mind so much," Simon said bitterly, "if I were guilty. It's being innocent that gets at me. It's so fucking unfair."

No words were ever more patently true.

Rhoda, totally convinced, felt her taut muscles relax. It was then, on impulse, that she told him about Clare. And couldn't have chosen a better moment.

Clare's disappearance, compared with Sally's, seemed to Simon of no great consequence. She had decided to go somewhere else – take a holiday – not send a letter – that was all. She hadn't left any blood anywhere, had she? The police weren't chasing Rhoda, were they? That she was Rhoda's sister and had been his father's mistress, the owner of the clothes in the wardrobe, was more disturbing.

218

"Why didn't you tell me before?"

"I didn't want to upset you."

He thought about it. Had things been normal he would have been upset. If you fling a pebble into a goldfish bowl the splash wets you and you might kill the fish. If you throw that same pebble into a large grey ocean it sinks without trace. Simon's ocean was very grey. He stood a good chance of drowning in it.

"I'm not upset," he said. "I've other, more upsetting things to be upset about. But I still wish my father had left the flat to you."

16

Mrs Mackay couldn't believe that Sally might be dying. She was drowsy all the time, that was all, too drowsy, maybe. She was too weak to get out of bed and didn't try. But if she were to get back to The Mount then it was necessary that she should walk, even just a little. Mrs Mackay couldn't carry her. And Sally would have to say where she had been – a story about being concussed and wandering around, she couldn't remember where. That had been the plan. Doctor Donaldson had used hypnosis with his patients to help them to find out where they had been. If he used it on Sally she might tell him. He might guess about the drugs. The pharmacist had gone down the corridor to speak to one of the nurses while she had waited for her cough linctus. "Only be gone a tick," he'd said. A tick had been about five minutes. Long enough.

So, all in all, it didn't seem wise to let Sally go back to The Mount yet. And she wasn't clamouring to go. She wasn't clamouring to go anywhere. Mrs Mackay wasn't sure if she could still speak or if she were just having her on. She had invited Mrs Hixon, during one of their many telephone conversations, to come to the cottage to see Sally, but she had declined. She had come to Macklestone for the Bradshaws' funeral, she said, and that had been enough. A once-and-only mission to put the pig's trotter in the wreath. That she had managed to put it in the Chief Constable's wreath had been an act of divine guidance. "Read her the story about Hagar in the wilderness finding the spring of water," she had suggested. "You are her spring of water. You bring her new life. She's in your loving care."

Love might be a many splendoured thing, but it is deadly dangerous too. Sally's wilderness was a land of growing menace where the springs gushed blood. She was pursued by phantoms and she longed for peace. The witch at her bedside was waiting to eat her. When she was fat. She kept hauling her up and trying to feed her. Her face was a frog's, it was smiling and mouthing: Eat a little, m'love – drink a little, m'love. M'love . . . m'dear . . . m'love . . . m'love . . . m'love . . .

Digging in the copse had diverted attention away from Simon's garden – apart from that, it didn't do any good. No severed hands were found hidden down a badger sett or a fox hole. They would never be found anywhere. Millington had fed them to his pigs.

That he had managed to be so calm after murdering the fifth Rapunzel was surprising. That he had murdered her was even more surprising. He hadn't thought he could do that. He hadn't thought he was that kind of man. Reading about the Rapunzel murders, in the early days before Hixon was caught, had made his body respond in a most peculiar way. He had half-hanged himself in the shed once; not out of remorse, he hadn't done it then, but out of a peculiar feeling of need. Something to do with sex.

He had been working on one of the badgers he'd trapped that summer evening when he had seen the bus stop down on the main road and Professor Bradshaw's fancy woman getting out. He had hoped she would walk to the Bradshaws' home along the road, but instead she took the path leading to the copse. The evening sun had been low in the sky, but it was still bright enough to show the shape of her body through her white dress. White was a see-through colour. It shouldn't be worn. Had he not been so intent on looking at the way her hips moved, gracefully like a young animal's, he would have remembered the badger's head that he had put to lie in the bracken behind him. Badger's masks, as the animal's face was called, were sold to the trade for good money if you had a contact who knew how to bargain, and you could sell a whole carcass to be stuffed for two or three hundred quid. He didn't think it was illegal, but he kept quiet about it because he wasn't sure. Dawn didn't know he was doing it. She wouldn't have liked it. There were times when he didn't think she liked him very much either, whatever he did. They hadn't slept together for a long time. All she liked doing was singing in the choir and serving in the pub and being a kind of mother figure to Radwell. It was no use her blaming him that they hadn't a child. You have to get together to do that.

Ever since the first Rapunzel had been found, he had been having disturbing dreams about lying with a woman with long hair. The woman coming up through the copse had hair like a rope. He had put his hands across her mouth to stop her screaming when she had looked at him, and then past him at the badger's head. Its eyes had been open – dead, of course, but open – and there had been blood on its snout. If she hadn't screamed he wouldn't have touched her, but once he'd touched her he couldn't stop. He had been too upset to have sex with her afterwards. It was necessary to get rid of her before someone came. If the police found her they would take her fingerprints to identify her, so he had cut her hands off with the badger knife. They might know her by her clothes so he had removed them. Kicking her head in had been the worst part of it – the memory had sucked at his brain like a leech. There had been no peace until it had finally gone. Radwell's finding the body had made the horror resurface, but it had faded again when Hixon was accused. Bradshaw, despite his immoral goings on and his nasty tongue, was supposed to be a good pathologist. If he thought Hixon had done it, then his own memory was a bad dream. A nightmare about something that hadn't happened. Having the police in the garden looking for Sally had given him a niggling pain in his stomach, but it didn't flash any signals to his mind other than wanting them off the premises. He wondered if the police would find anything in the copse now that they were digging there again. There was a bundle of torn up rags in a bag under the hay in his barn. He hadn't looked at them for a long time. If the dress

222

had once been white, it wasn't any more. Why should he think of a dress? And why white?

He needed a clear mind to do his farm accounts and this Friday evening it was particularly difficult to concentrate. Dawn suggested he should leave them for a while and do something else. She needed to borrow Mrs Mackay's trays to carry some pies to the Avon Arms. They wouldn't be as good as Mrs Mackay's flans, which was just as well or she'd lose her friendship for ever, but they were a stand-in until she was well enough to get back to her cooking. She felt guilty she hadn't been to see her, but Mrs Mackay had dissuaded her in case she caught her cold. She hadn't sounded husky on the phone, but not all that perky, either. "You might as well borrow the car," she had suggested, "it's adapted for carrying the trays and Mr Millington won't have to come in."

"You won't have to socialise," Dawn encouraged her husband, "if that's what's worrying you. Just collect the car and drive it back here."

But as that seemed rather callous – after all, she was accepting a favour from a friend who wasn't well – she called after her husband to wait a minute while she cut her some dahlias. "Just hand them in and say thanks," she said, thrusting the crimson flowers at him. He accepted them with sullen docility. It wasn't until he had gone that she realised he hadn't spoken a word.

Millington's moods were as sombre as the Towers of Silence of the Parsees. Birds chirruped in the hedgerows as he walked towards the cottage and the grass was brightly green after recent rain, but nothing cheered his spirits. He was a man to be made use of. A ⟨illegible⟩ when he reached the car, no keys. Mrs Mackay had forgotten to open it.

Carrying the flowers, ashamed of them, men didn't carry flowers, stupid women forgot to unlock cars, he went up the path to the cottage and rang the bell.

Mrs Mackay was down at the bottom of the long untidy back garden picking mint and didn't see him walking round to the back door, which she had left open.

He went in.

Sally moved restlessly and a strand of hair brushed her lips, which were dry and flaking. Afternoon sunlight was a pale wash over her dress, her first time to wear it. She had no recollection of Mrs Mackay forcing it on, but her voice droned in her head like a dirge: "It's lovely, m'dear . . . you're lovely, m'dear . . . it fits like a dream . . ." In Sally's forest a cat purred, a sleepy gentle sound; it was getting dark and the trees were closing in.

Sally died at five twenty-five on Friday afternoon, minutes before Millington touched her.

'If only' are two of the most helpless, useless words that anyone can utter. If only the pharmacist had admitted his suspicions about Mrs Mackay sooner. If only Donaldson had contacted Maybridge sooner and they had gone down to the cottage at once.

They went in through the back door and Maybridge smelt blood. His common sense told him he couldn't, but he did, he always did in cases like these. A premonition, salty on his tongue, making his heart race. There was a scatter of flowers on the kitchen floor and roughly cut mint on the table.

Millington was sitting on the stairs, a sunburst of red on his shirt. Mrs Mackay had bled heavily on to him. His own wounds were mainly scratches but he had twisted his ankle when he had moved backwards and fallen over the wooden tray. She had sprung at him when she saw the girl and he had wrenched it from her and slammed it across her face.

"I can't walk," he told Maybridge plaintively.

Maybridge pushed past him and went into the bedroom.

Mrs Mackay was crouched by Sally's bed. Blood from her head wound was running down her face and mingling with her tears. Droplets spattered Sally's naked breasts. Her dress had been ripped from throat to hem. She tried to tell Maybridge to cover her, that she wasn't decent, but it came out as a confused mumble.

"Oh, God," Maybridge said quietly, "Oh, dear God!" He felt for the pulse he knew he wouldn't find.

Claxby would have enjoyed interrogating Millington, his piranha instincts were aroused, but Maybridge had been at the scene of the crime and Claxby took the subordinate role.

224

Anger doesn't contribute to logical thinking, but in Maybridge's case it didn't detract from it, either. Sally was very clear in his mind. And so was his first sight of the lumpish, blood-soaked farmer sitting on the stairs. Moaning about his ankle.

Now, a few hours later, in the interview room in police headquarters and wearing a clean shirt, he was still moaning about it.

"Look, Chief Inspector," he said, rolling down his thick grey sock to reveal the bluish-black swelling. "I'm not deceiving you. It happened the way I said. I fell over the tray."

The interview was being taped. It was necessary to get the events in order, as far as possible, for the sake of clarity. And in Millington's words.

Millington's trivialising words. A dead girl. A battered woman. A sprained ankle.

Maybridge, outwardly unemotional, took Millington through the events quietly. "It happened in the bedroom. Why was the tray in the bedroom?"

Millington didn't know why Mrs Mackay had carried it upstairs, the thought hadn't occurred to him until now. He suggested that she might have heard him moving around upstairs and as she had it in her hand at the time, ready to give to him when he called, then she had just forgotten she was carrying it.

"So she knew you were there – walking about – and carried the tray up to you. Why did you go upstairs?"

"I was caught short."

"I see. You went to the lavatory. Why didn't she wait for you to come downstairs again?"

"I don't know. Maybe she didn't know it was me. I didn't have a chance to tell her. She wasn't there when I arrived. She must have been in the garden."

Maybridge gave the impression of thinking it over. "An awkward situation. Would it seem reasonable to suppose that she might have thought you were a burglar, and carried it defensively – like a stick?"

Millington agreed that she might have done.

"And that was the way you used it – on her. Why did she attack you, Mr Millington?"

Millington adjusted his sock. "I can't remember."

225

Maybridge turned to Claxby, who was seated next to him. "Isn't it amazing, Superintendent, the way memory plays one up now and then? After something rather nasty happens the brain takes a quiet forty winks or so before sorting things out. If it takes any longer then it has to be prodded – made to remember." Claxby agreed. Maybridge had enough strength of character to keep his anger in check, but he could be formidable. So far he was playing everything low key.

"Well, now," Maybridge said. "Do you think you might start to remember, or shall I help?"

Millington was silent.

Maybridge leaned back in his chair and seemed very relaxed. "Let's take it from the time you went into the bedroom. What is the first thing you remember when you went through the door?"

Millington tried to escape his gaze and couldn't. "The girl, I suppose."

"The girl, you suppose. Well done, we're getting there. Who was the girl?"

"Sally Loreto."

"Yes, Sally Loreto. The missing girl we came to your farm to enquire about. What was she doing?"

"I don't re –"

"Yes, you do," a quick thrust here, "keep it going, I'll help. She was what . . . walking around the room . . . sitting on a chair . . . looking through the window . . . reading a book . . . *what was she doing?*"

"Lying on the bed."

"Dressed or undressed?"

"Dressed."

"So Sally Loreto was lying on the bed, dressed. Did you speak to her?"

"No."

"Was she asleep?"

"She was lying with her eyes closed." He didn't want the memory that was creeping up on him.

Maybridge, sensing withdrawal, leaned forward and thumped the table sharply. "Come on – come on – come on – I want it fast – she might have been asleep – you don't know – you went up to

226

her and you – come on, I want it – and you'll give it – you touched her, didn't you? How? Where?"

"Her hair . . . I . . . it was a set-up . . . you lot set me up . . . I don't believe she was asleep . . . I think she knew I was there . . . and Mrs Mackay knew I was there . . . if it hadn't been a set-up she wouldn't have looked as she did . . . all tarted up . . . long hair like the other one and her hands on her frock, one hand on top of the other on top of her private parts . . . and then I . . ." He totally lost control. "You bloody bastards, what did you expect me to do . . . or try to do . . . I had to get at it, didn't I? . . . And I couldn't get at it with her frock on . . . and then she, Mrs Mackay, came in and went for me with the tray . . . and I tried to hold her off and it got her in the face . . . and she dropped it . . . and I stepped back on it and fell."

Maybridge spoke quietly and persuasively again: "So you think we – the police – set you up. You're an intelligent man and you wouldn't think that without a good reason, I'm sure. Tell me about it."

Millington shook his head.

"You mean you won't or you can't?"

"I can't remember."

Maybridge sighed. "You've given that excuse enough mileage, Mr Millington. Let it rest. Let's look at it together. You see a girl lying defenceless on a bed. You rip her dress because you intend to rape her. The police, with Mrs Mackay's help and – we assume – the girl's agreement, arrange for her to lie on the bed in order to entice you to commit a sexual offence. The police and Mrs Mackay and the girl – please note, not a policewoman, but a member of the milkman – the interior decorator – a passing tramp – none of those. *You.* Interesting. You arrive and are about to perform. Can you put me wise? Tell me more."

Millington was sweating heavily. He didn't answer.

"Well, then, let's assume you weren't set up. You mentioned just now – and we have it on tape, I advised you at the beginning of the interview that you would be recorded – you said that she had long hair *like the other one.* What other one?"

"I don't know." Millington was getting tired of the sparring

227

match. His head ached and his concentration was beginning to slip.

"I think you do and the sooner you tell me, the better. It has to be said some time, Mr Millington, even if it takes all night. This other girl with long hair – you mentioned her hands, one on top of the other. Who was she?"

Millington looked down at his own calloused hands. "I don't keep pigs." He thought he'd told Maybridge that before. It seemed important. He hadn't kept pigs for over two years. Nothing paid these days. That other girl, the one with the posh accent, had made sarcastic remarks about his battery hens. It was disgustingly cruel, she'd said, the things people did for money, and she'd told him he was charging too much for a nasty little bedroom and refused to pay for the night she hadn't slept in it. He began drifting out on that more recent memory, visions of blood floating before his eyes.

Maybridge allowed him rope for a moment or two then hauled him back in. There was more here, he sensed, than he had anticipated, and he was going to get it by whatever means he could. A squad of police were at this moment going over Millington's farm again, but thoroughly this time, inch by inch, inside and out. They should know something more by the morning. And by morning Mrs Mackay might be sufficiently recovered to be discharged from the casualty department of Bristol Royal Infirmary, where she was being kept overnight. If she were lucid and emotionally strong enough to be interrogated, she would have a lot of explaining to do. The stolen drugs, identified by Donaldson when he had gone into the bathroom in search of bandages and lint, had been left carelessly on a shelf. Maybridge guessed that she would eventually be convicted of manslaughter, rather than premeditated murder. Her anguish had been genuine when she had crouched by the body of the dead girl.

17

On the day that Sally died Simon and Rhoda made love. He hadn't known then that Sally was dead. There was no premonition. Nothing to trigger the panic attack. Rhoda had been about to leave him to go back to her own flat when he suddenly became terrified of being left alone. The police would come for him. He would never see her again. He felt the claustrophobic crushing of the nightmare bird on his face and he couldn't breathe. He tried gaspingly to take in air and began to shudder and sweat.

Frightened for him, she tried holding him, and spoke soothingly.

"It's all right, Simon. Calm yourself."

When he could speak he begged her not to go. To stay with him.

"As long as you want me to."

"All night."

"If that's what you want."

"I love you."

Oh, Simon, she thought, why did you have to say it? Emotions should be decently suppressed. The fourteen-year difference in their ages was strongly in her mind. But did it matter? What would Peter think of this – were he here to think of anything? What

229

should she do now? Tell him to go and lie down in bed while she warmed up some milk for him? Sit beside him on a chair all night? Play the maternal role – frustrate him even more? To sleep with him wouldn't be an act of seduction. He was already aroused. He had been wanting her a long time. So why resist him any more? Why make a moral dilemma out of a perfectly ordinary act?

With Peter and Rhoda the foreplay had been skilled, funny, occasionally rough and with moments of tenderness. With Simon it was wholly tender, very gentle. She didn't flaunt her body as she had with Peter, but she used it in every way she knew. For Simon this was an act of love in the truest sense. He fell into a long deep sleep afterwards and she held his naked body close to hers for most of the night.

Maybridge was told by the police officer on surveillance duty that he would find Simon and Miss Osborne at a wine bar in Regent Street. The lad had been acting like a tourist. Over the last couple of days he had visited the National Portrait Gallery and had sat for some while looking at the pictures. Miss Osborne had sat with him. And she had accompanied him to the V. and A. and to Harrods – the food department. They hadn't bought anything.

All these to Simon were ordinary things. And he was an ordinary person doing them. Doing them, perhaps, for the last time. He was absorbing freedom through his pores while he still had it. Nobody was noticing him or caring about him – only Rhoda. She had given him the photograph of his parents – and Clare – that morning. Rather warily and with apologies. She had nothing to apologise for, he told her. She couldn't help what other people did. For him she was perfection.

They were eating hamburgers and drinking lager at a corner table when Maybridge spotted them. It wasn't the best of venues to break the news, but where would be? The quiet ambience of a church, perhaps, but he couldn't ask them to accompany him outside and go somewhere else. Simon would think he was arresting him.

They looked at him, startled, when he approached.

He was tempted to say quickly to Simon: "It's all right – you're off the hook – I'm sorry you were ever on it," but Sally at this moment, in this crowded noisy bar, was a presence that was very real to him, a young girl to be mourned. He broke the news gently. "Sally has been found dead – of barbiturate poisoning – no, not suicide." He leaned over and touched Simon's hand. "I'll tell you more on the drive back to Macklestone. Just remember this – none of it was your fault."

And then he turned to Rhoda. "I'd like you to come, too."

"Of course." Simon looked sick with shock, he would need her company, her support. "I'm most desperately sorry." And then she read Maybridge's expression more accurately. His compassion now was for her.

She felt suddenly very cold. "You've found Clare?"

"We think so. We've found a body – and clothes."

"I see." It sounded calm. She heard but refused to see. This was unacceptable information. She wouldn't let it register.

Maybridge dreaded the drive back. Why was life so abominable for some? Why was there so much pain? When would her composure break? When someone was near to help, he hoped.

Tragedies tend to be built on trivial foundations and chance plays a part. Had Dawn been on the premises and not at choir practice she would have behaved sensibly towards Clare and Clare, in turn, would have been polite. She had booked a room for two nights at the farm as a gesture of independence. It was time, she believed, to declare herself. She wasn't a tart – or a nineteenth-century courtesan – or a red light floozy – or a . . . whatever Peter liked to call her. She was Clare, who loved Peter and lived with Peter – well, most of the time – not someone to be kept quietly under wraps. This was the twentieth century, damn it. She was Lisa's equal in every way except in marriage. She wanted to meet her. Peter had mentioned, casually, that he would be away for a few days in Birmingham assisting in a murder investigation, but that he would spend a few hours in Macklestone for the opening of the library extension where Lisa's mural would be on display. He felt he should be there. Clare had felt she should be there, too. Not brashly displayed as Peter's acquisition, but as a human being who didn't mind looking at murals. Or socialising with Peter's wife. Lisa needn't know she lived with Peter. But there was no harm in her knowing she existed. If everything went according to plan there would at some stage be a civilised divorce. She had told Rhoda this, many times, but not Peter. Peter had kept on living his dual existence in the bland assumption that she didn't mind.

A visit to Macklestone for the day would have sufficed. To stay two nights at the farm wasn't necessary. But she had seen it advertised in the local paper and it sounded rather attractive. She had booked in on impulse, without telling Peter, had stayed there the previous night and was mingling with the crowd around the mural when he arrived. He introduced her to his wife, coldly and very politely. Lisa responded even more icily before turning away for the group photograph. The row with Peter came later. He told her to cancel the room at the farm and go home. Which home? she'd blazed. She hadn't got a home. She had a bed in a flat. Lisa had a home. Lisa had everything. She wouldn't go back to the flat. She had other friends in other places. And he had better go back to his wife now. And stay. He'd told her brusquely that he had to return to Birmingham and do an autopsy. Which was true. Had he allowed himself more time, he could have gone to Millington's farm with her and then driven her to the station. Instead, he told her to call a cab. A few days later, when he returned to London, he wasn't too perturbed not to find her in the flat. She had walked out a few times before. She would come back, he believed, when she started liking him again.

Catching Millington in a bad mood was an unavoidable hazard and she had been too cross to sense the danger. When he had handed her the bill in his office, she had bent over the desk to read it before saying all the annoying things she had said. And he had looked at her breasts, seductive curves in her red and black dress, made more prominent by the way she stood. After paying him what she said was fair – the use of one bed for one night – and no cancellation fee – she walked out in the middle of his diatribe. And she walked the wrong way – past the shed where the hens were kept. She had stood in the doorway, her red straw hat in her hand, her long hair blowing in the evening breeze, and she had sniffed the fetid air of the shed and talked about money and cruelty, the rights of animals and the beastliness of man. Had she not taken a few steps inside the shed and made a sweeping gesture towards the hens, and caught him inadvertently across the face, she would have walked out alive.

Killing the woman in the copse had been swift and easy and terrible. Killing the woman in the shed had been marginally less terrible. Had he gone on killing, it would have been easier every time. A little manipulating of his memory afterwards, like twiddling the knobs of a television set to blur the picture, helped. But not when Maybridge was there.

Clare Warwick was found fully clothed under the cement floor of the dog kennels. She had been buried hastily, wrapped in sacking. Dawn was due back and Millington hadn't hung around. The area had been in the final stages of preparation for the kennels and the cement, already mixed, was not yet hard. Millington couldn't remember what he had done with her hands. He thought he had buried them somewhere else. With Maybridge's help he began remembering. "In the hens' shed," he said, "under the cage next to the door."

It would be an easy case to prove. Proving that he, and not Hixon, had murdered the fifth Rapunzel would take more time. Confessing to it wasn't enough. Clothes had been found in the barn and were being examined forensically, but it wasn't established and perhaps never would be that they were hers. Creggan's assertion that she was of Canadian origin would need to be verified. If correct, then her family might be traced and further evidence, such as date of birth and dental records, produced. Professor Bradshaw's testimony would have to be re-examined.

Maybridge, under Claxby's supervision, was organising an enquiry he found deeply troubling. Bradshaw wouldn't have deliberately misled the jury in order to protect Millington, so it must have been a case of incompetence. This was hard to believe. His earlier evidence was impeccable. And it was even harder to believe that he wouldn't have recognised a woman he'd known – probably intimately – in the past. The reconstruction had been a reasonably good resemblance of Trudy – alias Susan Martin – as far as Maybridge himself remembered her. Gross negligence or a deliberate effort to deceive had occurred. That Hixon had rightly been given a life sentence in the case of the other four murders and would continue serving his time, whatever the outcome of the enquiry, was irrelevant. The wrong man had been convicted.

Bradshaw's deliberate effort to deceive had taken a little while to germinate. When he had first seen the decomposing, mutilated body in Craxley Copse, it had just seemed another anonymous victim of violence. He didn't associate it with Hixon. Hixon's four Rapunzels, quickly found, had a pale marbled serenity and their hair was beautiful. This cadaver was more a 'thing' than a person. The long hair was there, but in a sorry state. She had been strangled manually and no strands of hair had been found embedded in her neck.

While her face was being built up for identification purposes, Bradshaw had attended to his own personal matters in London – a visit to a consultant neurologist in Harley Street – and had returned, self-absorbed and depressed, to be confronted with Trudy's face sculpted in wax, her features a little coarser than they had been in life, her eyes two mud-coloured orbs.

He was horrified.

His relationship with her, in the days when she had 'housekept' in Lisa's absence, hadn't been serious. She had been amusing company and he had been mildly fond of her. She couldn't see much harm in keeping his bed warm with him when Lisa was away, she'd told him. Neither could he. But when she'd confessed, after a drink too many, that she had been on the game for a while a few years ago, working in the Bristol area as Susan Martin, it had come as a shock. He couldn't have an ex-whore, charming as she might be, looking after young Simon in his mother's absence. He had seen her a few times after that, but not in his home. And not recently.

He should have identified her immediately, and probably would have done if he had been in a clearer frame of mind and feeling better physically. He had been too confused to think straight. The future loomed alarmingly and he hadn't yet planned how to cope with it. If any of the villagers identified her, the consequences wouldn't be pleasant. His relationship with her had been too overt. The police would come calling – looking for a motive. God knew what Lisa might say. Even now – years later – she referred to her as 'that bitch'.

That Trudy should be identified by a former 'client' as Susan Martin, after seeing a photograph of the reconstruction in his newspaper, had been more than he'd dared hope. It seemed the most amazing luck. The informant's name had been discreetly withheld from the Press and others had come forward in sufficient numbers to satisfy the police.

The de-personalising of Trudy had begun.

Bradshaw had linked the murder of Susan Martin, as he made himself think of her, with the murder of Hixon's fourth victim. Susan Martin had been strangled and buried shortly before or shortly after the body of the other woman had been found, he stated in his usual authoritative tone. Manual strangulation in both cases. No ligature, though an attempt might have been made with Susan Martin's hair, which was long enough. As for the mutilation – not part of Hixon's *modus operandi* – given the long period underground and the extreme disfiguration, it was difficult to be positive, but he had come to the conclusion whilst conducting the autopsy that the severance of the hands hadn't been caused by a knife, as had been suggested by his forensic colleague, but by an animal's sharp incisors, possibly a fox's. As for the depressed fracture of the skull – blows by a blunt instrument or kicks from a heavy boot, also suggested, would have been more than likely had the murder occurred in a different locality. But he had seen the body before its removal from Craxley Copse and thought that the damage might have been done by a falling tree branch. The area was strewn with them after recent gales. He had toyed with the idea of implicating Radwell at this stage, but had decided not to. The damage he'd caused by treading on the cadaver had been minimal. The goodwill of the police, even that of a gormless sergeant, had seemed politic under the circumstances. The absence of clothing had precluded forensic tests and he hadn't been called upon to comment. If they had been present, Hixon would have been acquitted. It was the accumulation of carefully prepared forensic evidence in the other four cases that finally influenced the jury. Already in the frame, he remained in it, despite his vociferous protests.

Bradshaw's conscience hadn't bothered him. He had protected his own family from scrutiny, that was all. Trudy – no longer Trudy, but Susan Martin, a long-haired Bristol prostitute – had been Hixon's fifth victim. The jury saw it that way. Why not? They could be right. The police hadn't come up with anyone else.

But Hixon's tirade after sentencing had been hard to forget: *When he shall be judged, let him be condemned: and let his prayer become sin. Let his days be few; and let another take his office.*

Uncomfortably prophetic.

Whoever took his office wouldn't have too happy a time sorting out his last lot of reports, he'd thought wryly. They had been deliberately brief. And inaccurate. He had knocked a few years off 'Susan Martin's' age to distance her from Trudy, though that would have made her a nymphet of about twelve when she had started whoring. Some of his actions weren't logical. He couldn't think why he'd suggested local burial and a tombstone – surely rather a risk? What had it been – a gesture of respect for Trudy or a final statement in stone that the deceased was 'Susan Martin'? Whatever his motive, the vicar and the villagers had gone along with it. There hadn't been one speculative glance in his direction.

On the whole, the period following the Rapunzel trial hadn't been bad. He'd had a loving relationship with Clare. It had been especially good in the early days, perhaps less so later. He and Rhoda were more mentally akin, a woman to go to in time of need as he had that night of Clare's celebration party. She had noticed the tremor when he'd held the glass of whisky and spilt some, and he'd nearly confided in her, but was glad later that he hadn't. The symptoms weren't too overt in the early stages, apart from a slight slurring of his speech. The medication the neurologist prescribed had helped to keep him fairly normal. He could still get around pretty well. And drive safely. The quality of life wouldn't be unduly impaired for a while, he'd been told; later he'd need more rest, more adjustment to physical weakness. And the right mental attitude. He had listened without comment. The later stages of the prognosis didn't form part of his scenario. All he had was the present and the immediate future. He wasn't going beyond it. A degenerative neurological disease had one plus point amongst a lot of negatives – you understood its course and could monitor it, and offload what you couldn't cope with. Clare had offloaded herself, and for both their sakes it was less painful that way. He didn't know where she had gone and had stopped being concerned about her. She was probably fucking someone her own age – as she should be. The flat would be hers when she decided to go back to it. He had no intention of willing it away from her. They'd had good times there together.

But his wife and his son were his immediate concern.

He'd called on Donaldson a few days before the final holiday with Lisa, making a bill for Lisa's therapy an excuse to talk to him. "I'm not querying it," he'd said abruptly, as he handed over the account with the cheque attached. "I just hope that the bank doesn't get stroppy over my signature. I get the shakes sometimes. Can't write straight any more."

And then he'd asked Donaldson the vital question: "If anything should happen to me – to use the acceptable euphemism – how would Lisa react? Would her attitude to Simon change? Or would she continue to be the antagonistic, emotionally unstable burden the lad couldn't take on?"

The even more vital question: "Is she dangerous?" couldn't be voiced. It had been at the back of his mind during the trial.

Donaldson, suddenly made aware of startling new vistas, hadn't known how to reply. His shocked expression, followed by deep embarrassment as he'd tried and failed to find the right words, had been answer enough.

In the few silent moments that followed, Bradshaw had realised that there would be no opting out. There would be no reassurances about Lisa to make him change his mind – there never had been – there never would be. Any more than his own illness would be miraculously cured. He had known it when he had sent Simon down the garden to say goodbye to his mother. And when he had hugged him he had tried to keep his emotions in check.

He knew that Donaldson would put Lisa in the best possible light if Simon came asking about his mother afterwards. And that was some consolation. If he could remember them both without pain, victims of an unavoidable accident it would be the best legacy he could leave him. Anyway, what other option was there? None, as far as he could see. He hoped he'd have the guts to do it when the time came. Lisa unaware. Unafraid. Somewhere quiet. No one else around.

Rhoda's memories of her sister would always be there. Stark and very frightening. Not a quiet death – a sleeping away into oblivion – but brutal. She was struggling through one of the worst periods of her life and trying to stay calm.

It was impossible for Cormack to make Clare's face acceptable for identification and she was spared that trauma, dental records would be sufficient, but seeing the articles of clothing was deeply distressing. Dusty and stained with the effluents of decomposition, they had been carefully arranged inside transparent plastic bags so that the worst parts were concealed. A ring which Millington had failed to remove from her severed hand was in a separate container and was the only item that had been cleaned and was bearable to look at. It was a square amethyst, not large, and inscribed with the date of her twenty-first birthday. Rhoda remembered giving it to her. Other, more expensive rings, gifts from Peter, weren't found. Perhaps she hadn't been wearing them.

She said: "Yes, they're Clare's. The same clothes as the ones in the snapshot. Were they on her when she . . . or did he . . ." She couldn't say it.

Maybridge cut in quickly. "She was fully clothed." He didn't have to be with her for the identification process, but she knew him better than anyone else, and he was trying to give her all the support he could. And so, he was relieved to know, was Alan Drew. He had phoned the solicitor with the news that Clare Warwick's body had been found, and his response had been immediate. He was waiting for her outside the building now.

She was going to stay with him in his Bristol flat for a few days but how he would be able to stand her, in her present mood, she didn't know. She wondered how Simon was. She hadn't enough strength to be supportive to him at this present time but she wished him well – was fond of him in a way – Peter's son. Peter, the pivot of this whole bloody merry-go-round of disaster.

She thanked Maybridge for being with her as they stepped outside. "You've been kind. It would have been even harder without you. Give my best wishes to Simon. I hope someone's with him, too."

Maybridge passed Rhoda's message to Meg, the only person that Simon would see. On returning to Macklestone he had been greeted by reporters who wanted his story – how does it feel to be an ex-murder suspect? – and so on. He had ignored them and gone up to the studio. After a few hours of waiting they had given up and left him in peace. Mrs Mackay's cottage and Millington's farm were more newsworthy areas.

Villagers who had come with kindly offers of help at the time of his parents' funeral began calling again – mainly out of a feeling of guilt. They had behaved badly towards him over Sally. They had gossiped. Believed the worst. What should they bring him as gifts of atonement? they wondered. Flowers? But flowers were for women – and for funerals. But there would be a funeral. But not his fault. What then? Most were relieved when he didn't open the door and departed with their booze and their chocolates. They had meant well, they consoled themselves, as they drank the one and ate the other.

Meg phoned to tell him that she was coming and to please let her in. She was calm, practical and brought food. If he wanted to isolate himself in the room at the top of the house, then that was his way of dealing with the trauma. It worried her but she accepted it and was prepared to wait. It was the long summer vacation from university and she could give him all her time. If he didn't want conversation then so be it, but he had to eat. He gave her his spare key and she came and went frequently, calling out before leaving, "Grub's up, Simon. Are you okay?" She needed a response, no matter how brief. He sounded all right, though he obviously couldn't have been. She was reminded of Lisa who had had these periods of isolation, too.

After three extremely anxious days, during which time she listened to his moving about – going to the bathroom – walking along the corridor to his bedroom, and then back to the studio – always back to the studio – he came downstairs.

It was six o'clock and the evening sun was golden in the room. He stood at the sitting-room door, blinking at her as if he had emerged from a long dark tunnel into the light. There were dark shadows under his eyes and a growth of stubble on his chin. He was wearing a grubby brown cotton shirt, the sleeves rolled up, and shorts. His hands were stained.

"I think I want you to see it," he said. It was hesitant. He didn't seem sure.

Meg was carrying a bowl of freesias she had just arranged. She put it down carefully and tried to sound matter-of-fact. "See what?"

He shook his head and then, changing his mind, "Yes – I think perhaps you – it's in the studio . . ."

She followed him upstairs.

He opened the studio door and stood aside for her to go in. The window was closed and the room smelt musty. The couch, pushed into a corner, was covered with a pile of rags stiff with dried paint. Water from the cold tap dripped into the sink, which held an assortment of brushes. And then she turned and looked at the wall where Lisa's mural had been and went rigid with shock.

It was Sally. A large, bold, fierce portrait painted in grief and with extraordinary brilliance. Sally running through a dark green landscape – Sally as she had been, every muscle working, head thrown back, lips parted, eyes looking towards something in the distance, something that enticed her, something good. Sally in a black skirt and a white T-shirt with patches of sweat under the arms. A girl of flesh and blood, unglamourised and so vitally alive Meg could almost hear her feet pounding on the forest path. She burst into tears.

Simon looked at her helplessly. "It was all I could do," he said. "What else could I do?"

It was the beginning of his future, though he didn't know it then.